Song For A
Scarlet
Runner

Julie Hunt
Song For A Scarlet Runner

ALLEN&UNWIN

SYDNEY · MELBOURNE · AUCKLAND · LONDON

SUPPORTED BY
Tasmanian
Government

This project was assisted through Arts Tasmania
by the Minister for the Arts

First published in 2013

Allen & Unwin
83 Alexander Street
Crows Nest NSW 2065
Australia
Phone: (61 2) 8425 0100
Email: info@allenandunwin.com
Web: www.allenandunwin.com

A Cataloguing-in-Publication entry is available from the
National Library of Australia
www.trove.nla.gov.au

ISBN 978 1 74331 358 9

Cover and text design by Ruth Grüner
Set in 11 pt Sabon by Ruth Grüner

This book was printed in January 2015 at McPherson's Printing Group,
76 Nelson St, Maryborough, Victoria 3465, Australia.
www.mcphersonsprinting.com.au

7 9 10 8 6

TO SUE MOSSCO

1

THE OVERHANG

Marlie and I lived at the Overhang, near the place where three roads met. One road went west to the Badlands. No one ever passed that way. It was the same with the road to the east – if you followed it you'd end up in the marshes, which stretched forever. Nobody went in that direction, and you'd never expect to see anyone coming from there. Only the road from Skerrick was used, and that was the one I watched, from high up on my ledge.

'Peat, get down. You won't make her come any faster by looking!'

I couldn't see my sister but I could hear her. She was in the yard below, putting hay in the bails and getting the buckets ready for milking.

'Come on,' she yelled. 'Come on, come on, come on ...' She was calling the cows, but she was also calling me.

I ignored her and stared along the road, following it over the hills until it became a narrow track that disappeared into the valley where Skerrick lay. There was only one person who used the road and that was Wim, our auntie. She came up every month to bring us supplies and to collect the cheeses we made. Sometimes, if the weather was clear, I could see her as a tiny dot in the distance; then I'd know she would arrive in two days' time, walking slowly because she always carried a heavy load – vegetables from her garden, flour, corn and lamp oil. Even with an empty pack, it would still take her at least four days to walk all the way from Skerrick.

Marlie and I longed for Wim's visits because she was the only person we saw. You might think it strange that two girls would live all by themselves up there at the Overhang, but that's the way it was. Our job was to look after the cattle. Every day we took them out to graze and every night we brought them back to the yard.

There were seven cows: Bella, Pem, Minka, Ellie, Creamy, Brown Cow and Skye. And each one had a calf except for Bella, who had the twins, Bright and Little Shy. Bright was my favourite even though he caused me a lot of trouble. He was brave and cheeky, and in the evenings when we locked the calves into the night cave, he was the one who always refused to come. Marlie lost patience with him but I thought it was funny the way he dug in his toes and wouldn't budge. Most nights Bella had to help. She'd walk right up to the entrance and pretend she was about to go in, even though she was much too wide to fit. Only then would Bright skip through. I'd have to close the gate behind him quickly before he changed his mind.

We separated the calves from the cows at night so we could milk in the morning. If the calves were on the cows all day and all night there wouldn't be any milk for us – not that it was really for us, it was for the people of Skerrick. We made the cheese for them.

Skerrick was the nearest settlement, the *only* settlement. You wouldn't call it a town, or even a village – it was just a scattering of huts with walls made of stone and roofs of sod. None of the huts had windows, because there was nothing to see.

Most valleys lead somewhere – they open up into new country. But the valley where Skerrick lay – Bane Valley, it was called – ended in a steephead, a solid rock wall. The huts were built at the base of it and the sides of the valley were so steep that no sun ever reached there.

It was much better to live at the Overhang, even if it was just a rock shelter. At least there was a view. From the ledge I could see the entrance to the Bane Valley, and if I climbed higher up the escarpment I could see the sandy country out near the Boulders.

I would never have wanted to live in Skerrick even if I had been allowed to, but Marlie would have gone back and lived there the next day if she could. She'd been born there – well, we both had, but she'd lived there for six years, and I'd only been there for a day.

'Peat, come down and help me!'

I took a last look at the road to Skerrick. The sun was in my eyes, so even if Wim was there I probably couldn't have seen her.

'Coming!'

2

LUCK

I got down the same way I'd come up, through the hole at the back of the ledge. It was a narrow gap and it led into the night cave. I squeezed through, then dropped onto the floor, pushing my way through the calves. Bright was standing in front of the gate blocking my path. Typical! I shoved past him and slipped out.

'Any sign of her?' Marlie handed me my bucket and stool.

I shook my head and sat down next to Bella. She was the lead cow and she always came in first.

'I don't know how Wim can bear to live in Skerrick,' I said, pressing my head into Bella's warm flank.

'Don't start that again. You've never even seen the place.'

'It's miserable. The sun never shines there.'

'It does. I can remember playing in the sun in front of our hut.' Marlie flicked her long hair from her eyes and set her stool down next to Creamy.

'It must have only been for two minutes at midday when the sun was right overhead.'

Bella shifted her weight and gave a low *moo* to show she agreed with me. Bright bawled a reply. He was restless, eager to be out with his mother. He bawled again and all the other calves joined in.

4

'You're wrong, Peat.' Marlie raised her voice above the noise. 'It was often sunny. Ma would sit in the doorway in the sun, shelling peas.'

'She never shelled peas. Peas wouldn't grow in Skerrick.'

'How would you know? You were only a baby. You're *still* a baby.'

I didn't reply. The calves settled down and the only sound was the milk squirting into my bucket.

My mother had made that bucket. She'd made a lot of things around the Overhang. I didn't remember her, but knew she must have been clever and capable. You could see it in everything she'd left us – this bucket, the spoons she'd carved out of blackwood, and the gate made of woven birch sticks that was strong enough to keep the calves in and the cows out. She'd made my wool dress too, and my trousers, and the felt vest I never took off. They'd belonged to Marlie until she grew out of them. And my mother had made the little cow charm that Marlie wore around her neck. It was carved from horn and it was my sister's most precious thing. She said it brought her good luck.

My mother hadn't been too lucky herself – or perhaps it was me who'd brought her bad luck. The trouble had started when I was born. There was a big man who lived in Skerrick. His name was Alban Bane and he was the boss of everything – the land, the huts, the people. He was especially the boss of my mother, because she was married to him. On the day I was born he took one look at me lying in my mother's arms and a fury ran through him. My hair was not brown, like his, or all the other people of Skerrick's. It was red. And my eyes were a different colour too, not dark like everyone else's. My eyes were even different from each other – one was brown and one was green.

When he saw me, Alban had strode outside and rung the bell. It was a huge iron bell mounted on scaffolding beside his hut, and it was rung whenever there was news to be announced, good or bad. Although I didn't think there would ever have been any good news in Skerrick – it wasn't that sort of place. Anyway, on my birth day, Alban rang the bell and told everyone that the baby girl was not his, but rather a child from the Badlands, a bastard child, and that my mother, sister and I would be leaving Skerrick that very day, never to return.

My mother took the only road out of the settlement – the track that led north, to the back country under the escarpment, where the cattle were kept. She knew about the Overhang because she and Wim had spent summers there when they were young. She knew where the water was and how to find food. She could make soup from nettle and hogweed. She knew where the mushrooms would come up and the places she was most likely to find mealy grubs and groundnuts. And the cows meant that every day we could have milk and cheese.

Marlie remembered the walk. She said our mother carried me in a sling on her back and that her arms were full of the few things she'd been able to collect and tie up in a blanket before Alban Bane had pushed us out of the family hut. The people who had been looking after the cows went back to Skerrick as soon as we arrived.

Marlie said those cow hands had left the Overhang in a terrible mess. She helped our mother clean it up. The first thing they did was collect fresh bracken to spread on the sleeping ledge, which was behind the cooking bench. Then they put straw on top, to make a soft bed. When that was done they built a rock wall between the living area and the yard, to keep the cows out. Before that, if the cows were in the yard and the weather was rough they would come right in under the ledge to get out of the rain. My mother also put a big stone on either side of the wall to help us climb over. She must have been strong then, to move stones that size.

I finished milking Bella and put my stool next to Pem. She was a strawberry-coloured cow, like her calf, Jiffi. Wim had told me that Pem was our best milker, because her milk was full of cream. She said our mother had made beautiful cheese from Pem's milk.

Our mother was a very good cheesemaker. The cows had liked her, so they gave her extra milk, and sometimes she had as many as six cheeses stored on the shelf against the back wall of the Overhang, lined up in the dark like little golden moons.

'Peas *did* grow in Skerrick,' Marlie said. 'Everything grew there – peas, corn, apples. And it still does. Ask Wim.'

I didn't answer. There was no point in asking Wim about Skerrick. She would just shake her head and change the subject. 'Don't worry about it, Peat,' she would sigh. 'It's no place for you.' Then sometimes she would add, 'It's no place for anyone, really.'

3

THE SHORT STRAW

When we had finished the milking I opened the gate of the night cave and headed out west with the cows and calves. I hoped Wim wouldn't come today because if she did I might miss her. I had drawn the short straw. Marlie and I always drew straws to see who would take the cattle out around the time when Wim was due to visit, and we knew we could expect her soon because there were four round stones and three pebbles on the slab in front of our rock pile. Pebbles were days and round stones were weeks. That was how long it had been since Wim was last here.

We loved Wim's visits. She'd sit down next to our cooking place and unload her pack while we told her everything that had happened since we'd last seen her – how Ellie was lame and how Bright was the naughtiest calf we had ever had, how he ran ahead when we took the cows out to graze and how we feared we might lose him.

'I'll bring you a bell to put on him,' Wim would say. 'That should help. Have you checked Ellie's hoof? She might have a stone in it, up high between the toes.'

Marlie had woken that morning certain that Wim was on her way. It wasn't just the stone pile: she had seen it in the glow beetles that moved across the roof of the Overhang. She said you could tell the future with them – that they were better than stars. Early that morning she had seen a bright one twinkling overhead. I was half asleep when she'd nudged me.

'See it, Peat?'

It was still dark, almost dawn. I'd opened my eyes and looked up. A bright beetle was flashing every few seconds. The light was blue-green and it was moving towards the back wall.

'She'll be here today for sure.'

'That's what you said yesterday.'

Marlie's glow beetles weren't always right, and this flashing beetle was starting to fade.

'She will come this afternoon,' she'd said with complete certainty.

I hoped she'd been right. If Wim came in the afternoon she would stay the night and both of us would see her, but if she came in the morning she might be gone by the time I returned with the cattle.

I put my arm on Bella's neck and we walked along the road. The other cows followed, their calves trotting behind. The road ran along the base of the escarpment. There was grass growing beside it, not rich green feed for the cows, just spindly dry grass under a few stunted trees. Beyond that, there was scrub.

Bright was worse than usual this morning. He ran ahead and was soon out of sight. I didn't know how Bella had come to have a calf like him. She was steady and thoughtful, and if Bright was my favourite calf, she was my favourite cow.

'What are we to do with him?' I asked her.

She looked at me with huge calm eyes and gave a soft *moo* as if to say, 'Let him be – he'll come back.'

As we walked along I thought about the straws. I wasn't sure Marlie had been completely fair. She had rustled about in the half-light then shoved her fist in front of my face with two bits of straw poking out of it. One was long and wispy, like she was, and the other was short and strong. I liked it better when I had two the same size to choose from.

I'd studied the straws carefully. It seemed too obvious to pick the long one, but the short one could have been long as well. I decided I wouldn't be fooled and chose the short straw, plucking it out of Marlie's fist. It was as long as my finger. She laughed and opened her hand. The long straw went forever. The rest of it had been hidden up her sleeve.

So here I was. I decided not to go far today. If I stopped at the Boulders and let the cattle graze there, I'd be back in time to see Wim even if she came in the morning.

Our mother's grave was near the Boulders. It was just a circle of stones, and they were always getting knocked out of place. One of these days, I thought, I would build a fence around it to keep the cattle out; then I would plant things on it – rockrose and daisies. When we reached the Boulders I began straightening the stones.

Marlie said she talked to our mother every time she came this way. She told her how we were going and that our hearts were good and strong. Our mother had worried about our hearts because she'd been born with a hole in hers. It hadn't bothered her in Skerrick, but once she moved to the Overhang the hole got bigger and the cold winds blew through it in winter, Marlie said. Our mother started coughing, and she grew so weak that Wim had to come up and help with the work. Wim stayed and looked after us when our mother died, and she would have stayed forever but Alban Bane made her go back to Skerrick as soon as Marlie was old enough to take over. After that, our aunt had got the job of picking up the cheese.

I fixed up the circle of stones and then settled down in the shade of a boulder. Bella called out once or twice, and I heard Bright reply. It was getting hot, and there seemed no point in chasing him. He wouldn't go far. That's what I told myself anyway, but as the morning wore on I began to worry. I looked at the escarpment and considered climbing up a way to see how far he had gone, but it was steep and crumbling. At the Overhang the rock face was solid and there were plenty of handholds. You could climb as high as you dared.

'Come on, Bella,' I sighed. 'We'd better find him.'

I headed along the road with Bella and Little Shy. The other cows followed, their calves trailing along behind. I could hear Bright's bell, but it was growing fainter.

Wim said if you followed the road far enough you would eventually come to the Gap, which was a narrow break in the escarpment. It led to the Badlands and, in the old days, it used to be guarded to stop thieves coming in and stealing the cattle. She said whole herds had been driven through, and if you went out there you could still see their hoof prints: the ground that had once been mud was now stone and the hoof prints were there forever.

I had never been far along the road. It was overgrown, and there wasn't much feed out that way, but this was the direction Bright seemed to have taken. Soon we were pushing through saplings and small shrubs, and the ground became rough underfoot. I couldn't see if it was caused by potholes or the hoof prints of ancient cattle, because the undergrowth was too thick. I called Bright, but he didn't answer and soon I could no longer hear his bell at all.

It must have been past midday when the cows began behaving strangely. Bella moved out from under my arm and ran ahead, bellowing, and the others followed. Then she propped, and the group stopped dead behind her and stood staring.

Cows are curious creatures, and they are easily spooked, but I was more spooked than they were when I caught up and saw what they were looking at.

4

THE STRANGER

We'd reached the Gap. I couldn't believe we had come so far. It was only as wide as a cow, and the sides were sheer. Bright was standing in front of it. I would have liked to go nearer and look through, but someone was there – a stranger, a man with long fair hair and a bag slung over his shoulder. He was tall and thin, and he was scratching Bright behind the ear while the calf moved his head up and down and leaned against him. I had never seen Bright act in a way that wasn't wild before, but that wasn't what shocked me – it was the fact that someone was there at all. In the nine years of my life, I had never met anyone while I was out with the cattle.

'I thought he must belong to someone,' the stranger said. 'Where are you from?'

I gaped at him, too stunned to speak. He must have thought I didn't understand, because he repeated the question slowly. He spoke in the western tongue, a language Marlie and I knew because our mother had spoken it. Wim had told us it was long since banned in Skerrick, because it was the language of the Badlands.

I pointed back along the road, never taking my eyes off the man. He wore a long loose shirt made of some fine sort of cloth that seemed to change colour in the light.

'Is it far?' he asked.

I nodded.

He sat down next to Bright, still scratching his ear.

'Ah,' he sighed. 'I was hoping I was almost there.'

'Almost where?' I asked.

'Wherever the next place is.'

'The next place is Skerrick,' I told him.

'Is that where you live?'

I shook my head. 'Marlie and I live at the Overhang. We look after the cattle.'

The man was quiet for a moment. Then he asked, 'Which is closer – the Overhang or Skerrick?'

'The Overhang,' I replied.

'Well, I'll go there, then, if it's all right with you?'

I didn't know if it was all right or not. The only visitor we'd ever had was Wim.

The stranger stood up, leaning slightly on Bright. He had the clearest eyes I had ever seen and he wore a thread around his neck.

'Are you from the Badlands?'

The stranger threw back his head and laughed. It was a high, windy sound.

'Badlands? Where's that?'

I pointed towards the Gap and he laughed again.

'No. I'm a traveller,' he said. 'I come from lands a long way from here.'

He began walking down the road. The cows parted to let him through and Bright looked rather annoyed, as if he had expected the stranger would stay scratching him all day.

'Come on, Bright,' I said, taking hold of his ear.

Bright refused to move, so I got behind him and gave

him a push. It did no good. When Bright wasn't being wild, he was stubborn; Marlie said he was like me in that respect.

'Do you want some help?' the stranger called.

I pushed Bright again and this time he moved, but not in the right direction. He took off towards the Gap and probably would have gone straight through if the stranger hadn't whistled. Bright stopped immediately and looked over his shoulder.

'Come,' the stranger called.

I stared, amazed, as Bright trotted up to the man and rubbed his head on him. The stranger took a rope from his bag and held it out for me to take.

'Use this, or I'll have to be whistling and calling all the way.'

'He doesn't know how to lead,' I said when I'd caught up.

But Bright surprised me. He didn't object when I put the rope around his neck, and when I started walking he walked beside me – I didn't even have to pull him along.

'Do the cows belong to you?' the stranger asked, as we walked along the road.

'No. They belong to Alban Bane. Everything belongs to him – the cows, the cheese, the land, even the Overhang.'

'But you don't belong to him,' the stranger said.

I stopped in my tracks.

'What makes you say that?'

He shrugged. 'I'm new to this country, but to me you look much like the people in the land I have just left.'

I was shocked.

'I look like a robber or a cattle thief?'

The stranger smiled. 'Not everyone in your so-called Badlands is bad,' he said. 'They have the same colour hair as you do, only theirs is less wild. Maybe they comb it.'

'What's it like there?' I asked him.

'The cattle are bigger than yours.' He held up his hand to show me how high. 'And the corn grows taller than me.'

I gazed up at him to see if he was lying, but if he was his face showed no sign.

'How much milk do the cows give?' I asked.

'A full bucket each. Sometimes more.'

That couldn't be true. Our cows gave less than half that.

'It's a fine place,' the stranger said. 'But there's a sickness there. I had to pass through quickly.'

He fell silent after that, and he didn't speak again until we reached the Boulders. There, he paused and looked up, his eyes following the line of the escarpment.

'This place feels closed in,' he said. 'Is there nowhere to get a view?'

'There's a good view from the ledge above the Overhang,' I told him, although I wondered if he'd fit through the hole at the back of the night cave. 'From there you can see the road heading east towards the marshes. You can see Bane Valley and the path that leads to Skerrick.'

'I will go to Skerrick tomorrow,' he said. 'And find work.'

I told him I didn't think strangers were welcome there, especially if they spoke the western tongue.

'What's the next village after Skerrick?' he asked.

'There isn't one. The valley ends in a wall.'

'Ah, a blind valley!' The stranger scratched his chin. 'I've heard of such places. The wind blows up and meets itself coming back.'

It was late afternoon now, and the Boulders threw long shadows on the ground. 'Do you mind if we rest for a while?' he asked.

'I think we had better keep going. Marlie will be worried.'

'Who is Marlie?'

'My sister.'

The stranger gave a little sigh and continued walking. I asked him what work he did.

'I'm a journeyman. I can do anything – work with cattle, till the soil, grind grain, make bread. I can build and sew and work with metal and stone.'

There seemed no end of things that the stranger could do. I wanted to ask him all about these things, but he seemed to be short of breath so I held my tongue.

❧

By the time we reached the Overhang it was almost dark. A big pile of wood was heaped against the fence, which meant the glow beetles had been wrong – Wim hadn't arrived, and Marlie had spent the day collecting wood. I handed Bright's rope to the stranger and ran ahead.

Marlie stood and stared, gaping in the same way I had when I'd first seen him.

'Who is he?' she gasped.

'I don't know. A traveller. A journeyman.'

'You shouldn't have brought him here. We'll get into trouble.'

The stranger took the rope off Bright, who trotted straight into the night cave. The other calves followed. Marlie's mouth fell open.

'I can't believe it,' she said, as she shut the gate behind them.

By then the stranger was standing in front of the Overhang, leaning on Bella.

'Let me help you with that wood,' he said. 'I'll chop it and stack it.'

Then slowly he sank to the ground and sat with his head on his knees. I realised he was exhausted.

Marlie hesitated for a moment, then she went to the stranger.

'Help me take him inside, Peat.'

The stranger was tall but he wasn't heavy. With one of us on each side we half carried him into the Overhang, where we propped him up against our cooking bench. Marlie had made soup. He watched quietly as she poured it into bowls and seemed surprised when she offered him some.

'Most grateful,' he whispered.

'Where are you going?' Marlie asked.

'East, eventually,' he said. 'To the marshes and beyond.'

'Beyond!' Marlie was shocked, and I was too. 'There is no beyond,' she told him. 'The marshes go forever.'

'That's what you think,' he said. 'There is always a beyond.'

Then he laughed and, although he was weak, the sound echoed through the night cave and came back stronger than it had begun. We had never heard anything like that laughter before. It was a wonderful sound, high and wild, but it frightened me and I thought it frightened Marlie as well.

'Shhhh, you mustn't,' she said, looking over the wall as if she feared the sound might echo all the way down Bane Valley to Skerrick.

The stranger took no notice. He sipped his soup.

'Life's short,' he said. 'And the world is larger than you think. Come with me if you like.'

'We have to look after the cattle,' Marlie said.

'Tomorrow I will go to Skerrick.'

'Skerrick!' Again Marlie was shocked. 'No one has visited there for years.'

The stranger pulled himself up on the cooking bench and took a few unsteady steps forwards, then he saw our sleeping ledge and slumped onto it.

'Would you mind if I rest for a while until I get my strength back?'

He put his bag under his head and lay down, staring up at the glow beetles on the roof.

'This reminds me of Hub,' he sighed. 'The lights of Hub.'

Marlie and I stared at each other.

'Haven't you heard of Hub?' he asked.

We shook our heads.

'Hub is the centre of the world. From there you can go anywhere you want. A hundred roads lead out of Hub, and a hundred rivers too, and each river leads to the sea. The only problem is choosing which way to go.'

He laughed again, and then he started coughing. His eyes shone with a feverish light.

'Are you ill?' Marlie asked.

I was wondering the same thing. He was either ill or a bit mad, raving about the lights of a place called Hub.

'I'm just tired. I've come a long way, and I have a long way to go.' He closed his eyes. 'Like all of us,' he added.

Then he went to sleep, wheezing slightly.

'What should we do?' I asked Marlie.

She looked at the glow beetles.

'Nothing,' she said. 'We'll sleep by the fire tonight. Tomorrow he will head back the way he came.'

—◆—

As usual, the glow beetles were wrong. The stranger seemed better when he woke the next morning. He thanked us for our kindness, chopped and stacked the wood with surprising speed then left, taking the road to Skerrick.

As soon as he had gone I climbed up onto the ledge above the Overhang and watched. He walked with long easy strides, heading down the valley. At that rate it wouldn't take him long to get to Skerrick, less than four days.

It was one of those mornings when the sky was full of moving clouds. Bane Valley looked darker than usual and soon the stranger would be lost in the distance.

'Wait!' I called. 'What's your name?' But already he was out of earshot.

It had rained in the night, and when a flash of sunlight lit the road it looked like a silver thread. I wished I could wind it in and bring the stranger back. Why hadn't we asked him more questions while we'd had the chance?

'We should have invited him to stay,' I told Marlie when I came down.

She was milking Bella, and for once Bright wasn't bawling.

'Maybe we'll see him on his way back,' she remarked vaguely. She was staring into the bucket as if she was in a trance.

'Peat, look at this.'

The bucket was three-quarters full. Bella had never given that much milk before, even when the grass was plentiful, and yesterday she had spent more time walking than grazing.

I took my stool and placed it next to Pem. It was the same with her – the milk just kept coming.

＊

Wim arrived two days after the stranger had left. It was evening, and we both ran to her, eager to be the first to tell her our news.

'I know,' she said, before we could speak. 'I met him on the path. You shouldn't have shown him the way.'

She handed her pack to Marlie and put an arm around each of our shoulders.

'I tried to convince him to turn back, but he wouldn't listen. That poor young man.'

I hadn't thought of the stranger as a young man, but I supposed that to Wim everyone was young. Wim was quite old, older than our mother would have been – perhaps forty. Her boots were worn out with walking, and she looked worn out as well. I took her hand.

'He tamed Bright,' I told her. 'And the cows are giving more milk.'

'Well, that's something,' she said grimly. 'But I fear for him. He'll get no welcome in Skerrick.'

———

Wim always worried about us, but that night she seemed more worried than usual, and the next morning she lingered instead of leaving at first light. When Marlie took the cattle out to graze, Wim stayed and helped me with the work, straining the curds for the cheese while I cleaned out the night cave.

'When the stranger returns you're not to speak to him, Peat,' she said, as she was leaving. 'Just let him go on his way.' But she looked doubtful, as if she wasn't sure which way that could be. Perhaps she feared he wouldn't return.

———

Marlie and I kept an eye on the road, waiting for the stranger to come back. Whenever it was my sister's turn to take the cattle out she brought them back early, and I was up on the ledge looking out whenever I could.

When he didn't return, we began to wonder if we had dreamed him. In our minds he grew taller and his hair grew longer.

'What colour were his eyes?' Marlie asked. 'What did he have in his bag?'

I went over every word the stranger had said to make sure I hadn't forgotten anything from our conversation on the road, and when Marlie kept asking questions I began to make up the answers.

'His bag was full of treasures from the places he'd been.'

'Did you ask him where he came from?'

'He didn't come from anywhere. He's always been a traveller. He said his people were wandering people and he was born on a high mountain pass somewhere north of Hub.'

'Did he tell you that?'

I nodded. 'The air was so thin up there that his mother had to speak to him in whispers so as not to waste her breath. She told him the world was vast and full of wonders. She whispered that in his ear.'

'How could he remember if he was only a baby?'

'The stranger remembers everything,' I said.

Marlie was chopping up potatoes for our dinner. She put down her knife and stood up, gazing over the rock wall. 'I wonder if he'll remember us,' she sighed.

<hr>

We waited for ten days, although it seemed longer, then suddenly one morning the stranger was there on the path from Skerrick. I saw him from the ledge. His shirt was torn. He had lost his bag and he wasn't walking with the same easy strides he'd left with. When he reached the crossroads he stopped and waved, then he hesitated. I thought he was going to come and speak to us but he must have changed his mind because he waved again and the next moment he was gone, heading east, his light hair streaming behind him.

5

GLOW BEETLES

'What do they say?' I stared at the glow beetles on the roof.

'Today is the day.' Marlie lay beside me on our sleeping ledge, holding the cow charm that hung around her neck. 'You see that cluster to the south?' There was a cloud of twinkling beetles near the entrance to the Overhang. 'That means Wim will definitely come today.'

She sounded as if she was trying to convince herself.

It was ages since Wim's last visit. Two full moons had passed and our supplies had almost run out. We had a couple of handfuls of corn and a few slivers of dried meat left, and as well as the milk and cheese, we were eating whatever we could find – wild turnips and nettle, the odd mushroom that came up after rain. Most of the time it was enough, but this morning I had woken up hungry and cranky.

'She's never been this late before.'

'Don't keep going on about it,' Marlie snapped.

'Maybe she's sick,' I said. 'Or tired.'

We had always worried that one day Wim wouldn't come anymore. It was a long way from Skerrick to the Overhang and we were afraid the journey would get too hard for her.

'Maybe Alban Bane won't let her come.' I regretted speaking as soon as the words were out.

'Stop it,' Marlie cried. 'Of course he'll let her come. She has to get the cheese.'

It was getting light. I looked at the cheeses lined up on the shelf. Usually we only made three a week, but since the stranger had come we'd been making five or six. The cows had kept up their generous milk supply, and there were dozens of cheeses waiting for Wim to collect them. There were too many to fit on the shelf, so we had stored some in a box at the back of the night cave.

'She'll never carry them all,' I said.

'We could help her,' Marlie replied. 'We could help her carry them back.'

That was a foolish thought, but I didn't say anything.

'If something's happened to Wim they'll send someone else,' Marlie said.

The thought of someone other than Wim coming to collect the cheese made tears prick in my eyes. I knew Marlie felt the same way. I heard her sniffing.

'Are you crying?' I asked.

'No.' Marlie threw back the blanket. 'Come on. Get up. I'll take the cows out today.'

'Don't you want to draw straws?'

She shook her head. Her face had a sharp, pointed look.

'If Wim comes you'll miss her,' I said.

We milked in silence – the only sound was the calves moving about inside the night cave.

After a while, Marlie spoke. 'Maybe we should give up milking.'

'What?' I gasped. 'Why?'

'We're spending too much time milking and making

cheese when we should be out looking for food.'

'Wim would want us to keep milking,' I said. 'It's what we do.'

'I know it's what we do, but how long do we keep doing it? We could milk one cow instead of all six.'

'Wim will come. She'll probably come today.'

But Wim didn't come that day, or the day after. Both of us became frayed and short-tempered. Another week went by, then one morning we woke and found the flashing glow beetle was back on the roof – the same one we'd seen the day the stranger arrived. I thought Marlie would be pleased, but she wasn't.

'It's a bad sign,' she said. 'Wim's not coming. Not today, not ever.' She turned to me in the dark. 'I wish you never brought that stranger here. It's something to do with him. I know it. It's your fault.'

'How can it be my fault?'

'Didn't the stranger say you looked like the people of the Badlands? Perhaps your father is from there. Maybe you're half bad.' Marlie had started to cry.

'I'm not half bad,' I said. 'It's not my fault!'

I took the cattle out past the Boulders. I had a sick feeling in my stomach. Maybe it was hunger, or maybe it was because of the fight with Marlie. Bella stayed close to me. I could tell she didn't like what Marlie had said; when I sat down to rest she came and breathed on my face.

'I won't go home to the Overhang,' I told her.

There is a blue-black shadow in every cow's eyes and

I felt Bella was offering me hers. It was deeper than the night cave. I wished I could hide in it. I started to cry.

'It's all right, Bella,' I said. 'Everything will be all right when Wim comes.'

⟶

I didn't go home that night until long after dark. Marlie was waiting by the fire.

'I saved you some soup,' she said. 'I was worried that you weren't coming back.'

I sat down and ate, not even bothering to shut the calves in the night cave.

'Wim will come soon,' Marlie said gently. 'Not just to collect the cheese but to collect us as well.'

'Do you really believe that?'

She didn't answer. Instead she came and hugged me.

'I'm sorry, Peat. I didn't mean what I said this morning.'

Marlie had always been thin, but now I could feel her bones.

'You're getting skinny, Marlie.'

'You too,' she said.

My sister was six years older than me, but that night she seemed younger. When we climbed onto the sleeping ledge she snuggled close to me.

'Tell me the story, Peat – the old story.'

I knew which one she meant. It was a story she'd used to tell me when I was smaller; then I'd taken it over and changed it and she hadn't liked it anymore.

'Where do you want me to start?' I asked.

'The feast. The meal they prepare to welcome the girls back.'

'It was meat,' I said. 'Goat's meat. It was roasting in the fire pit.'

'What else?'

'There were corncakes with honey, and nuts that were part of the hoard they found hidden under the floorboards of Alban Bane's hut.'

'What happened to him?' Marlie asked. 'Did he die?'

Sometimes I killed Alban Bane. I had him fall from the steephead while he was looking for birds' nests, or I let him stumble into a sinkhole at night. I didn't really care what happened to him in the story, or in real life, but Marlie cared because he was her father.

'Give him a change of heart,' she said. This was her favourite ending.

'Alban realised his mistake.' I spoke quietly. 'He should never have sent the girls away. He wasn't angry anymore, and all the badness in him turned to good. He helped cook the feast, and he said there should be singing and dancing.'

'And the flowers?' Marlie asked. 'Tell me the bit about the flowers.'

'The girls wore flowers in their hair – yellow orchids that grew out near the Gap, and bunches of violets plaited together.'

Marlie knew as well as I did that no orchids grew anywhere near the escarpment, and that even if they did the cows would trample them. Violets were something Wim had told us about but we'd never seen.

'And did the girls dance all night?'

'All night,' I replied.

I heard Marlie sigh with satisfaction. Then her breathing grew steady, and in a few minutes she was asleep.

I lay awake staring at the roof of the Overhang. The flashing glow beetle was still there. I knew glow beetles probably signalled to each other and not to people – but that blue-green light seemed to be flashing right at me, sending a warning.

6

THE ESCARPMENT

Later that night one of the cows started bellowing.
I wasn't asleep; I was still staring at the roof of the Overhang, although the glow beetle I had been watching was
gone. The cattle were usually quiet in the evening. I sat
up and looked out over the wall. There was a light at the
crossroads.

'Marlie, someone's coming.'

I jumped down from the sleeping ledge as my sister
struggled to wake up. The cattle were tramping around
outside in the yard, and the light was getting closer. Then
I heard a voice calling in the dark.

'It's all right. It's me.'

'Wim! I knew you'd come.' Marlie sat up so quickly
she hit her head on the roof. 'I was telling Peat—'

'Shhh!'

Wim put her lamp on top of the wall and climbed over.
She was pale and breathless, and she was carrying the
stranger's bag instead of her pack full of supplies.

'What's happened, Wim? Why are you here now, in the
night?'

Wim didn't speak at first. She sat down next to our
cooking fire and stared into the coals. I was about to
throw some wood on when she caught my hand.

'No, Peat. Listen to me. That stranger . . . he was carrying

30

a disease. People in Skerrick are ill and Alban is blaming you.'

'What?' Marlie cried. 'That's not fair. It's not Peat's fault!'

'We saw him,' I told Wim. 'His shirt was torn.'

'I tried to warn him.' Wim spoke in a hurried whisper. 'He knocked on Alban Bane's door and asked for work. Alban wanted to know where he came from, and when the stranger pointed to the west Alban flew into a rage and called him a thief and a bandit. *Do you think I have work for the likes of you?* he cried. *In the old days your people stole our cattle, and now you'll steal anything you can get your hands on. How did you find your way here?*

'When the stranger mentioned you Alban knocked him down, then he rang the bell so that everyone came running. The stranger wasn't strong, but he was quick and clever. He got up and ran, and he was lucky to get away, to escape with his life.'

Wim took both my hands.

'And you must do the same, Peat,' she said. 'I came as soon as I could. Alban forbid me, and had me watched. Marlie, help me pack this bag. I managed to grab it when I snuck away. Get whatever supplies you have left.'

'We've run out.' Marlie's voice was trembling.

Wim took her lamp to the back of the Overhang and quickly gathered a few things – a knife, a cup and a blanket.

'There's bread in the bag,' she said. 'I didn't have time to get anything else.'

She scooped a cup full of milk from the bucket by the cooking bench and handed it to me.

'Drink this. You must leave immediately.'

'But where will she go?' Marlie cried.

'West, through the Gap.'

'The stranger went east,' I said.

Wim paused. 'The poor fool.' She put her finger to her lips. 'Shhh. We have to be quick.' She wrapped a cheese in cloth and put it in the bag, then she turned to Marlie, holding the top open. 'What else?' she asked.

Marlie looked completely bewildered. She cast her eye around the Overhang and, finding nothing, put her hand to her neck and took off the cow charm.

'Take this, Peat.' She put it over my head.

Outside, the cattle grew more restless. Two or three cows were bellowing now, and we could hear them rushing about in the yard. Wim blew out the lamp.

'They're coming,' she breathed. 'I tried to get here sooner.'

<hr>

After that, things happened quickly. There was a shout and the cattle were running. I heard them break through the fence, and then their hoofs were pounding on the road and my heart began to pound as well.

'Go. Go now!' Wim slipped the bag over my shoulder and pushed me towards the stone wall; then we both stopped, because there were lights beyond the yard – lanterns, flickering a short distance from the Overhang. They were coming closer, and they seemed to be coming from all directions. We heard voices, an argument.

'That brat should never have been born. Look what she's brought on us.'

'Leave her, Alban. She's just a child.'

'She might be a child, but she's trouble. She knew what she was doing.'

'How could she have known? Let her go.'

'Let her go? Three people have died already. A dozen are ill. We could all catch the disease and you say let her go! She caused this and she'll pay for it.'

'It's true,' a third voice joined in. 'She sent him to us as revenge.'

'Revenge for what?' came the second voice.

'Her mother's death,' the first voice snapped.

'Alban, you're not well. You're delirious…'

The voices went on, but I stopped listening. Marlie took my hand and pulled me to the back of the Overhang.

'The night cave!' she whispered, as we slipped through the open gate.

It was pitch dark inside, but I could see light coming from the hole at the back of the cave. I couldn't remember climbing through it – sometimes you move faster than thought. Suddenly I was out on the ledge, looking back down at Marlie.

'Block it off,' she whispered. 'Block off the hole so they can't see the light from in here!'

I took the blanket from the bag and began stuffing it in the hole. The last thing I saw was Marlie's face, looking up at me.

'Go well, Peat,' she said.

Then I heard Wim shouting into the darkness. 'She's gone. The child is gone, Alban. You're too late.'

'If we don't find her I'll take the other one instead!' the man yelled back.

'No, you won't!' Wim cried.

I crawled across the ledge on my belly and looked down. Below me were half-a-dozen lanterns, and there were more in a long line coming up the road from Skerrick.

'Out of my way!' A voice echoed in the Overhang. I heard a bucket being knocked over and a *clang* as our cooking pot hit the back wall.

'Leave our things alone!' Marlie cried.

There were footsteps in the night cave. I held my breath.

'Why aren't the calves locked in? You'll get no milk if the calves are with the cows.'

Then the voice was outside again, giving orders.

'Find her! She'll have gone towards the Gap. I want her back here by morning, and find the cattle as well.'

Some of the lights began moving along the road, heading west.

'Make a fire,' the man shouted. 'A big one.'

I could hear branches breaking as the people helped themselves to our woodheap. It was dark on the ledge, but if they built up a fire I would be seen. I looked up at the escarpment towering above me. It reared into the sky like a dark wave; I couldn't see the top. Without thinking, I began to climb, feeling my way, finding handholds. The blood thudded in my ears.

When I reached a crevice in the rock, I lodged myself there and adjusted the weight of the stranger's bag. I didn't dare look down. A slight wind blew, pressing me into the rock wall, and when I started climbing again the updraft seemed to help me.

Soon I was high above the ledge. The smell of smoke faded, and there was nothing in my mind except where to put my hands and feet. I had always been strong. The soles of my feet were tough, and my toes gripped the rock like fingers.

I was dimly aware of the moon rising and hoped I was high enough to be out of sight. From below I was probably no more than a speck on the escarpment, a tiny insect crawling on the face of the rock. As I moved up, I had the strange feeling that I was climbing out of my past and into my future.

Eventually the way was blocked by a jutting outcrop of rock. I paused and looked down. The fire was a red circle far below. I closed my eyes and took a deep breath, then I began moving east across the cliff face, with the idea of getting far enough away from the Overhang by morning to climb back down to the road. I couldn't go west because Alban Bane had sent his people that way.

———✦———

All night I climbed across the escarpment. At last I found a crack in the rock wide enough to wedge myself into and stopped to rest. My arms and legs were shaking. The wind whistled past, and I was suddenly cold. Somehow a small tree had taken root in the crevice, its trunk just as thick as my arm. I reached into the stranger's bag. The rope was there; the same rope I had used on Bright. I tied one end around the tree and the other around my waist, then I squeezed myself further back, away from the drop. There was a blanket in the bag as well, not a rough felt blanket like the one I'd left in the hole in the back of the night cave, but a light sort of rug. I wrapped it around myself.

The moon had moved across the sky. Soon it would be

dawn. In my exhaustion, I thought I heard the stranger's voice on the wind. I tried to make out the words, but they weren't in any language I understood. I pulled the rug close and closed my eyes. In my mind, I was following the stranger through the world. I wore a thread around my neck like his, and the wind blew the tangles out of my hair so that it flowed out behind me like his did. It was evening and we were in high mountain country. In the distance I could see lights. He bounded ahead of me, and when we reached the top of a rise we were suddenly looking down on Hub, with all its roads and rivers leading in a hundred directions.

I must have fallen asleep for a while. I stirred, and became aware that the wind had dropped. In the silence, I could hear water trickling somewhere in a crevice behind me. I opened my eyes and put my hand to my neck. The stranger's thread wasn't there but Marlie's cow charm was. I hoped it was lucky, because the sun was high in the sky and a huge drop yawned beneath me.

THE SLEEK

The view from high up on the escarpment was breath-taking. I had never seen so far before, or even dreamed that so much country existed. I could see the steephead where Bane Valley ended, and mountains beyond it. In the east I could make out the marshes. They were grey-green and they stretched away into the distance.

I felt light-headed with the vastness of it all, and a bit giddy; then, without warning, I was sick. I held onto the tree and leaned out so as not to get it on the blanket. The road was far below. It was the same road that went past the Overhang, but it looked different here – it was narrow and grassy. The sight of it made me dizzy. I leaned back into the crack between the rocks and closed my eyes, my throat burning and my mouth tasting foul.

There was no wind this morning, and the only sound was trickling water. I discovered a gap in the rocks behind me, wide enough to poke my head right into. It was dark inside, and had a musty smell, but the water sounded close and I wanted to wash my mouth out, so I got the cup out of my bag and reached my arm in. The gap wasn't big enough to put my head in as well as my arm, so I couldn't see what I was doing.

I felt something swipe me. Oh, did it sting! I lurched back and would have fallen if it hadn't have been for the stranger's rope, which held me as I dangled over the cliff edge.

I scrambled back to safety and looked at my arm. There was a fine trail of blood from my elbow to my wrist.

Cautiously, I peered into the hole again. For a moment two small bright eyes met mine. There was a chittering sound, then all was quiet. I tore a strip off the blanket and wrapped up my arm before reaching into the hole again. The creature spat, but if it tried to scratch me again I couldn't feel it. The cup hit rock. I held it the right way up and heard water running into it.

'That's all I want, little one,' I whispered as I pulled my arm out.

I drank the water. When I looked into the hole again, I saw a fierce little face. The animal opened his mouth and showed me a set of tiny teeth before backing away. His tail came into sight: a red plume tipped with white. I heard him spit at me again, then chomping sounds came from within. On the floor of the cave I could see a scattering of fine white bones. I would have liked some more water, but I decided I wasn't game to put my arm in again.

I looked at the road below. There didn't seem to be an easy way down to it. Cling-vine was growing out of the rock face, but I doubted it was strong enough to take my weight. I decided I needed to eat before I tried to make my descent.

As soon as I took out the bread, something shot past my shoulder and leapt into the tree. A face peered down at me through the leaves: a sharp, narrow face fringed with reddish fur. The eyes were bright and mean. If the creature sprang at me now I could fall. I broke off a small piece of bread and threw it, and he caught it in midair.

'There, we're even,' I whispered. 'Bread for water. Now go away.'

I put half the bread back in the bag and began eating the rest. The creature ate too, then moved closer, wanting more.

'I need this. I have a long way to go.'

He blinked and held my gaze. His eyes were grey-green, like the marshes.

'I have to eat. I have to get down from here,' I told him, as I threw him another piece of bread.

The creature caught it, then he ate slowly, looking deep into my eyes.

'What are you?' I asked. He wasn't like any animal I had seen near the Overhang. He wasn't a rabbit or a fox.

'You're small and sleek,' I said. 'And you are not to be trusted. I'll call you a sleek.'

The creature blinked and closed his eyes as if satisfied, then suddenly he sprang, snatching the remaining bread out of my hands and disappearing down the rock face. I held onto the tree and leaned out over the drop, but I couldn't see where he'd gone.

I cut myself a hunk of cheese and had another drink, then I undid the rope, packed it away with the blanket and began the climb down.

The cling-vine was stronger than I'd expected, so I used it to lower myself a little way at a time until my feet found a narrow ledge, then I paused for a moment before carefully lowering myself further.

Suddenly I heard a high-pitched cheeping sound from above. I looked up and saw the sleek – then I heard the same sound below; he was now crouched on a rock beneath me, and his fur was standing on end. I hadn't see him move – he'd simply disappeared from above and appeared below – so I wasn't sure if he was actually the same creature or another one.

When I continued lowering myself towards him he shrieked in alarm, so I froze. I tried to find a foothold and realised there was nothing beneath me.

'Thank you, little sleek,' I gasped, as I pulled myself back up to the ledge.

The sleek went quiet and stayed where he was. His fur settled. I climbed along the wall and began coming down a different way.

Luckily I had always been a good climber. I'd found the hole in the night cave and climbed up onto my ledge at the Overhang before I was old enough to walk. Marlie had always been scared I would fall – so scared that in the end she'd put a rope on me and kept me tethered to the cow-yard fence when she was busy.

I adjusted the weight of the bag on my back and decided to only look as far down as the next foothold. I was glad the face of the escarpment was solid here and not the crumbling rock I had seen out near the Gap that day I'd met the stranger.

Eventually I found a long groove in the rock wall and squeezed into it; then, bracing myself with my hands and feet, I made my way down the groove like a person coming down a chimney.

The sun was low in the sky by the time I reached the bottom. I was surprised to find the sleek waiting for me. He looked friendlier than he had on the escarpment. He was no bigger than a cat, but he was finer. His ears were pointy and his fur shone in the last rays of the sun.

When I sat down on the ground, he sat down, too.

'You saved my life up there, Sleek.'

He looked so soft and silky that I thought I might touch him, but when I reached out he spat and scratched me just as he had done in the hole. Then he turned and skittered away. I saw the white tip of his tail disappear into the long grass. I tore off another piece of blanket, and after I had bandaged my hand, I slung the bag over my shoulder and began walking along the road.

After a while the road left the escarpment and wound through trees and open fields. The ground was soft and springy underfoot, nothing like the hard ground near the Overhang and the road that led to the Gap. There weren't many stones about, and those I saw were covered in moss. Lichen grew on the tree trunks and some sort of feathery vine trailed from the lower branches into long grass.

Not good cattle country, I thought. *Plenty of feed, but their hoofs would rot in this wet ground.*

I decided to stop and have a proper look inside the bag before the sun went down. The stranger had travelled light. Apart from the rope and blanket and the things Wim had added, there was only a wooden bowl and a spare shirt, like the one he had been wearing.

I took out the bread. Immediately there was a rustling in the grass nearby and the sleek appeared, his eyes fixed on the food. I held out a small piece. He snatched it from my hand and gobbled it; then he watched me suspiciously, waiting for more.

'That's all for you,' I said. 'I've got to make this last.'

When I took out the cheese, the sleek didn't wait for me to eat it in front of him. He sprang at me, as he had on the escarpment, snatching the whole cheese from my hands. He was tremendously strong: the cheese was nearly as big as him, and he was gone with it in an instant, disappearing into the grass.

'You're not getting away with this!' I cried and ran after him.

The sleek might have been strong, but the cheese was heavy and hard to hold in his mouth. After a while he slowed down, and when he did I lurched towards him and grabbed it. He darted away, then he stopped, staring back at me defiantly.

I put the cheese in the bag. 'Shoo, Sleek! Go away!'

He flattened his ears, stood up on his hind legs with his nose in the air and made a clicking noise – the same sound that Marlie sometimes made when she disapproved of whatever I was doing.

I clapped my hands and the sleek dropped onto all fours and ran off, heading, it seemed, for the road. I was still cross with him, but when he paused and looked over his shoulder I followed. It wasn't like I had any other company.

The sleek moved easily in front of me, weaving in and out of the long grass. As we walked, the grass became taller. Soon it was almost too tall to push through. I was about to turn around when I fell forward into what looked to be a large nest. It was made of sticks and reeds and lined with soft grass.

By now it was getting dark, so there seemed no point in going any further. I turned my back on the sleek and ate out of the bag, biting off chunks of cheese and gulping them down. Then I took out the blanket and, putting the bag under me so the sleek couldn't steal the rest of the food, I lay down inside the nest. I was exhausted from the climb and from my escape the night before. I put my hands behind my head and watched the moon rising, the same moon I had seen from the escarpment. That seemed ages ago.

I wondered about Wim and Marlie and hoped Alban Bane had gone home by now. It would be terrible if he and his gang were camped outside the Overhang waiting for me, and worse if he took Marlie back with him. Poor Marlie. One way or another, I had always brought her trouble. I put my hand on the cow charm and tried to remember the last thing she had said to me. *Go well, Peat.* Tears stung my eyes and my throat felt tight. I thought about the cows. Who would look after them if Marlie was taken?

The sleek watched me with lazy eyes from a small distance, his head between his paws.

'I don't know what's going to happen, Sleek, but I know one thing for sure – I can't ever go back to the Overhang.'

He yawned and closed his eyes. After a while he curled up and went to sleep.

Things could be worse, I told myself. *At least I'm alive.*

It was true: I was alive and safe; I had food in my bag, Marlie's cow charm around my neck, and a companion, if not a friend, in the sleek.

The only problem was that I was heading for the marshes.

8

THE GREEN ROAD

The next morning the sleek led me through tall grass until we found the road. It was green and narrow and so overgrown in places that it was barely there. It was the sort of road you could see better with your eyes half closed than open. It wound in and out of trees and shrubs, sometimes looping back on itself. Occasionally I caught a glimpse of the escarpment through the greenery, but it was far away. Birds twittered above, and the bushes on either side of me were full of small rustlings. At each sound the sleek hissed and spat.

'Are you always this angry?' I asked.

The sleek stopped and glared at me as if he could understand what I said.

'No harm meant,' I muttered. 'Let's go.'

He didn't move. His red tail flared and seemed to grow brighter.

'Look, I didn't mean anything…'

I tried to step past him and suddenly he sprang, sinking his teeth into my leg. He was only small, but the weight of him and the shock of his attack knocked me over. I clutched my leg with both hands and tried not to cry. When I looked up the sleek was sitting in the middle of the path grooming his tail, which had settled back to normal size.

I lifted my hands and examined the bite. The tooth marks were deep. Blood ran down onto my foot, and my whole leg was hurting even though the wound was just below the knee. I found the strip of blanket I had used to protect my arm earlier when I'd reached into the hole and bound my lower leg with it. The sleek watched me from the corner of his eye with a bored expression, then he turned and continued along the path. I limped along behind for some time, until I decided to eat the last of the food. When I stopped the sleek did, too. He sat on his haunches and sniffed the air, his ears twitching, then he put his head between his paws, his eyes on the bag.

I suppose he'll want half, I thought.

The moment I opened the bag, the sleek sprang. He took the last of my bread and was gone.

'Good riddance!' I yelled.

There was nothing to do but continue on alone. The path grew spongy underfoot, and it passed by a series of small ponds. Sometimes it skirted the water and other times it went straight through. The undergrowth on either side was thick, and the water in each pond seemed deeper than the last. By mid-morning I was wet and hungry and miserable. My leg-bandage was muddy and bits of weed were caught in the hem of my dress. I wished Marlie was here. However hard my life had been at the Overhang, I'd always had my sister by my side.

When the path disappeared into a large pool, I decided to try to find a way around rather than wading through, because the water looked as if it would be over my head. I put down the bag and followed a vague animal track that soon petered out. When I came back, something had been through my possessions. The blanket was half pulled out, the cup lay on the path and the cheese was gone.

'Sleek, you wretched creature!'

I slumped on the ground and looked at the water in despair. A nose broke the surface: the sleek was swimming towards me with my rope in his mouth! He dropped it at my feet, backed away and waited. I pulled the rope. It was snagged on something. When I pulled harder, what seemed to be a piece of the bank broke free. I hauled it towards me and found it was a nest, like the one I had slept in the night before. *If only I had a paddle I could use it as a boat*, I thought.

I picked up my things and tested it with my foot before carefully stepping in. The nest pulled away from the shore. The sleek had the rope in his mouth and he was towing me. His strength surprised me.

'Good little sleek!' I said when we reached the other side. He dropped the rope and spat at me, then he dived back into the water.

Soon he reappeared with something in his mouth. He placed a long green tuber at my feet and stared, as if daring me to pick it up. It looked like a long potato, and when I nibbled one end I found it was crunchy and sweet. After I had finished it, he turned and ran up the path.

I didn't trust the sleek. He had helped me down the escarpment, but he had also scratched and bitten me. He had given me food, but only after he had stolen what I had. Still, I decided to follow him until I worked out whether he was a friend or an enemy. It was better to have a companion than to have nobody at all.

In the late afternoon he left the path. A mist came down

and it started to rain. The sleek went a short way, then he stood aside to let me pass and I walked ahead. I had not gone far when a little hut appeared before me through the soft rain. It stood on stilts and was made of woven reeds. From a distance it looked flimsy, and as I drew closer it looked even more flimsy. I had never seen a building like that before. It had a ladder made of twigs that were only as thick as my little finger. I was sure they would snap as soon as I put my foot on them, but I gave it a try and they didn't. The ladder creaked as I climbed up. A hessian bag hung over the doorway, and when I pulled it aside I could see a fishing net, a woven mat and a bed made of bundled reeds. Everything had a greenish tinge. I thought at first that it was mould, but when I touched the floor I found it was actually a fine layer of dust, green dust. No one had been there for a long time, and the hut had taken on the colour of the marshy country around it.

The sleek didn't follow me up the ladder. He turned and disappeared into the mist. I crawled inside the hut, sat on the bed and looked out.

At the Overhang Marlie and I had liked misty days like this. We couldn't take the cattle out in case we lost one, so we would light the fire and sit by it, and Marlie would sing the songs she'd learned from our mother. They were old songs, and although the tunes were sad, the words were happy.

I put the stranger's blanket around my shoulders and hummed to myself.

If the sleek doesn't come back, I won't care, I thought. *I could stay here forever. Maybe I could catch fish and dive for the long green tubers.*

But the sleek returned at dusk. He had something in his mouth: the pale shoots of a plant. Each one was the size of your finger. He dropped them on the mat and watched me eat. The shoots were delicious – sweet and crunchy, like the tubers.

'Thank you, Sleek,' I said.

He disappeared down the ladder and didn't return until dark. This time it wasn't wild food he was carrying but some sort of cake with seeds in it.

'So it's not just me you steal from?' I muttered. It gave me a strange feeling to think there were other people around; I hoped they weren't like the people of Skerrick.

The sleek looked at me out of the corner of his eye, then he curled up and went to sleep.

9

AMOS LAST

The mist continued for days, so I stayed in the stilt hut. I was glad we weren't moving because my leg had swollen up from the sleek bite and it hurt every time I put my foot down.

The sleek came and went, bringing me food: more cake, an apple, a piece of cooked meat. I was beginning to think Marlie's cow charm really was lucky – I would stay here and the sleek would look after me.

On the third day, however, the mist lifted and the sleek grew restless. He spat at me and looked at the ladder. When I refused to pack my bag he crouched against the reed wall of the hut with his tail spreading behind him. I watched it change colour from reddish-brown to a deep crimson before I picked up my things.

This time the sleek did not lead the way. Instead he kept a distance behind me, as if making sure I wouldn't double back to the stilt hut, which was exactly what I wanted to do. I found a path and limped along it. My leg hurt with each step and I wanted to rest, but the sleek wouldn't let me – he drove me on, nipping at my heels whenever I slowed down, and when the path joined up with the road his nipping got worse.

I was almost in tears when I came around a corner and found the roadway blocked by a donkey cart. Startled, the donkey leapt forward and lost half his load, which was made up of long green tubers like the one the sleek had given me.

'Halt, Bray!'

A man appeared from the undergrowth. I backed away. He was covered in mud and his arms were full of tubers. He was tall – almost as tall as the stranger. His grey hair was close-cropped and he had a thick black beard.

'How many times do I have to tell you? Steadfastness in the face of adversity,' he said. The donkey put down his head and started grazing.

The man turned to me. 'Not your fault,' he said. 'He's always been flighty. It's the breed. But you can help me pick these up. Would you mind?'

I shook my head. As I put down my bag I noticed the sleek sliding away into long grass.

'Would you be a Morrow or an Ebb?' the man asked. 'You have the look of an Ebb, but seeing as you are here, lost, you must be a Morrow. So careless, those Morrows. You're the second child of theirs I've picked up this season.'

'I'm not either,' I said.

The man looked at me in surprise, then he gave a crafty smile.

'You're a Morrow if ever there was one. Do you know how I know?'

He didn't wait for a reply.

'Because all Morrows lie!' He roared with laughter, and the donkey joined in. 'See? Even Bray likes your joke!'

Although I hadn't made a joke, I laughed as well. I was so glad to find a kind and friendly person.

'Had your lunch?' The man reached into a basket at the front of the little cart and pulled out some cake just like the sleek had brought me. 'You'll be wanting a ride, I expect? Well, I can't be taking you home until after the Third Mist. No point in setting out unless there's a chance of reaching the destination, eh, Bray?'

The donkey raised its head.

'So, to be on the safe side, you should stay with us until all the mists are done.'

'How many mists are there?' I asked.

The man looked startled for a moment, then he wagged his finger in front of his face as if he'd been caught out. 'Now that's a Morrow question if ever I heard one. Everyone this side of the marshes knows there are three mists.'

'What about the other side of the marshes?' I asked.

The man laughed so much that he had to put his hand on the cart to steady himself.

'There *is* no other side of the marshes,' he cried, wiping his eyes. 'Hop in!'

As I climbed into the cart, among the strange vegetables, I saw a flash of red. The man glanced over his shoulder. 'Just you, not your vermin,' he said.

'He's not mine.'

'Of course he's not yours. But you are his,' the man sighed. 'That's the way it is with them.'

For some reason I thought it best to own up about the stolen cake, so I told him that I'd already had some of his food.

'What the vermin does is no fault of yours.'

The man clicked his tongue and the donkey began

walking very slowly along the road. The man walked beside the cart. He had a slight limp.

'What did you think of the First Mist?' he asked conversationally.

'I liked it. It made me feel safe.'

The man laughed as if I had made another joke.

'I always enjoy the First Mist,' he said. 'But not the second. What's your name?'

'Peat.'

'A grand name! It's rich and deep and will keep you warm all winter. My name is Last, Amos Last.'

The man had a peculiar way of talking, but I liked him. Wim had told me she'd heard there were people who lived on the edge of the marshes. She thought they spoke a different language. Amos Last's words were the same as ours but his accent was different. His voice went high and low, and there was a softness to it, as if the mist and rain had seeped in and taken away the hard edges.

We had not gone far when the road straightened and a rise appeared ahead. The donkey stopped.

'My apologies, Bray.'

Amos motioned for me to step out of the cart. When I was on the ground, the donkey began walking again.

'That's our Bray for you. He's not one for hauling people up hills.'

We walked along in silence for a while. I leaned on the cart so as to take the weight off my leg.

'Finest Bray. Most handsome of donkeys.' Amos gave me a wink. 'Here you are, walking ahead on four strong legs, and we're coming behind with only two good ones between us.'

The donkey paused and flicked his ears, then he began walking again.

'But that's the way of the world, eh, Bray?' Amos Last said cheerfully. When the donkey snorted, he added, 'Nothing to forgive, my friend.' He turned to me. 'It's his nature. It's in the breed.'

I wondered if the sleek was following, or if he had gone back to his hole in the escarpment. For a moment I thought I would miss him.

'Did a stranger pass this way?' I asked.

'And when would that have been?' Amos chuckled.

'About two full moons ago.'

Amos Last smiled and scratched his chin. 'Can't say I saw him. One of the children might have. You can ask them.'

'Children?'

For some reason the thought alarmed me; I had never met any children before.

'I had a dozen or so at last count,' Amos said. 'It's hard to keep track of them. Gilly would be about your age, or was it Ula?'

We reached the top of the rise. The road stretched ahead, with wild grass on one side and neat fields on the other. In the distance it turned sharply to the right and went up a steep hill. Perched near the top I could see a small wooden shack.

'That's our place. The end of the road.' Amos Last sighed, and his shoulders slumped. His good humour seemed to have left him at the sight of the shack.

When we reached the spot where the road turned, he unhitched the donkey. 'Thank you, Bray,' he said. He turned to me. 'Bray doesn't like hills, and he doesn't like my wife,' he explained.

A cross-looking woman appeared outside the shack. 'No. Absolutely not!' she yelled. 'We've got enough mouths to feed.'

Amos Last looked up the hill. 'It's only until after the mists,' he called.

'One night,' his wife yelled back. 'And no more. If the Morrows can't look after their own, why should we?'

Then she clapped her hands and a big group of muddy children came out of the shack and ran down the hill. There were so many of them it seemed like an avalanche. How could they have all fitted inside the hut?

I quickly stepped behind the cart, and this made them laugh.

'Not yet,' they cried. 'First, let's get this lot up.'

They loaded each other with the tubers, and they loaded me up as well.

'Come on,' they said. 'We'll play later.'

I wondered what they meant by 'play'. Marlie and I had only ever worked. There was no opportunity to find out. When we reached the shack, Amos Last's wife was waiting outside.

'Pay up,' she said. 'What have you got?'

Her eyes were fixed on my cow charm, but I wasn't going to give her that. I had nothing else except the things in the bag. I took out the stranger's shirt and she snatched it.

'Go and wash your face and hands, you dirty Morrow!'

'I'm not a Morrow,' I said.

The woman glared at me.

'You're an Ebb?' she demanded.

I shook my head.

'Well, you're not a Last,' she said. 'And there are only three families in this district – the Ebbs, the Morrows and the Lasts.' She put her hands on her hips.

'I'm not from this district. I'm from Skerrick.' It seemed easier to say that than try to explain about the Overhang.

'Never heard of it!'

An old woman with bright-blue eyes poked her head from the door of the shack. 'I've heard of it,' she said.

Amos Last's wife regarded me shrewdly. 'You can stay tonight and go back to where you came from tomorrow.'

'I'm not going back,' I said. 'I'm going on.'

'You little fool,' she said. 'There's nowhere to go. We are the Lasts, and this is the end of the road. Beyond us there are only the marshes.'

She grabbed my hand and pulled me further up the hill, past the hut. The pain in my leg made me cry out.

'Don't play your foreigner tricks on me,' she snapped as she turned me around. 'Look out there! If you go *on*, that's where you'll end up. All the muck of the world drains into those marshes.'

I looked where she pointed. The marshes were vast. They began with lowlands of trees, grasses and ponds. Further away I could see fields of reeds and then a complicated maze of islands and waterways that seemed to move as I watched, although perhaps it was just the reflection of clouds in the water. Islands seemed to join up, then separate. It was mesmerising. In the distance, the land seemed to fray off into the sky.

'Is that the coast?' I asked.

'There is no coast. There are only the marshes.'

'There must be ocean somewhere,' I said.

'If you believe there is anything beyond the marshes, you're dreaming,' the woman sneered. Then she turned and went down into the shack, slamming the door behind her.

10

THE LAST CHILDREN

As soon as their mother was gone, the Last children ran up to me. They were full of questions.

'What happened to your leg? How did you get here?'

'Did you come down the river?' a girl about my size asked.

'How could she come down the river? She's got no craft,' someone else said. 'How old are you? Where did you say you were from?'

A tall boy fingered my cow charm. 'What's this for?' he asked. 'It looks like two horns.'

'It's for luck and making wishes. It belongs to my sister, and I'm going to give it back to her one day.' A lump formed in my throat.

The boy closed his eyes. 'Make Ma happy,' he said. 'And let Bray go up hills!'

Everyone laughed. 'Does it work?' they wanted to know.

I nodded, blinking back my tears.

'Of course it works,' the tall boy declared. 'If you hadn't found Pa and Bray, you could have wandered into the marshes. You're not from here, so you wouldn't have known.'

'Known what?'

'About the swamp hags.' He lowered his voice. 'They

take children. They lure them into the marshes.'

'Don't scare her, Bryn.' An older girl stepped in front of the boy. 'My name's Hennie,' she told me. 'Don't listen to him.'

'I'm not scaring her, Hen. I'm probably saving her life,' Bryn said quietly. 'We'll show her later, when it's dark.'

I would have liked to hear more about the marshes, but Amos Last's wife yelled that it was dinnertime.

Amos sat at the head of a rough-hewn table and the grandmother sat at the other end. A small fire burned in the fireplace. There wasn't much food for a big family: a few oatcakes, some cheese and a pile of tubers. My stomach rumbled. I had only eaten one oatcake since the sleek and I left the stilt hut that morning.

When I reached for the cheese, a forked stick came down over my hand and stayed there, pinning me to the table.

Amos's wife glared at me. 'Wait!' she yelled, then she nodded to her husband and he began mumbling into his beard.

'Preserve us from mud, pestilence, illness, accident, swamp hags, muck and bad mists,' he said. 'Deliver us from leaf-rot, bindweed, marsh fly, swamp fever and the treacherous bog.'

'If it wasn't for bindweed, you wouldn't be here,' the grandmother interrupted.

'Not now, Mother,' Amos muttered.

'No, it's true,' the old woman continued. 'If one of those ladies hadn't bound your bones up with it, they would never have knitted.'

Bryn was sitting next to me. He leaned close and whispered in my ear. 'Bray kicked Pa and broke his bones. But he's all right now.'

'Save us from vermin, swamp waifs and vapours,' Amos continued. He didn't look as if he enjoyed saying the words. 'Protect us from bogwort and the green fog. For that is the Lore.'

'For that is the Lore,' everyone repeated.

'*Now* you can eat.' Amos's wife released my hand and everyone tucked in. I was shocked at how ravenous they were. They grabbed the food and gulped it down without chewing.

'Bog in quick, or you'll miss out,' Hennie said to me.

Amos Last's wife was worse than any of them. She snatched a tuber out of the old grandmother's hand and shoved it in her own mouth.

I had never seen people eat so fast, but I supposed the only people I had eaten with were Marlie and Wim and we hadn't had to race each other.

———

When the food was gone and the meal was over, the Last children took me up to the top of the hill. It was dark so they walked slowly. I was glad about that, because my leg was worse than ever. It felt hot and tight and it was throbbing. When we reached the top Bryn stared into the night.

'Sometimes it takes a while to see them,' he said.

'See what?'

I looked where he was looking. There were lights far

away in the marshes, very faint and blurry. Perhaps they were shining through mist.

'Are they the swamp hags' houses?' I asked.

He shook his head.

Hennie took my hand. 'They are waif lights,' she whispered. 'Watch them. They move.'

The lights did seem to be wavering.

'Are there people out there carrying torches?' I asked.

'Those lights are the souls of lost children,' Bryn said. 'They were probably Morrows.'

I gasped. 'You mean the swamp hags killed them?'

'Killed them and made medicine out of them,' came the solemn reply. 'Every night you can see the lights of those poor children. They wandered out into the marshes. They thought they heard voices; someone calling them. And they heard drifts of song on the breeze.'

'And they saw flowers,' said one of the younger girls. 'Beautiful flowers that glowed in the dark. Flowers that had such a lovely perfume the children wanted to pick some and take them home.'

'But the flowers were always just a little bit ahead of them.' Hennie leaned close to me. 'And every time they reached out to pluck one, it disappeared.'

'So they got caught, you see,' Bryn said. 'And now they are trying to get back to solid ground, but it's too late.'

There and then, I decided I would not go anywhere near the marshes. But I would also not go back to the Overhang.

'Have you ever heard of a place called Hub?' I asked.

'Everyone's heard of Hub,' they replied. 'It's the centre of the world.'

'I want to go there,' I said.

'You're too young to go to Hub,' Bryn answered. 'You should stay here with us.'

'Yes, stay with us.' A little girl with a round face took my hand.

'Your mother wouldn't let me.'

The children sighed. They knew they were too many for their mother already.

'The only way to Hub is by river,' Bryn said. 'You'd have to go back to the river and follow it upstream.'

'I didn't see a river.'

'It's like that,' he said. 'Hard to find. Some days it's there and some days it's not, depending on the fog.'

'You would need a craft,' one of his sisters said.

'Where do I get one?' I asked.

'They are hard to find, like the river. They look like nests but really they are reed-boats.'

'But I have found two already!' I exclaimed.

Hennie raised her eyebrows. 'Really?'

'Are you sure you're not a Morrow and telling lies?' Bryn asked, and everyone laughed. 'Grandmother has only found two in all the years of her life. Pa has found one, and Ma has never even seen one.'

'I definitely found them. I slept in one and I went across a pond in the other.'

A clanging noise came from the hut. It sounded like someone bashing a tin drum.

'That's Ma,' one of the younger boys told me. 'It means it's bedtime.'

Amos Last and his wife slept in a back room. The grand-mother and all the children slept under the table. When I lay down at the end of the row next to Hennie, she put her arm around me the way Marlie had sometimes used to.

I felt better about continuing my journey. I knew exactly where the last reed-boat was. All I needed to do was follow the green road back the way I had come and I would find it. Then, if I could find the river, I would be on my way to Hub.

11

THE SECOND MIST

The next morning the Second Mist arrived. It wasn't like
the mist I had experienced in the stilt hut. It was thick and
white and cold as ice. You could see it pouring under the
door and rising up to the roof.

'It's come early.' Amos Last's wife looked at me accusingly. She turned to her husband. 'See what happens? You
open the door to strangers and invite in the disasters of
the world.'

Amos Last put a small knot of wood on the fire.

'That's right, burn all my wood!' his wife shouted.
'And who's going to chop more?'

The mist filled the shack. Soon I could hardly see my
hand in front of my face.

'What do you do in a mist like this?' I shivered.

'Sleep,' one of the children murmured.

There seemed nothing else to do but lie down and drift
back to sleep.

That morning, in Amos Last's shack, I had a wonderful
dream. I was in a reed-boat paddling up a river. Giant
cows grazed on either side and corn as tall as people
waved gently in the breeze. The sleek was curled up on
my lap, purring like a cat.

The river was slow and wide. I rounded a corner and came across a town built into a steep hillside. Hundreds of steps led to the houses, and bright gardens grew on the roofs of all the buildings. There were trees everywhere, and baskets full of flowering plants hung from their branches. Beyond the houses I could see terraces, where rows of peas were climbing over frames made of birch sticks. The scent of their purple flowers filled the air. Birds sang in the trees and I could hear the sound of a waterfall cascading somewhere in the distance. I saw the stranger sitting on the riverbank, and he waved and called people to the water's edge to greet me. They knew my name and said they had been expecting me.

'This will be my new home. I will work here,' I said. 'I will look after your cattle.'

'Of course,' the people replied. 'But first, tell us your story.' They sat down on the riverbank and waited for me to speak.

I would like to have heard what I said in the dream, but at that moment I was woken up by Amos Last's wife.

'Out!' she cried. 'I said *one* night. You're not staying here till the end of the mists. They could last for weeks.'

'Don't send her away, Ma,' I heard Bryn's voice say.

Some of the younger children whimpered, perhaps in their sleep.

I felt for my bag, and Amos Last guided me to the door.

'I'm sorry,' he said, once we were outside. He put some-thing in my bag and tied a rope around my wrist. 'Come.'

I felt a little tug and began walking behind him. I couldn't see him but I knew he was just ahead. We went uphill. With each step the pain shot up my leg. After we had walked some distance I heard sobbing.

'What's that? Who's crying?' I asked.

'The mist,' he replied.

The sobbing grew louder. It was all around us. Amos had to shout over the noise. 'Take no notice. It always does this.'

'Why is it crying?' I called out to him.

'Who knows?' he yelled in reply. 'Sometimes it sobs, sometimes it laughs, but whatever mood it's in, it will chill you to the bone. Put your hands over your ears.'

We went over the hill and down the other side. Soon we were climbing again. Amos walked in silence. The sobbing quietened, then it stopped and I could just hear his footsteps. The mist muffled all sounds and I couldn't see a thing. It was the sort of mist in which you could disappear and cease to exist. I suddenly needed to hear the sound of my own voice.

'Amos Last, I had a marvellous dream,' I shouted.

'People often do,' he answered. 'The mist is known for its dreams. But they are unreliable. Once, during the Second Mist, I dreamed my wife had a loving heart.'

I thought I heard him laughing but I wasn't sure. We kept walking uphill. I was cold and damp and the bag was heavy. When Amos Last stopped, I ran into him.

'Here it is,' he yelled. 'Drip Cave. Mind your head.'

Drip Cave was dry, and the mist wasn't as thick inside as out. Amos undid the rope. I could see his shape as he moved about and made a fire.

'Don't let it go out,' he said. 'Hopefully there will be enough wood to last you. If you do use it up, don't go outside looking for more.'

He shook my hand. 'There's food in your bag. Stay here. I will come back and get you when the mist ends. Try not to sleep too much. The Second Mist can be dangerous. You can go to sleep and not wake up.'

'Will you be able to find your way back home?' I asked.

'Most likely.' He didn't seem pleased at the idea.

I opened my bag and found he had put bread and oatcakes in there, along with a thick sheet of something sweet and leathery.

'Thank you, Amos Last,' I called as he left me, but my voice was swallowed by the mist.

12

DRIP CAVE

I sat down and watched the fire. The mist gave it a halo, which filled the cave with an eerie sort of light. It was only a little fire but it crackled bravely. I wanted to build it up. There was a small stack of logs at the back of the cave, along with some brushwood. I wished I had asked Amos how long the Second Mist might last. *He must come up here to get away from his wife*, I thought as I put a log on the fire.

To make the food last, I decided I would only eat a small amount at the end of each day. But it was hard to know day from night: I wrapped myself in the stranger's blanket and waited for it to get dark, but nothing changed. From time to time I went to the cave entrance and looked out. All I saw was white. The Second Mist seemed to have its own light, and the first day went on and on.

Finally I ate some oatcakes and lay down. There was no sound except water dripping. I dozed, careful not to sleep for too long. Part of me hoped I might dream again of the city with its beautiful gardens, but I had no more dreams. The white mist seemed to seep into my mind, and just as it was hard to know whether it was day or night, I could barely tell whether I was awake or asleep.

The water dripped and the fire burned low. Like a sleep-walker, I got up now and then and put more wood on. I was afraid the fire might go out; if it did, I had no way of lighting it again.

The mist seemed to get thicker. I could feel the weight of it pressing on my chest. Soon I had only one log left.

'You'll be all right, Peat.' I spoke aloud to myself, but my voice seemed to come from far away. The sound of the dripping grew muffled.

I felt in the bag for more food and found a little pouch of something soft. It didn't feel like food. I sniffed it. Tobacco! Did Amos Last think I smoked? I put it in my pocket, then I ate more oatcakes and half the sweet leathery stuff. It must have been dried fruit, or perhaps it was made from the tubers. I lay down again, holding the cow charm.

'Oh Marlie, Marlie, Marlie,' I whispered. I kept saying my sister's name to stop other thoughts coming into my mind – thoughts about how my life could run out along with the wood and the food.

I thought of Alban Bane and the mob. Wim would have to go with them when they went back to Skerrick. I hoped they hadn't taken Marlie. Poor Marlie. How could she live at the Overhang all by herself? Maybe she would try to follow me – but she had to mind the cattle. If nobody looked after them they would run wild and Bright would get into trouble – he'd fall down a hole, or get himself caught in the thorn bushes that grew at the foot of the escarpment. There'd be nothing that Bella could do to save him. I wished Bella was with me now. She could lie down next to me, and I could lean on her the way

Bright did. I longed for her warmth and her dark eyes.

I drifted into a dreamless sleep, and I might have kept on sleeping if I hadn't heard a voice in my head, the stranger's voice.

Wake up! it said. *Get up. Move!* I wasn't sure what language the words were in, but I understood them perfectly.

I sat up with a start. The fire was almost out. I put the last piece of wood on and realised I would have to go outside and find more. I knew that Amos Last had advised me not to, but what else could I do? I tied one end of the rope to my bag and the other end to my wrist, then I went to the entrance. Before I went out, I ate the last of the food.

Something had happened to the mist outside Drip Cave. It was so thick I could barely push my way through it. I crawled along the ground and found a couple of bits of wet wood. The weight of the mist made breathing difficult, and I was soon soaked to the skin. I quickly followed the rope back into the cave.

When I put the wood on the fire it smouldered and the smoke stung my eyes. I thought that I should have tried to get more wood earlier, before the fire got low. Then I could have dried my clothes and whatever wood I found.

'Too late now,' I muttered.

Never too late, came the voice of the stranger. So I stumbled outside again and found a few sticks. The fire did its best, but there were hardly any embers, and finally it sighed and went out. There was nothing I could do. My teeth chattered, and soon I was shivering all over. The only warm part of me was my leg, which was still throbbing. I lay down under my blanket and tried to fill my mind with warm thoughts: Marlie and me by the fire in the Overhang, the warm breath of the cows, sun shining on the corn that grew on the riverbanks in my dream. The thoughts didn't help. Soon I was so cold I couldn't think. Then the shivering stopped and I didn't feel anything anymore.

I lay facedown and tried to stay awake, and if the stranger spoke to me I didn't hear. The only sound was my own breath, and it was rough and noisy. *I don't usually breathe like that*, I thought vaguely, then I realised the breath wasn't mine. Something was in the cave, some animal. I felt it sniff the back of my neck, and I should have been afraid, but I was too drowsy to care. What did it matter if a wolf or some wild creature got me? I didn't have the energy to fight. A little whimper came out of me, a kind of sigh like the fire had made before it went out, then something stepped lightly onto my back. I heard a rattling sound and felt warmth. It slowly spread through my body, and I felt as if I was coming back to life. I tried to sit up, and when I moved the rattling sound stopped. Something spat at me. The sleek!

He hissed and leapt away, disappearing from the cave. I looked up and found the mist had lifted. Drip Cave was light and clear, and a ray of sunlight was falling on the floor at the entranceway. Stray drifts of mist were floating through it, evaporating as I watched.

I got to my feet and staggered towards the entrance, peering out. There was still mist in the valley below, a great white sea of it, swirling in on itself. It was receding like the tide going out, and one by one treetops were appearing. Birds began singing, loud and clear.

There was a path leading downhill. *To Amos Last's place*, I thought as the sleek appeared on it, running towards me with a tuber in his mouth.

'Thank you, Sleek. Thank you,' I sighed as I gobbled it down. 'You're a true friend. And thank you, Marlie.'

I reached for the cow charm, but it wasn't there. The leather thong it was attached to must have broken!

In a panic I searched the floor of the cave on my hands and knees, but I couldn't see it. Perhaps I had lost it when I went outside to get wood. I had to find it – the charm had kept me safe this far. I got to my feet, feeling slightly dizzy.

Then I heard a little clinking sound and the sleek dashed past me out of the cave, dragging the cow charm with him. He stopped not far from the entrance. I was weak and couldn't move very fast. When I was in reach of him and the charm, he ran off again. I followed, leaving my bag and blanket in Drip Cave.

'Thief!' I cried, as I stumbled down the hill after him.

The sleek didn't take the path. He scampered under the trees then crisscrossed his way down the steep slope, keeping a short distance ahead of me.

When we got to the bottom, the ground was wet underfoot. I stopped and looked back up the hill, but I couldn't see which way we had come. There was no sign of the Last house.

The sleek stopped, too, and stared at me with shining eyes, as if he was daring me to come closer. I studied him warily. He had saved me with his warmth, but I was not going to follow him into the marshes – not after what the Last children had said. Still, I wanted Marlie's charm. The sleek trotted on, casually, as if he didn't care one way or the other.

Then the charm got snagged on a bush. I saw my chance and grabbed it.

'Got it!'

I tied a knot in the leather thong and put the cow charm back around my neck. The sleek watched me with a blank expression on his sharp little face.

I turned around, trying to decide whether it was worth trying to go back to Drip Cave for my things or whether I should just find the road and follow it back to the reed-boat.

But it was too late to do either – not because it was getting dark, but because the Third Mist had arrived.

13

THE GREEN MIST

How to describe the Third Mist? It wasn't like either of the mists before it. Long wisps settled like scarves over the low trees and shrubs nearby, then bits of it drifted towards me. It was green and seemed to be full of whispers. I caught snatches of conversation.

'...listen...she's just a gossip...'

'...and that messy old shag's nest...disgraceful...'

The sleek flicked his ears as if he was trying to get the whispers out of them. I crouched down and listened.

'...it's just a rumour...'

'...she was jealous...'

Then the mist began whispering recipes.

'Three parts bog water, one part swamp weed and one part bone meal...'

'Swamp hags!' I gasped. I clutched my hands to my chest and tried to calm myself. Maybe I was hearing things. I was weak from my time in Drip Cave. I may even have caught the sickness the stranger was carrying.

'Add a drizzle of bogwort...' said the mist.

'Not bogwort. Bogwort is a recipe for disaster...'

The mist seemed to be arguing with itself. I looked up. The hill had disappeared into green.

'...no fool like an old fool...' the mist whispered. Then it began laughing, a strange wispy sound.

'Shhh, stay in the shallows…' it sighed.

The words made no sense.

'I'm getting out of here,' I told the sleek. I staggered back the way we had come – or the way I thought we had come. My leg was paining badly. The sleek followed me with his ears down. The gleam had left his eye and he had a hunched, frightened look. When the voices returned, he cringed.

'…she's a cheat…it's become a mud-slinging match…'

'…last time I was beaten by a whisper…'

The green mist only lasted long enough for me to get truly lost. By late afternoon it had cleared and the only sounds were frogs, honking waterbirds and the occasional splash of a jumping fish. There was no path to follow and there were no hills in sight.

Ahead were the burnt-out remains of a stilt hut. The ladder was gone and most of the walls had fallen away. A bird with black feathers was nesting inside the framework. It stretched its long neck and made a low croaking sound when I approached, then it flew up onto the roof and watched me pass with bright-green eyes.

The ground underfoot was boggy, and every step was difficult.

'I blame you, Sleek,' I muttered.

I tried to take notice of the direction of the sun. It would set in the west, and I knew I should be travelling that way, back towards solid ground. I faced the sun and limped on through the marsh. My shadow trailed behind me, long and wavering. It felt like something heavy, dragging me back.

'I have to find somewhere dry to sleep,' I told the sleek. 'If I could find a tree with a low fork I could sleep in that.'

The only trees in sight were on what looked like a small island, although it was hard to tell land from water. Everything was a shade of green.

Suddenly the sleek raced ahead and dived in. He swam to the island and scrambled up the bank, turning to face me as if expecting me to follow.

'That's all very well, Sleek. It might be dry over there, but what's the point if I have to swim?' My clothes were still damp from the white mist. I didn't want to get drenched.

The sleek moved further along the bank, then he stepped out onto the water and walked towards me. He arrived some distance ahead, and I discovered he had used a narrow walkway that was just under the surface. It was made of twigs. I stepped onto it with caution, but it took my weight.

The island was surprisingly dry. It even had a little path leading up into the trees.

Things were looking up. 'Thank you, Marlie,' I said and touched the cow charm.

Suddenly a rope pulled tight around my ankle, and in a second the world was upside down. Something popped inside my leg. I screamed, and the sleek did, too.

My feet were in the sky and my head was facing the marshes. I struggled to look up and saw there was a noose around my foot – I was hanging from a tree, caught in a snare. A fiery pain tore through my leg. It was excruciating. The charm fell over my head and landed on the ground with a *plop*.

The noose looked as though it was made of sinew rather than rope. *Probably part of some lost child*, I thought. *A Morrow.*

The sleek stared up at me as if waiting for directions.

'There's nothing to be done,' I wailed. 'Go. Get away.'

He scampered back down the path and dived into the water.

I swung from the tree. The blood was pulsing in my head, and the pain in my leg settled into a deep ache that spread through all of me. Would the swamp hags come for me today, or in the morning, or would I be left hanging for days? I wondered what sort of medicine they would make out of me.

I waited for it to get dark. *Let the hags come sooner rather than later*, I thought, and the tears ran down my forehead into my hair.

I must have fainted, because the sleek woke me with a clicking sound. He was on the ground below me and he had a very long tuber in his mouth. He stood on his hind legs and reached up. He was trying to feed me, but I was too high above him.

'Bad luck, Sleek,' I cried. 'It's no use. Just go. Go back to wherever you came from.'

My tears dripped onto the sleek. He shook himself and sat down. He ate the tuber with a wet crunching sound, then he curled up and went to sleep. When the moon rose and shone on his reddish coat he looked like a small fire burning beneath me.

I hung upside down as the stars moved over the sky. My leg went numb. When I heard a voice I thought I was dreaming – either that, or the green mist had returned.

'Lily? You can't fool me. Own up and I'll let you down.'

A light was moving across the water. I heard panting and the slosh of heavy footsteps on the walkway.

'Lily!' the voice insisted.

Someone was moving towards me – a strange lumpy-shaped figure that seemed to have things growing from it. I smelled smoke and fish and herbs.

'This'll teach you to come snooping around...'

It was a woman's voice. As she came closer I saw that the light came from a burning branch she held. The sleek shrieked and fanned out his red tail.

'Scat!' she yelled, throwing a handful of mud at him.

The sleek ran off, and the burning branch came closer. I closed my eyes rather than look into the face of a swamp hag.

14

THE SWAMP HAG

'It's not Lily,' she cried. 'Damn! Hold this.'

The swamp hag thrust the flaming torch into my hands and disappeared out of the light. Then – 'Ow! Ow! Ow!' – I was lowered to the ground in a series of painful jerks.

'Surely you're not a Morrow,' she said. 'Even a Morrow would not be foolish enough to wander into the marshes. You're lucky you got caught in my snare. If you hadn't, you would have been lost.'

She took back the torch and peered into my face. 'Swamp waif,' she decided. 'Not a Morrow. One green eye and one brown. You're of mixed breed.'

The swamp hag loosened the rope around my ankle and squatted beside me to examine my leg. 'Infected puncture wound,' she gasped. 'The snare didn't do this. Well, not all of it. Razor-vine? Snide bite? Or perhaps you were staked?' She put both hands around my foot and gave my leg a short, sharp tug. I screamed as the pain shot threw my body.

'Sorry,' she said. 'It had to be done. Your leg's broken, and if I don't straighten it the bones won't knit. Hold this.'

Again she handed me the torch. I watched her out of the corner of my eye. The lumpy shape of her was actually a garment – a shaggy old coat. It was full of bulging pockets. Bunches of leaves sprouted from several places, and a vine was growing from under her collar. A bundle of sticks poked out of one sleeve.

'Now, what have I got on me?' she asked, patting herself up and down. 'It's hard to remember where I put things.' She opened the coat, revealing more pockets on the inside. 'Bindweed must be freshly harvested. I don't carry it. But bogwort will help with the pain.' She pulled out a handful of something and pressed it to my leg.

Bogwort! I thought.

'Yes, yes, yes,' she replied. 'A recipe for disaster.'

I hadn't spoken aloud.

'Take no notice of things you hear,' she muttered. 'This place is full of lies and whispers.' She took the torch out of my hands. 'The wound really needs a swamp-balm poultice. Isn't it always the way, how the very thing you need is the one you haven't got?'

I wondered why she was bothering to patch me up when I was going to be killed.

'Of course, they'll all want a piece of you once we get back to the huts,' she said. 'But you're mine. I found you. You were caught in my trap, so it's up to me whether I share you or not.'

I shuddered and closed my eyes. I might as well have stayed at the Overhang to meet my fate, rather than come all this way only to be taken by swamp hags.

'How dare you call us that!' The woman grabbed my wrist. 'I've a good mind to let you wander off into the Far Reaches. We're marsh aunties, not swamp hags and my name is Eadie!'

She was silent for a while. When she spoke again she had calmed down. 'I suppose you're delirious, poor little sod.'

The marsh auntie sat down heavily on the ground beside me. 'What's this?' she asked, picking up my cow charm.

'That's mine.'

'Ah, so you speak aloud as well as to yourself.' She held up the charm. 'A cow herder. Where are you from, girl?'

'Skerrick.'

'Can't say it rings a bell. Now *this* is more interesting!'

Eadie held up the tobacco pouch. It must have fallen out of my pocket when I was hanging upside down. 'You've come from Amos Last!' she declared.

She passed me the charm and pulled a long curly pipe from somewhere inside her coat. She began stuffing it with the tobacco.

'He's all right, Amos,' she said. 'He could be a mud uncle if he tried. But he's under the thumb of that wife of his. Do you know she has lived on the edge of the marshes all her life and she's never seen a skiff?'

I wasn't listening, because I was staring at her pipe. It was made of bone! A thigh bone or an arm bone.

'Yes, it's a humerus,' she said. 'Do you know what a humerus is?'

I shook my head.

'It's the name of the bone. Funny, don't you think?'

I didn't think it was funny at all.

'This bit is the humerus,' she said, pointing to the stem of the pipe, 'and the rest is made of pipe clay. Myriad makes them. She makes pots as well. You'll meet her at the Welcoming.'

She lit the pipe with the torch, sucked on it and blew a thin trail of smoke into my face.

'Imagine never seeing a skiff in all your life. They're

scattered around like seed pods. They're everywhere you look. And when it rains and the tracks flood, they all float inland on the tide. That Last woman is thick as a ditch.'

Eadie sucked on her pipe again and blew out three little boat-shaped puffs of smoke, which sailed into the night.

'How are you feeling?' she asked.

'My leg is tingling under the bogwort, and it's not hurting me now.'

'We'll need a splint to get you home, then tomorrow I'll collect the bindweed. It's marvellous for bone-setting.'

She puffed on her pipe and leaned back. 'Just listen to those frogs,' she remarked. 'All talking at once, and saying the same word over and over. Doesn't it drive you mad?'

She seemed to be waiting for a reply. I was trying to think of one when the air was pierced by a scream.

The marsh auntie put down her pipe and stood up. 'That'll be Lily. It serves her right. Stay here. I can't deal with you at the moment. I've got bigger fish to fry.'

She lumbered away with the torch, leaving me in darkness. I heard her feet squelching in the swampy ground then some branches breaking as she crashed through the undergrowth. If I was going to make a run for it, now was the time.

I got onto my hands and knees and struggled to my feet. My leg didn't hurt, but it immediately gave way under me. I crawled towards the water, thinking it might be easier to swim rather than cross the walkway. Getting wet was now the least of my worries. I could hear the marsh auntie shouting.

'I should leave you hanging there. It's what you deserve.'

'I wasn't snooping,' a shrill voice replied. 'I came here to practise, just like you.'

'That's a filthy lie, Lily, and you know it. The marshes are endless and you choose the same island as me? Do you expect me to believe that?'

'Believe what you like. Just let me down. The blood is running to my head and ruining my complexion.'

'Let it run to your head. It might feed your brain!'

I reached the water and was about to crawl in when something flapped overhead. There was a deep honking sound, then wings brushed my face. It was the bird I had seen earlier. And its claws were grabbing at my hair!

'Get out!' I screamed, waving my hands about my head to fight it off.

The bird circled then dived for me again. Eadie hurried back, clapping her hands.

'Beat it,' she yelled. 'Shoo! Shoo!'

The bird flew off with a plaintive cry.

'It won't hurt you,' she said. 'It's just after hair for its nest. Now listen...' She put her face close to mine. 'I told you to stay put. You'll undo all the good I've done. Do you understand?'

Her eyes were very dark and I could smell fish on her.

I nodded. Anything to get her away from me.

'You don't understand at all. If you wander into the marshes you will get lost and die. Is that clear?'

I'm going to die anyway, I thought.

'Yes,' she agreed. 'But not yet.'

'Let me down!' cried the voice of Lily in the distance.

'Anyway, it's your decision. If you wander off and die you'll have no one to blame but yourself.' She stood up and sighed. 'Waifs! They can be so difficult at times!'

Eadie headed back up the path and I heard snatches of the conversation that followed.

'...scarf...torn silk...ruined...' The shrill voice was lower now, and Eadie was no longer shouting.

'...teach you a lesson,' she said. '...swamp waif...'

'Swamp waif?' Lily's voice went up. 'Show me at once!' she screeched.

15

LILY

'This is my sister, Lily,' Eadie said gruffly.

The second marsh auntie was tall and thin and she was wearing layers of some fine fabric that shimmered as she moved.

'It's called glimmerweb,' she said. 'Divine, isn't it?'

Her face was pale, and her long fair hair hung to the ground in tendrils. I couldn't help thinking how unalike the two sisters were.

'That's because we're not from the same family,' Eadie muttered.

Lily knelt down beside me. 'Call me Lil,' she said with a wink. 'What's your name, sweetie?'

'Peat.'

'Can you spell it?'

'Of course she can't spell it,' Eadie snapped. 'She's only just arrived in the marsh.'

'P-e-a-t,' I said.

Lily laughed, a high tingling sound. 'No, *spell* it,' she said. 'Look, I'll show you how. My name is Lily. Watch me.'

She put her hands together as if she was saying a prayer. Then she closed her eyes and slowly opened her fingers. For a moment I thought I saw a pale lily opening from a bud. Then she clapped her hands, giving herself a little round of applause.

'You see? Now it's your turn.'

I was suddenly very tired. I hadn't eaten for ages, my leg was broken and I had been in fear of my life for too long. If they were going to kill me, I just wanted them to get it over and done with. I didn't have the energy for this game.

'We need to find something to make a splint with,' said Eadie.

'Splint? Why?' Lily had a breathy way of speaking. Everything about her was light.

'Because the swamp waif is injured and we can't stay here all night.'

Lily came closer and looked at me. I could smell some sweet fragrance on her – so sweet that I took a deep breath.

'Like it?' she whispered. 'I call it Essence of Limelight.'

She turned to Eadie. 'You've broken the poor waif's leg. See how dangerous your snares are? That could have been *me*.'

'It was *meant* to be you. Come on. Help me find some splint wood.'

Eadie headed back along the bank and Lily followed, holding her garments up and stepping carefully.

'I'll take the swamp waif,' Lily said. 'She'll be my apprentice. I'll teach her to make perfume.'

'She's mine. I found her and I'm having her.'

'We'll ask the Great Aunt,' Lily said airily. 'She can decide.'

I heard a branch snap in the dark, and before long the two of them returned. Eadie had split a small tree bough in half. She bound my leg between the two flat sides of the wood.

'Go and get a skiff, Lily,' she said. 'Make yourself useful.'

Lily stepped delicately across the surface of the water. She was on the same walkway the sleek had used.

'And be quick about it,' Eadie barked. 'The swamp waif is getting cold.'

'I'm not a swamp waif,' I said.

'Of course you're a swamp waif. All children who wander into the marshes are swamp waifs. But most aren't as lucky as you. Most aren't found. Swamp waifs grow up to become marsh aunties. But not all marsh aunties were swamp waifs.'

I closed my eyes, tired of all this talk I couldn't understand.

Lily came back with a reed-boat. She and Eadie had just lifted me into it when the honking bird returned. This time it went for Lily. When it clutched a clawful of her hair she squealed and quickly pulled a tiny bottle from the shimmering folds of her dress. While the bird was still pulling her hair, she unscrewed the lid and held it up. The bird immediately let go. Its eyelids drooped and it flapped to the bottom of the boat and sat there with its head under its wing.

Eadie snatched the bottle. 'What's that?' she demanded.

'Swoon,' Lily replied. 'It's from my latest collection. Like it?'

Eadie took a sniff. 'It stinks.' She handed it back and began paddling vigorously. 'And what's more, it doesn't work!'

'I'm still perfecting it.' Lily slipped the bottle into her dress. 'So far it only works on creatures.' She turned to me. 'When you are my apprentice, Peat, I'll show you how to make magical perfumes. Would you like that?'

'No, she wouldn't. I told you, she's *mine*.'

'We'll ask Hazel,' Lily sighed, running her hands over her head. 'I wish I had a mirror. I'm all messed up.'

She studied one long lock of hair. 'Really, Eadie. That wretched bird of yours has broken some of my finest strands.'

'It's not *my* bird,' Eadie said sharply. 'Start paddling.'

Lily began stroking the surface of the water with a paddle, pausing from time to time to gaze at the patterns she was making.

'Moonshine?' she wondered. 'Or perhaps Swirl. It's hard to know what I'll call my next perfume. What do you think, Peat?'

I didn't answer. The motion of the boat was making me drowsy.

'Can't you see the waif is exhausted?' Eadie cried. 'Leave her alone.'

I closed my eyes and went to sleep to the sound of the marsh aunties arguing.

16

EADIE

I woke up inside a stilt hut exactly like the one where the sleek and I had stayed, except this was lived in. It was crammed full of shelves and bottles. Bundles of herbs hung from the ceiling, and jars of coloured liquids were stacked against the walls. There was a little stove with a pile of sticks on one side of it and a low table on the other. A jar of everlasting daisies was wedged into a hole in the table.

The hut had a musty smell. An old hessian bag hung over the doorway, and when I heard a splash I wriggled across the floor and looked out.

Eadie was sitting on a small walkway below, cleaning fish and throwing the guts into the water, where they were immediately taken by the shag. He dived for them then flapped up onto a post at the end of the walkway, stretching his beak skywards as he gulped them down.

'Don't move,' Eadie said, without looking at me. 'You're meant to be keeping that leg completely still. I'll be up in a minute.'

The hut swayed as she climbed the ladder. She slapped two fish down onto the floor and stood up, wiping her hands on her coat, a knife between her teeth. She reached behind the stove and pulled out a chopping board, then she spat out the knife and chopped the fish into thick chunks, throwing them into a pot. One bit missed and landed under the table.

How messy the hut is, I thought.

'It's not a hut, it's a hide,' said Eadie.

And what is she hiding from?

'The other aunties,' she replied, as if I had asked the question out loud. 'They'll all want you, but you're mine.'

Suddenly the hut, or hide, tilted to one side and righted itself again. A couple of jars slid off the shelf. Eadie caught one of them. The other smashed to the floor.

'That's Healbane! Do you know how hard that is to find?' She glared at me as if it was my fault, then she stirred the pot with a stick. The smell of the cooking made my stomach growl.

I noticed that my leg had been bound up. The splint was gone, and in its place was some sort of mud pack wrapped around with long green tubing.

'I had to go out early to gather the bindweed stems. You have caused me a lot of trouble. Are you hungry?' she asked. 'Here's your breakfast.'

Eadie handed me a steaming bowl and I took it eagerly.

'Fish soup and wild marsh rice flavoured with duck-weed and charmwort,' she said. 'Duckweed will help heal your snide bite, and charmwort will be good for the break.'

The soup was delicious. I'd never tasted anything like it. Marlie and I had made soup in the Overhang but it wasn't delicious like this. Eadie refilled my bowl, and it was only when I had finished my third helping that I looked at her properly.

Her coat was huge and lumpy and sprouting all sorts

of greenery. It was made of fur or fleece, and there were bulging pockets all over it. The surface of it was slightly glossy in places, as if it had been slicked with fat to keep out the weather.

'Like it?' She smiled at me and I saw she had a tooth missing. Her face was wide and her skin looked like polished leather. She had a brown moustache and her eyebrows met in the middle.

'It's taken me a lifetime to get it to this point.' She stroked the coat as if it was an animal, and her eyes gleamed with pleasure.

'All the pockets are full,' she said proudly. 'And if I need more, they appear.'

She opened the front of the monstrous coat and I saw that the inside had even more pockets than the outside.

'Isn't it heavy?' I asked.

'Of course it's heavy!' she said. 'But I'm very strong. Do you want more soup?'

I shook my head. Eadie was a lot less frightening in the daylight. She bent down to pick up my bowl, and I had a close look at her hair. It was like her coat – dark and matted, with things growing from it. I recognised a piece of cling-vine.

'Pull it out, will you?' she said. 'I haven't got time to be weeding my hair.'

She kept her head low. There were other things in her hair as well – seeds, small bones, and some white mess that smelled of fish.

'Shagmuck,' she said. 'I shouldn't let that bird land on my head.'

I pulled out the cling-vine.

'You could wash your hair,' I suggested, although I didn't see how that would be possible, because her hair had grown into her coat. It was hard to work out where one ended and the other began.

'My hair doesn't like water!' she snorted. 'Now, I must grind some swamp-balm seed, because your poultice will need changing this evening. I want to get it done before the Welcoming.'

She took a bottle from the shelf and poured some seeds into a bowl, and then she began grinding them with a round stone.

'I have remedies for everything,' she told me. 'How old are you, Peat?'

'Nine.'

'Thought so,' she said. 'You're small for nine. You must have been stunted. Well, there's no quick remedy for that.'

'Are you a doctor?' I asked.

'Something like that.' She added a drop of pale liquid to the seeds and continued grinding. 'All marsh aunties have the healing skills. Well, they've got to be good for something, haven't they!' She laughed, and her face crinkled up into a hundred wrinkles. She poured the ground seed mix into a jar and secured the jar to the shelf with string.

'This hide moves,' she explained. 'At times it's inconvenient. There are breakages. That's why I should always tie my jars to the shelf. But I can't be remembering everything. Not at my age.'

I wondered how old she was. She looked ancient, but she moved like someone younger than Wim. Her hands were sure and steady, and she was full of energy.

'You wouldn't believe me if I told you,' she said. 'And there's no point in asking the others because they haven't got a clue. They think they know everything, but they know nothing.'

Just then I heard voices outside.

'Eadie?'

'Are you there?'

Eadie crouched down next to the stove.

'Ignore them,' she said quietly. 'There's no skiff underneath the hide. There's nothing to tell them I'm here.'

'Eadie?'

'She's not home. Let's come back later.'

'No, we'd better check.'

I heard the splash of paddles. The hide shook slightly as something bumped against the stilts.

'Look at the state of her ladder. You'd think she'd do some repairs...'

17

THE MARSH AUNTIES

'Ah, there you are, Eadie!'

A face appeared in the doorway – a little crinkly face with keen eyes. The woman was small and wiry. She had a string bag slung over her shoulder and there was a rope coiled around her waist. She stepped off the ladder and took in everything in Eadie's hide.

'Hazel says you're to bring the swamp waif at once, and the Welcoming will be held in the Reed House.'

'No,' said Eadie. 'We'll hold the Welcoming on one of the floating islands.'

'Well, don't say I didn't deliver the message.' The woman sat down on the floor. 'Hazel's in a shocking mood already.' She leaned out the door and called down, 'Eadie wants to have the Welcoming on one of the islands.'

'Hazel won't be pleased,' came the reply.

The marsh auntie turned to me and looked me up and down, then she picked up one of my hands and studied it critically.

'Hmm. Working hands. Can you tie knots?' she asked. I nodded.

'This is Ebb,' Eadie said to me. 'She's your auntie.'

No, she's not, I thought.

'I make the nets,' Ebb said. 'I also make rope and twine and string. And I do most of the fishing.'

'There are people called Ebb who live on the edge of the marshes,' I said.

'Shut up,' she hissed. 'I don't want to hear of them. It's enough that I've got the name!'

'They drove her out,' said Eadie. 'Most of us have been driven out of somewhere.'

Something about the angry little woman made me angry as well. 'You've got the wrong name!' I blurted out. I didn't know why I'd said it or why the thought had come into my head.

The marsh auntie turned and glared at me. 'What did you say?'

'You've got the wrong name. It's making you wild. You should change it.'

'To what?' she demanded.

I looked at her stringy hair and the knotty muscles in her neck, and her hands, which were small and strong and callused. She was the sort of person who could put things together and fix them, but she could also tear them apart.

'Nettie,' I said. 'Nettie would be a good name for you.'

'Nettie.' She repeated it with a bitter look on her face, as if she was tasting something sour.

Eadie looked at me in surprise. 'Very good,' she said.

'Nettie.' Ebb tried the word again, looking at me warily. She leaned out the door. 'Come and see the swamp waif,' she yelled. 'She's got a mouth on her like razor-vine.'

Another marsh auntie clambered up the ladder. She was a large, soft-looking woman with wavy grey hair, and she wore a tunic made of woven reeds. She was carrying a big teapot and a plate of cakes.

'This is Flo,' Eadie said.

Flo devoured me with her eyes. 'You'll be useful,' she murmured.

Eadie laid out four small bowls and Flo filled them with green tea.

'Marsh cake?' Flo asked, holding out the plate.

The cakes looked like small green parcels. A trail of steam rose from each one and settled above the plate in a little cloud of mist. 'You can eat the wrapping. It's seaweed.'

I took a bite of the cake. Oh, so spicy and sweet! I had never tasted anything so marvellous.

'Like it? Plenty more where that came from.' Flo lowered herself to the floor. 'If you come with me you can have marsh cake for breakfast, dinner and tea.'

'She's not going with you,' Eadie said.

Flo ignored her. She leaned close to me and said, 'Little swamp waif, I make the skiffs. If you come with me I will make one especially for you, and I will teach you the art of making them. You will be my apprentice, and you'll live on marsh cakes and sweet tea.'

I sipped my drink. It was as delicious as the cake.

'She's staying with me,' Eadie said. 'I need to heal her.'

'Don't be ridiculous. You can't bring up a waif in these conditions.' Flo swept her hand around, gesturing to the hut's clutter. 'Besides, any one of us can fix that leg.'

'No,' Eadie insisted. 'She's mine. I found her and I'm keeping her. I'll teach her the stories.'

'She's too young for the stories and you know it, Eadie. We'll see what Hazel has to say.'

How many marsh aunties are there? I wondered.

'Seven,' Eadie answered. 'And that's six too many. Me,

Lily, Ebb, Flo, Olive, Myriad and Hazel. You'll meet them tonight.'

'There could be more in other parts of the marshes,' Flo remarked. 'There have been sightings...'

'But seven is enough,' Ebb said. 'We don't want more competition.'

Competition for what? I thought.

'For you,' said Eadie.

Flo began rocking back and forth. It took me a while to realise that she was trying to heave herself up from the floor. She was a big lady and it took her several goes.

When she was upright she leaned down and touched me lightly on the cheek. Her fingers were smooth and cool, like reeds. 'Goodbye, little swamp waif,' she said. 'Think about my offer. I'll see you at the Welcoming.'

The other auntie left without saying a word. They climbed down the ladder and I heard them paddling away.

'Ha!' Eadie cried. 'Did you see the look on Ebb's face? You're game, Peat. I'll grant you that. Nettie! Ha!'

She poured herself a jar of some frothy black liquid that looked like brackish water but had a rich, sweet smell.

'Marsh ale,' she said. 'Builds your blood and makes your coat shine.' She gulped it down and licked the foam from her moustache. 'I'd give you some, but you're too young for this strong brew.'

'Is the Welcoming for me?' I asked.

'Of course. Hazel will give the speech and tell you the rules.'

'Who's Hazel?'

'Hazel is the Great Aunt.'

'Is she the boss?'

'She thinks she is. She lives in the Reed House.' Eadie spat out the doorway. 'I'm going out now. I have plants to collect. Can I trust you to stay here and rest?'

She didn't wait for an answer before she disappeared down the ladder.

18

EADIE'S HIDE

With Eadie gone I had the chance to have a look around.

Apart from the herbs, there wasn't so much in her hut – the stove and little table, a bed made of bundled reeds, a woven mat, a box with sheets of fine bark stacked on top of it, and a few pots and pans.

The bed had an old blanket strewn over one end and a sack-pillow at the other. The pillow had a hole in it and was leaking feathers. *If I had a needle I could stitch it up*, I thought.

A fishing net hung from a hook on the wall, along with a leather bag and an assortment of woven baskets. The floor was covered with lumps of dried mud and seeds that had fallen from a bunch of pods that was hanging above. There were fur balls as big as your fist under the table. *Probably from Eadie's coat*, I thought. *Maybe it moults in summer.*

The hide reminded me of the Overhang, except for the mess. Marlie and I had kept the Overhang in order. Our things had been stored neatly on the shelves, and we'd swept the floor every day with a broom my mother had made from split corn stalks. I decided to tidy up for Eadie.

There was a bucket of water near the door, so I rinsed out the bowls we had drunk the tea from and put them away on a shelf, along with the knife and the grinding stone. Then I scraped the remains of the soup into a clean dish and filled the pot with water. I would have liked to take the pot outside and clean it properly, but I didn't think I could manage the ladder with my leg bound up. I washed the chopping board, and then I swept the floor and wrapped the sweepings in a sheet of bark. All this I did without standing up.

Next I began to explore the jars on the lower shelves. Most were so covered in dust that I couldn't see what was inside. I took some of them down, wiped them and put them back. The labels were peeling off and the writing was so faded I could barely read it: Holdfast, Hushweed, Samphire, Eyebright.

When I opened the lid of the box I found hundreds of small packages inside. Each package was wrapped in bark, tied up with string and labelled. There was Hare's Breath, Walkwell, Heart's Ease, Bladderwrack, Glibwort, Delirium and lots more.

There was also a jar in the box that was full of handy things: nails, wire, fishing hooks, a bag needle, twine, thread and buttons. I sewed up Eadie's pillow, then I shook the mat and blanket out the door. A reed-boat floated past with nobody in it. Further out, I saw a flock of wildfowl landing on the water.

Eadie's ladder was even more rickety than the one on the hut where I'd stayed with the sleek. The rungs looked rotten, and the two top ones were broken. I picked some better sticks from the pile next to the stove and replaced the top rungs, wiring them firmly into place. Then, because the bag over the door was flapping in the breeze, I sewed a stick along the bottom to weigh it down.

If she doesn't like it she can take it off, I thought.

Once I had finished, I sat on the bed and considered my situation. I had somewhere to live, food to eat and people who wanted me. I wasn't quite sure *why* they wanted me, though, and was about to think more on that when Eadie returned.

'Had a good old poke around, have you?' she called out.

I lifted the door flap to see Eadie tying a reed-boat to the walkway. It was laden with dried branches and piles of rushes.

'They're for tonight,' she said, hoisting herself up the ladder, bunches of herbs tucked under her arm. When she reached the top she stared at the floor.

'Where are the bean seeds?' she demanded. 'They were right here.'

I unwrapped the bark bundle of floor-sweepings, picked out the seeds and gave them to her. She stuffed them into one of her pockets, muttering, 'I wish people wouldn't touch things they know nothing about. I hope you haven't put any weight on that leg.'

She looked cautiously around the hide, and when her eyes fell on the bed I thought what a good job I'd done. I had folded the blanket and set the pillow straight. Eadie picked up the pillow and turned it over.

'I hope you put that needle back,' she said. 'I need that for mending my coat.'

She began tying the herbs into bundles and hanging them up, mumbling to herself. I was tired after cleaning the hut, so I sat on the bed and watched.

After a while I closed my eyes and thought my own thoughts. I went over everything that had happened to me since I'd left the Overhang. I remembered what the stranger had said – *Life's short and the world is larger than you think*. How right he was!

'He came here, you know,' Eadie said.

I opened my eyes with a start.

'Don't look so surprised. He was sick. I cured him. He had the catching disease. Who knows how many people caught it from him along the way. You and Marlie didn't get it because of the cattle.'

I stared at her. How did she know about Marlie and the cattle? I might have snooped around in Eadie's hut, but she had been snooping in my mind!

'I don't mean to eavesdrop,' she said. 'It's just that I can't help hearing everything that goes through your head – yours and everyone else's. That's why I need to live alone – to get some peace.'

'What do you mean about the cattle?' I asked.

'People who work with cows are immune to the catching disease. It's a medical fact.' She let out a honking laugh. 'It's a pity the aunties didn't come snooping around while that fellow was here – I could have got rid of them; wiped them all out with the pox in one fell swoop.'

'Why didn't *you* catch the disease?'

'Me!' She seemed to think the idea was hilarious. Her honking laughter sounded a bit like the shag. 'I don't catch diseases. I never get sick. I would have died decades ago if I was delicate!'

She finished what she was doing and turned to me. 'He

left me this,' she said, holding out a thread. It was the one the stranger had worn around his neck. It was fine and shot through with silver.

'Nice, isn't it?' she said. 'Silk, plygrass, cotton, and I think the silver is hair, probably from a horse's tail, although it could be some sort of web. Have it, if you like.'

'Thank you, Eadie.'

I held the thread up to the light. There was no knot in it. It was made all in one piece.

'Where did he go?' I asked.

She shrugged. 'Hub, I suppose. Wherever you're going, you have to go to Hub first.'

'Have you ever been to Hub?'

'Many times. In the old days I was always travelling.'

I put the thread around my neck along with the cow charm.

'Enough chattering,' Eadie said. 'You'll be late for your own Welcoming. I'll have to do the poultice later. No time now.'

She picked me up, threw me over her shoulder, and climbed down the ladder without wasting another moment.

I was surprised by how strong she was. My face was pushed into a pocket of herbs on her back. They crackled under my nose and the herby smell made me sneeze.

'Don't worry, it's only snoop grass,' she said. 'A sniff of that will do you good.'

19

THE ISLANDS
OF FLOATWEED

'Some days the marsh is all water and other times it's mainly land.' Eadie scanned the horizon. 'This is one of the water days.'

We had travelled a long way from the hide. The reed-boat sat low in the water with the weight of the load of rushes, and paddling was hard work. I was panting and sweat ran down my face.

'Aren't I meant to be resting?' I asked.

Eadie ignored me. 'Usually I would have caught a current by now,' she muttered. 'Ah, there it is!'

She pointed to some greenery that had appeared ahead and I recognised the island from the night before.

'Is this where the Welcoming will be held?'

'Of course not,' she replied. 'I just need to check my snares before we go any further. I won't be long.' She stepped out of the boat and sloshed through the water, then she disappeared up the bank.

'Nothing,' she called. 'Lily can count herself lucky.'

I wondered why Eadie wanted to snare Lily.

'She annoys me,' Eadie said when she returned. 'She's always snooping around, and when I'm practising I like to be alone.'

'What are you practising?'

'The stories. For the competition.'

'What stories? What competition?'

Eadie sighed and cast her eyes skywards. 'Swamp save me from the endless questions of the waif!' She took a deep breath and began paddling. 'The marsh aunties hold competitions,' she explained. 'To see who's the best. My stories usually win.'

'Does Lily tell stories, too?'

'Lily? She couldn't tell a story to save herself! She just creeps up and listens in. She wants to check to see if my stories are better than her perfumes.'

'Why?'

'Mother of Marsh Aunties, is there anything else you want to know!' Eadie looked at me over her shoulder. 'We're not moving very fast. Put in some effort, will you?'

<hr/>

When the boat was far out on the water, Eadie paused and looked around. The island had disappeared behind us and there was no land anywhere.

'See anything?' she asked.

'What am I looking for?'

'Islands,' she replied. 'Floating islands.'

I put down my paddle and shielded my eyes. The sun was setting, and the water was blood-red and glittering. In the distance, I saw a dot.

'There's something.'

'Ah! The sharp eyes of a waif!' Eadie looked to where I pointed. 'It's the shag,' she said. 'The shag means land.'

We paddled towards the dot and arrived near the burnt-out hut I'd first seen the shag nesting in just before dark.

'We're back at the edge of the marshes,' I said.

Eadie snorted. 'Yesterday this was at the edge of the marshes. Today it could be anywhere.'

The shag circled overhead and landed awkwardly on the side of the boat, making it tilt. He stared at Eadie.

'Get your own,' she said. 'I'm not feeding the likes of you.'

The bird blinked and glared. Eadie stared back.

Any minute now he'll go for her head and pull out some hair, I thought.

'Shhh!' Eadie snapped. 'I'm trying to hear.' She leaned towards the shag. 'He thinks there's floatweed to the south,' she said, taking up her paddle. 'Shoo. Off you go!'

The bird squawked and flapped away. It seemed that she could read the minds of birds like she'd read mine.

'Bird brains are worse than humans',' she said under her breath. 'But sometimes they're good for advice.'

Once we'd paddled a short distance from the shag's ruined hide, the boat started moving easily by itself. I put down my paddle and lay back on the branches, trailing my hand in the water. The boat skimmed along, despite the weight.

'Ah, that's better,' Eadie sighed.

'Once you find the island, how will the other aunties find it?' I asked.

'By the smoke. We'll light a fire and they'll head towards it.'

We travelled for a long time across the dark water. The stars came out, and when a big moon rose over the horizon Eadie gave a sharp cry. She reached over the side and pulled up a glistening heap of green stuff.

'Floatweed! Ha! We're nearly there.'

The boat slowed down and wove in and out of the floatweed. Soon we came to rest in still water. Eadie stood up in the boat and looked around.

'We need a decent-sized island,' she said. 'And one that will hold our weight.' She pointed to a mass of heaped weed. 'That one will do.'

The island wasn't much bigger than the craft, and it didn't look very solid. When she stepped on it, it dipped low in the water and made a sucking sound.

The noise and movement seemed to attract more weed, though. Stray clumps floated towards the island Eadie had chosen and attached to the edges. The island was growing. Soon it was large enough to hold several people. More floatweed must have gathered underneath, too, because it began to rise out of the water like a small hill.

Eadie lifted me out of the boat and put me on the floating island. Then she unloaded the wood and the reeds.

'Tie these in bundles, Peat, and put them around the edge for seating,' she said. 'I'll make the fire.'

Soon a long pillar of smoke rose from the island. Eadie sat down and gazed out over the water.

'Now we wait,' she said, taking out her bone pipe. 'I must warn you, the aunties will try to win you with gifts – but you mustn't be swayed.' She stuffed the pipe with tobacco. 'And when the Great Aunt asks you to give your speech, you must say that you belong to me.'

'But I don't belong to you...' I began.

'You don't now, but you will once I begin training you, and I'm going to start immediately.'

She dug into her coat and pulled out a little leather pouch. 'I have collected the things in this bag over many, many years. They are small, but they are powerful.' She gave me a steady look. 'Lesson one, Peat – always open and close your stories. If you don't, the characters can come out into the world. I hope you're paying attention.'

'What is this training?' I asked. 'What are you training me for?'

'For the stories. You're going to be my apprentice.' She put her fingers in the pouch and drew out a bent nail.

'What's this?' she demanded, holding it up. Flames leapt from the fire, and the shadow of the nail fell on her face. 'It's a weapon,' she said. 'A sword.'

She turned the nail around so that she was holding the point and not the head. 'Now it's a club. Can you see that?'

I nodded.

'Good,' she said. 'Now the story can begin.'

20

THE BARGAIN

'Once, long ago and far from here, there lived a warrior. His name was Pike, and he was afraid of nothing. He slept with a battleaxe tucked in his belt. Every night he dreamed of fighting, and every morning he woke with the battle light shining in his eyes.'

Eadie's face gleamed in the firelight, and she stared into the flames as if something was there.

'Pike lived in a rough stone fort at the top of some cliffs, and his enemy, a giant called Scabbard, lived in a sea cave at the bottom. Each day they met on the path and fought. You'd think one would have killed the other, but the two were equally matched. Every day when the sun reached its peak overhead they stopped fighting, and each went home to sharpen his weapons and polish his shield.

'Are you listening carefully, Peat? I'm going to ask you to repeat this story.'

I nodded, pulling a pile of reeds up behind me so I could lean back and get more comfortable.

'One night Pike dreamed he lost the endless battle,' she continued. 'He dreamed Scabbard speared him straight through his heart and he fell from the cliffs into the swirling sea. This frightened the fearless warrior. He was so afraid for his life he decided to seek advice.

'There was a wayfarer who came to the coast every year – an age-old man known as the Siltman. He came to pan for tin and to trade the silver trinkets he made. He would set up camp at the river mouth and people would visit him there. They believed he understood the language of fish and birds and had supernatural powers. Pike decided he would take his dream to the Siltman.'

Eadie turned to me and frowned. 'Lesson two, Peat. See the story in your mind, and the audience will see it, too.' She took a deep breath.

'The Siltman had always been old, and he never grew any older. He arrived each year in winter just after the waders and barnacle geese had left for warmer shores. His footprints and those of his dog would appear on the beach three weeks before he did. Pike found him sifting silt at the river mouth.'

Eadie's face grew thin and pale. Her eyes were deep hollows. She lifted one hand and her fingers looked bony. *Is it a trick of light from the fire or is she actually changing?* I asked myself.

'Shhh,' she said, and her voice was dry and wispy.

'The Siltman listened to Pike's dream. *You will certainly die*, he said. *Unless I save you.*

'The warrior was afraid of the Siltman. The old man's voice was like wind blowing through the rushes, and his eyes looked clear through to the next world.

'*Save me?* asked Pike. *How can you save me?*

'*I can split your spirit from your body and put it away for safekeeping. Then you can never be killed.*'

Is this a true story? I wondered.

'Of course it's true,' Eadie snapped. 'Do you think I'm a liar?'

I didn't know.

'Just listen,' she said, and she went on with the story.

'*Do it*, said Pike. *Split my spirit from my body.*

'*There's a price*, said the Siltman.

'*Name it*, said Pike, who had a strongroom full of gold back at the fort.

'*I don't want gold*, the old man whispered. *I want something more valuable than gold.*'

Eadie whistled through her teeth and a tremor of fear ran through me. She leaned close.

'Do you know what he wanted?' she asked.

'No,' I breathed.

She was quiet for a while, then when she spoke again it was in the voice of the Siltman. '*Give me a child*, he said. Your *child*.

'*It's a deal*, said Pike quickly, because he had no wife and he had no child.

'The Siltman reached up and put his hand on Pike's chest.' I watched the firelight flicker through Eadie's out-stretched fingers. 'He took Pike's spirit from his body and put it in a bag at his feet.

'The Siltman's dog had recently given birth to a litter of puppies. They were in that bag. The spirit went straight into the nearest puppy, then the old man drew out the little pup and gave it to Pike.

'*Keep him safe*, he said. *And you will live forever.*'

Eadie's brow creased, and she stopped talking.

'Go on,' I said. 'Did he live forever?'

She pointed to the water and put her finger to her lips. Our island was surrounded by lilies, glowing in the darkness. I hadn't noticed them before. Eadie leaned towards me.

'Spies,' she hissed. 'The Listening Lilies.'

Immediately the lilies closed up and sank beneath the surface.

'Blast them!' Eadie cried. 'I should have been more careful.'

'Do they belong to Lily?' I asked.

'Lily, Flo, Olive. Any of the marsh aunties could have sent them.' Eadie spat the words out.

'Does it matter what they hear?'

She sucked on her pipe and blew smoke from her nostrils. Her coat seemed to be swelling, and bits of fur were sticking up in tufts.

'Those aunties raise my blood pressure and my hackles,' she snorted. 'But they won't stop me. Where was I?'

'The Siltman put the spirit of Pike into a puppy.'

'That's right,' she said. 'Pike slipped that puppy inside his cloak and went home. He called him Shadow, and the pup followed him everywhere.

'Shadow grew up into a giant wolfhound. He was fierce and fearless, like his owner. He guarded the fort when Pike went out into battle. And Pike fought as never before. Do you know what happened?'

She looked hard into my eyes. I shook my head.

'Spears passed through him and went out the other side without leaving a scratch. Deathblow after deathblow glanced off him. The giant Scabbard could not kill him.'

Eadie fell silent and stared into the fire. She was silent for so long that I thought the story had ended. I could hear waves lapping at the shores of our small island and faint voices across the water.

'I think they're coming,' I said.

'Typical,' Eadie replied. 'The aunties always arrive at the wrong time.'

She began speaking quickly, trying to finish the story before the others reached the island.

'Years went by. Pike married and had a son. Shadow loved the child with all his being. He taught him to walk by standing close and letting the boy pull himself up with handfuls of wiry hair. When the boy was big enough to climb onto Shadow's back, the dog took him riding, and together they explored the country beyond the cliffs.

'Pike gave no thought to the bargain he had made with the Siltman. He didn't tell his wife about the deal and, in time, he forgot about it completely. One day, Pike's wife went away to visit her family, and while she was gone the Siltman returned. For the second time in his life, Pike was afraid.

'*The boy's not here*, he told the Siltman. *He's out riding his dog. When he comes back I'll bring him to your camp at the river mouth.*

'The Siltman turned and walked away without saying a word. Pike had no intention of honouring his promise. When the boy returned his father hugged him tight then, leaving Shadow to guard the fort, he picked up his son and ran.'

———

The voices on the water were getting nearer. I could hear shouts and a wailing sort of song. I wished they would go away, because I wanted Eadie to finish the story.

'Later.' Eadie held up the nail. 'The tale isn't over,' she said. 'But I will close it anyway.'

She put the nail back in the little bag and tied up the string. Then she heaped more wood on the fire and the flames leapt high.

21

THE WELCOMING

I couldn't see the aunties in the darkness, but I could hear them. Someone yelled words I couldn't understand, and there were howls of laughter.

'Don't speak Marsh. The waif won't know what you're talking about!'

There was arguing and cursing and singing – a strange song that had no tune. One voice rose higher and higher until it became a scream, while someone else made a low honking sound.

'That's Olive,' Eadie said. 'She's got a beak on her like a barnacle goose and a laugh to match.'

I couldn't believe there were only half-a-dozen marsh aunties. It sounded like many more.

The island rocked about as the aunties clambered up. They were carrying heavy bundles and their faces were flushed with excitement. Lily rushed to me and kissed me on both cheeks.

'I've got you a present, Peat,' she whispered, slipping a little bottle of perfume into my pocket. 'I've perfected the Swoon.'

She sat very close, as if she was claiming me. Another auntie put herself between me and Eadie.

'I'm Myriad,' she said. 'How is your leg? Eadie's not the only one who can cure, you know.'

Myriad's hair was gold and it fanned out around her head like a halo.

'Welcome to the marsh,' she said.

'*I* will do the Welcoming!' came a booming voice.

The Great Aunt took her place by the fire. She was an enormous woman, and she seemed to be trailing a long shawl, but when I looked closer I saw that it was mist – a white mist that reminded me of the one in Drip Cave. When she sat down, the mist slipped from her shoulders and gathered in her lap. Her eyes were green and seemed too large for her face.

'Sisters, Marsh Aunties and Women of the Wetlands.' She spread her arms wide. 'We are gathered here to welcome the swamp waif Peat!'

There were murmurs of agreement.

'It has been many years since we've had a swamp waif in our midst.'

'Thirty,' said Myriad. 'I was the last.'

'Thirty years!' the Great Aunt cried. 'And now at last we have some new blood.'

New blood. I don't like the sound of that, I thought. *What do they need the blood for?* I remembered what the Last children had said.

Eadie leaned across Myriad and spoke in my ear. 'Parents tell children all sorts of stories to stop them wandering into the marshes and getting lost. You are quite safe.'

'We are lucky to have a swamp waif,' continued the Great Aunt. 'She will stay with us and live in the marshes forever, and when we die she will take our place.'

Forever? I thought.

'Shhh.' Eadie silenced me.

'Is there any marsh business to declare before we proceed with the Welcoming?' the Great Aunt asked.

Lily stood up. 'I'd like to declare that the Green Mist was marvellous,' she said in her breathy voice. 'There were so many strands, so many layers. It was just...' She was searching for the word. '...tantalising!'

The Great Aunt nodded. 'Thank you, Lily.'

'It was one of the best mists you've ever raised, Hazel,' Lily added.

Eadie leaned in front of Myriad again. 'She's trying to flatter the Great Aunt. She wants Hazel to give you to her. But it's not up to Hazel.'

'I have a declaration.' Another auntie stood up. She had a large nose and was wearing a tunic made of bags and feathers. 'I would like to declare the Far Reaches out of bounds. The Churn is particularly active at the moment, and we wouldn't want the waif to get lost in it.'

'Declared,' said the Great Aunt. 'Thank you, Olive. Next?'

Ebb jumped up. 'I wish to declare that I've changed my name to Nettie.'

Ebb – or Nettie – gave me a tight little smile.

'She's decided she wants you,' Eadie whispered. 'If you go with her she'll work you to the bone and you'll be making fishnets to the end of your days.'

'Declared,' said the Great Aunt. 'Is everyone here?'

'Flo is missing,' said Lily.

'She's always late,' the Great Aunt muttered. 'We will start without her. I will deliver the Rules and proceed with the Welcoming.'

The Great Aunt rose to her feet, and the island lurched.

She glared at me with her huge green eyes. 'These are the Rules of the marshes,' she said. 'They will become the rules of your life.

'Rule One: No marsh auntie or swamp waif may leave the marsh without the permission of the Great Aunt.

'Rule Two: The Great Aunt will rule until the night of the Eclipse.

'Rule Three: All new swamp waifs will be apprenticed to the marsh auntie of their choice.

'Rule Four: That marsh auntie will care for the swamp waif and protect her from danger.

'Rule Five: After the Welcoming, the marsh auntie will teach the waif her special skill.

'Rule Six: The marsh auntie will own the swamp waif until the day of her death.'

Whose death? I wondered. I didn't know if I liked these rules, but when the Great Aunt asked me if I understood, I nodded and said nothing.

'Each auntie will show you her special skill in turn. Afterwards you will make your choice and give your speech. Are there any aunties you don't know?'

I didn't feel that I knew any of them, but I pointed to Olive.

'Olive makes clothes,' said the Great Aunt. 'She would teach you the arts of dying, weaving and sewing. When she opens her bundle you'll see an array of fabrics and threads.'

Olive smiled at me and nodded.

I pointed to Myriad.

'Myriad makes pots and pipes. She has hands that can shape clay.'

'What do you make, Great Aunt?' I asked, although I knew I wouldn't choose the Great Aunt Hazel because something in her voice reminded me of Alban Bane.

'I make the mists,' she said. 'If you come with me, I will teach you the art of weathermaking. You will learn how to make mists and rain and winds and storms. Now we will start. Let the aunties prepare themselves.'

The Great Aunt sat down and the island sank a little then bounced back up. The other aunties began unpacking their bundles.

Olive rushed over to me and pressed some cloth into my hands. 'For you, little waif,' she said. 'A beautiful dress.'

The dress was my size and it was made of fine brown linen with feathers over the breast. My own dress was ragged, and there were holes in my vest, but I could never give up the clothes made by my own mother.

Nettie handed me a fish. It had rainbow scales and its tail was bright orange.

'It's called a Golden Galaxia,' she said. 'They're very rare. When you are my apprentice, I will show you how to make a net so fine it can catch anything you want.'

I don't want to be caught in your net, I thought.

The marsh aunties were all over me. They were hungry for me. It was good to be wanted, but they wanted me too much.

'You're crowding her,' Myriad cried. She picked me up and stepped away from the fire.

'Don't go with Eadie,' she whispered. 'Eadie is not to be trusted.'

'Bring her back!' the others yelled. 'You're stealing her.'

'Order!' yelled the Great Aunt.

Myriad set me back down on my bundle of rushes.

'Swamp waif, is there anything you want to say before the aunties begin?' the Great Aunt asked.

'Yes.'

I didn't know if I should stand to address Hazel, but I had something important to say, so I put my hands on the shoulders of the aunties next to me and, keeping my leg straight, I got to my feet.

'Great Aunt, I don't know if I want to stay in the marshes forever and follow your rules. And I don't think I want to belong to anyone.'

The Great Aunt gasped, and there was a general grumbling among the others. Someone clicked her tongue and hissed, 'Ungrateful waif!'

The Great Aunt stared at me with a face like thunder. 'You haven't got a choice,' she said. 'If we let you go, you will wander into the Far Reaches and be lost. You might be swallowed by the Churn. What else have you got to say?'

'I would like to thank Eadie for fixing my leg,' I said hesitantly.

'But *she* broke it!' Lily cried.

'Enough!' said the Great Aunt. 'Eadie, you may go first.'

'That's hardly fair,' I heard Lily whisper under her breath.

Eadie pulled out her story bag and moved closer to the fire. She picked out a glass bead, let it glint in the firelight, and put it back. Then she took out a leaf.

'Tell the one about the herb queen,' someone suggested.

'No. Tell *The Bad Wish*.'

'How about the story of the very first swamp waif?' Myriad asked. 'I love that tale. It always makes me cry.'

'Everything makes you cry,' Olive said. 'What about *The Fickle Thread*?'

All the aunties were talking at once. Eadie returned the leaf to the pouch and produced a wishbone.

'No, not *The Bad Wish*,' Ebb cried. 'Tell *The Tale of Lucky Fish*—'

'Silence!' The Great Aunt stared around the circle. 'Let the storyteller choose the story.'

Eadie dropped the wishbone back in the pouch and took out the nail. She gave me a wink that said she had known all along which story she would tell.

'Sisters,' she said. 'On a cliff far from here is an ancient stone. It's taller than a man, and its surface is worn from the storms that blow in from the western sea. This stone was once a man, a giant called Scabbard, who loved battle more than anything else in the world. His enemy was a warrior called Pike, who lived in a stone fort that looked over the ocean.'

The aunties settled back to listen. There were murmurs of approval.

'Scabbard lived in a cave at the bottom of the cliff. Every day he and Pike met on the path and fought. They fought fiercely with swords and battleaxes, and the clash and clamour of their struggle rang out across the ocean.'

I looked around the faces in the firelight. Except for the Great Aunt, everyone was watching Eadie. Now that they weren't looking at me they didn't seem so worrisome. Olive had a kind face, like somebody's grandmother, and Lily and Myriad looked harmless. Still, I didn't want to be owned by any of them. *What will happen if I don't choose?* I wondered.

The Great Aunt, meanwhile, had fixed me with a fierce stare. I tried to ignore her.

'Scabbard had a burning rage inside him,' Eadie said. 'If the cold waves hadn't washed over him each night, he would have burned up. Every day he vowed to defeat his opponent, Pike, but the two were equally matched. Then, one night, the warrior Pike dreamed that he lost the endless battle...'

I stopped listening to the story and tried to make a plan. If I took my chances in the Far Reaches, perhaps I wouldn't get lost. Perhaps I would find my way out of the marshes. Perhaps I would find my way to Hub, and from there I could go anywhere I wanted.

Eadie was standing in the circle of marsh aunties. Her face had the look of a mad warrior in battle. 'Spears went right through him without leaving a mark,' she cried. 'Deathblow after deathblow glanced off him. Pike could not be killed.'

The fire crackled and a spark landed on Eadie's coat, igniting a bunch of dried leaves that poked from a pocket. She let it flare for a moment before slapping it out.

'Years passed,' she said. 'Pike married and had a son...'

The marsh aunties listened intently. I glanced at Hazel then quickly looked away. Her green eyes frightened me. I wondered if she could read my thoughts like Eadie could. I closed my mind and listened to the story.

'When the Siltman came to the door, Pike knew what the old man wanted, and he was glad that his son was away from the fort at the time riding his great hound over the hills inland from the coast. He promised to deliver the child that evening. The Siltman turned and walked away without saying a word.

'As soon as he could, the fearless warrior took the child and ran. He ran across the country in the direction his wife had taken. He ran all day and all night.

'When Scabbard came up the path the next morning, Pike was not there to fight him, so he kept going. He reached the top of the cliff and came to the fort. The place was deserted, except for the dog which stood guarding the door. Shadow growled and leapt towards the intruder. Without a moment's hesitation, Scabbard speared the dog straight through the chest. At that moment, the warrior Pike fell dead.'

The aunties gasped.

'And the boy?' cried Olive. 'What happened to the little boy?'

Eadie lowered her voice. The aunties had to lean in to hear what she was saying. They had forgotten about me for the moment. But the Great Aunt had not forgotten. I felt her eyes on me.

'The boy fell to the ground,' Eadie said. 'He tried to wake his father. He was too young to understand what had happened. In his desperation he cried for his mother, and when she didn't come he called for his dog. Shadow was dead, poor beast, but his ghost heard the boy crying. It glided silently across the country, and when it reached the child, it picked him up and gently put him on its back. The boy stopped crying immediately. The ghost dog put its phantom nose to the ground and followed the scent of the boy's mother.'

The marsh aunties sighed and sat back. Eadie looked around at her audience, then she put the nail back in the pouch.

'A beautiful tale, Eadie,' said Lily.

'A rescue story,' Olive sighed. 'I love a good rescue.'

'So loyal, that Shadow, even as a wraith.' Myriad dabbed at her eyes with the hem of her dress.

Eadie sat down and tucked the pouch inside her coat. The aunties clapped loudly, but the Great Aunt looked unimpressed.

'Next!' she said, raising her palms to stop the applause.

Olive put her hand on my knee. 'I'll go next. I'll show the waif how I weave my magical cloth.'

She reached into her bag and pulled out balls of coloured thread, but before she could start the Great Aunt stood up and looked out over the water.

'Stop!' came a voice. 'Stop the Welcoming! Someone has cheated!'

'Flo,' the Great Aunt cried. 'You're late!'

The island bobbed up and down as Flo climbed onto it. She had a lily in her hair, and she was holding one in her hand.

'The Welcoming cannot proceed,' she panted as she bustled into the firelight. 'Eadie has broken one of the rules.'

'Which rule?' the Great Aunt demanded.

The moon disappeared behind some clouds and a breeze blew up around the island.

'Rule five,' Flo replied. 'Eadie has already begun teaching the waif her special skill. She began training the waif *before* the Welcoming.'

The Great Aunt frowned and the wind grew stronger. I could hear the reed-boats knocking together.

'Is this true?' she asked.

More clouds appeared from nowhere. The air grew cold.

'The lilies don't lie,' Flo answered. 'Eadie has been teaching the waif how to tell stories.'

The Great Aunt turned to Eadie. A sudden gust blew the fire apart and I heard a moaning sound, as if a great wind was gathering somewhere over the marshes.

Eadie leaned towards me. 'Not over the marshes,' she whispered. 'It's right here. Hazel is furious!' And, with that, she picked me up and threw me over her shoulder.

'Put her down!' the Great Aunt roared.

Eadie ignored her. She tipped me into the reed-boat just as the island began to shake and buck.

'Here comes the rain!' someone yelled.

Thunder rumbled in the distance and the rain poured down. The aunties gathered their bundles and hurried to their crafts.

'Paddle for your lives!' I heard someone shout. 'The island is breaking up!'

Eadie steered the boat into a swift current and we were swept along before the blast of the storm.

'How will you find your hide?' I shouted.

'I don't need to,' she cried. 'We're leaving the marshes!'

'But the rules—' I yelled.

'Forget the rules! You're mine!'

'But I didn't choose you,' I cried.

A flash of lightning lit up Eadie's face. Her eyes were wild and her smile was fearsome.

'All the aunties want a waif,' she yelled. 'But I am the only one who *must have one*!'

Strands of vine whipped around her head. Her hackles were raised. She turned her back on me and I watched her coat grow huge in the darkness, until it was all I could see. The cold rain pelted down and the wind howled as we were blown into the night.

'What happened to the boy?' I cried. 'Did Shadow's ghost take him to his mother?'

Eadie turned to me and roared with laughter.

'Lesson three, waif,' she shouted. 'Don't finish the story until you get to the end! They reached a river, and the ghost hound lost the scent. He didn't know which way to go, so he headed to the river mouth, where the Siltman was waiting.'

22

THE RIVER

'Here we go – swamp-balm seed. It's not hard to find,' said Eadie as she waded through the marsh with a handful of long yellow pods. The sun was rising through the mist, and there was no sign of the wild person Eadie had been the night before, just as there was no sign of the storm, except for some wreckage floating on the water – a broken ladder and some tree branches.

Eadie climbed into the boat. She opened the pods and put the seeds in her mouth.

'I'll fix your leg first, then we'll get you out of those wet clothes. I haven't got my grinding stone,' she said, 'so I'll have to chew these.'

She spat the pulp into one hand, took some dried herbs from a pocket in her coat with the other, and rolled them together.

'You've been asleep for a long time,' she said. 'I don't know how you slept through that gale.' She began un-winding the bindweed from my leg.

The night before seemed like a dream. It was as if the storm had blown the memory of it about in my mind, and it took me a while to put the pieces back together – the marsh aunties, the story, the Great Aunt's green eyes full of rage, and Eadie's wild face.

I was soaked through, and so cold that my hands and feet were numb.

'Did I cause the storm?' I asked.

'It was Hazel's storm but yes, you were the cause of it.'

'I don't know if I want to go with you, Eadie.'

'Suit yourself.' She shrugged. 'We can part company as soon as we reach the river, if you like.'

'What river?'

'There are many ways into the marshes but few ways out. Either we go towards the Far Reaches and risk the Churn, or we find the river. The river goes to Hub.'

Eadie put the bindweed aside and looked at my leg. There was a mud pack underneath and it was hard as rock.

'I wish I had my stone. I need something to knock it open with.'

She took up the paddle and tapped along the length of the mud casing until it cracked, then she gave it a sharp knock and it fell apart in two pieces. She removed some white crumbling paste from my leg and replaced it with the newly chewed pulp.

'It's healing well. You'll be walking in no time.'

She leaned over the side and scooped up a big lump of mud, which she slapped down in the bottom of the boat. Then she wiped her hands on her coat.

'Where is the Holdfast?' she asked herself. 'That's right, heart pocket.' She plunged her hand into a deep pocket over her chest and pulled out what she needed.

'Without this, the clay could take days to set.' She packed the fresh mud around my leg and sprinkled it with

Holdfast, then she secured it with the bindweed. 'Ah, here comes the sun. That will help. Give me your dress.'

I didn't want to take off my clothes, but before I knew it, Eadie had me out of my vest and was slipping my dress over my head.

'Use that until yours dries.' She nodded towards the bottom of the boat. The dress Olive had given me was there, and so was Nettie's fish. Eadie must have thrown them in when we left the floating island.

I put the new dress on, wondering how it hadn't got drenched in all the rain. It was dry and warm.

'I don't know how she does it,' Eadie said. 'All her fabrics are like that. The clothes she makes always fit perfectly, too, and they never wear out.'

She threaded her paddle through the arms of my dress and my vest, then she reached over the side of the boat and picked up a long pole that was floating past.

'I'll hang your clothes up to dry,' she said, tying the paddle to the pole with bindweed so it formed a cross-piece. She then set the pole upright like a mast and my clothes were high in the air, hanging like an empty version of myself – a Peat scarecrow. But if it was a scarecrow it didn't work, because the shag landed on top and gave a honking cry. Eadie glanced up.

'How did it end then?' she muttered. 'Everyone get home all right?'

The bird looked into her eyes without blinking.

'Well, it's only what she deserved, the old cow.' Eadie spat over the side.

I wondered what had happened.

'Marsh auntie business,' she said. 'Hazel got blasted by

her own storm, and it caused a power shift. They're bringing forward the Eclipse. Keep still while I go and get you some breakfast.'

She stepped out of the boat and waded through the water, the shadow of her coat moving in front of her like a strange rippling creature. When she disappeared into some rushes, I began thinking about the story she had told the night before – the boy, the dog and the bargain with the Siltman. Somehow, I felt it was connected to me... but surely that was a foolish idea. How could I have anything to do with those fighting men and the stone fort on top of the cliff? I went through the story in my mind, and I was halfway through telling it to myself when Eadie returned.

'Excellent,' she said. 'You'll be ready to perform it by the time we reach Hub.'

Her arms were full of small round fruit. She handed them to me and threw one up to the shag, then she got into the boat and began paddling. When the boat caught a current, she set down the paddle and put her hands behind her head.

'Ah, this reminds me of the old travelling life,' she said. 'Before I came to the marshes.'

The shag spread his wings but stayed put, crouching above us as the boat skimmed over the water. Now and then we swerved to avoid some floating pieces of walkway. We passed the roof of a hut, then the current took us up a channel that wound through a thick field of reeds.

'How do you know this is the right current?' I asked.

'The water level has risen with the rain. All channels lead to the river. That's the beauty of a storm like that – it lets the marsh leak out into the world.'

I wondered where Eadie had lived before she came to the marshes. The Badlands?

She smiled to herself. 'It's so long ago I can hardly remember it. A lifetime ago. Many lifetimes, actually.'

I looked into her face and wished I could read her thoughts the way she could read mine. She could be telling me anything and I wouldn't know whether it was true or not.

She gave me an easy smile, but the fierce look I had seen on her face in the lightning flash was still vivid in my mind.

'You worry too much, Peat,' she said. 'Chew on these.'

She handed me some freshly picked green leaves. She must have gathered them when she got the fruit.

'Worrywort,' she said. 'Also good for flavouring soups and stews.'

I chewed the leaves slowly and a crisp, peppery flavour filled my mouth.

The warmth of the sun and the gentle rocking of the boat made me think of the river I had dreamed about at Amos Last's house. I hoped that was the river we were heading for.

After some time the channel widened and the reed field was replaced with low scrub. The sun was warm and Eadie's coat steamed, giving off a pungent smell. The shag settled his wings.

'His feathers are dry now, and your clothes should be, too,' Eadie said. She lowered the pole, causing the shag to screech and take flight. I put my clothes back on over the top of Olive's dress.

When we reached the river I gasped at the expanse of

it. I gazed across, but I couldn't see the other side. The sky was wide, and the deepest blue I had ever seen, and the water was smooth as glass. The warm air was alive with insects. Very far out, a white bird glided across the surface then dived into its own reflection.

I leaned over the side of the boat and got a shock at the girl looking back at me. Her face was wide and brown, and her hair was so bright it might have been alight. Something disturbed the water and flames wavered around her head.

'Enough looking,' Eadie said. 'This is where the work begins.'

She threw me the paddle. 'We can't expect to find a current that will take us upstream, although we might get some backflow if we stick near the shore.'

We began paddling steadily, Eadie in front and me behind, trying to keep in time with her strokes.

'Your friend's back,' she remarked.

I looked behind us and saw a nose poking out of the water.

'Sleek!'

I knew the sleek had caused me a lot of trouble but I was so pleased to see him that I laughed aloud.

The sleek ignored me. He swam alongside the boat with his eyes fixed straight ahead. It was as if we were fellow travellers who happened to be going in the same direction and nothing more.

23

THE HERB QUEEN

We paddled all day, keeping close to the riverbank. When we passed a row of upturned baskets at the water's edge, Eadie paused for a moment.

'Hives,' she said. 'I'm surprised they're still here.'

The baskets were old and falling to pieces, but bees swarmed around them.

'Olive made those,' Eadie told me. 'Back in the old days when marsh aunties came and went as they pleased. Ah, smell the air!'

She paddled on with long steady strokes. I was getting weary. In fact, I was so tired that I was just pretending to paddle. I wished we had a rope on the reed-boat, because if we did the sleek could give us a tow.

'Fat chance,' Eadie said. 'But you can try if you like.'

She handed me a length of bindweed. I held one end and threw the other to the sleek, but he took no notice, and when I tried it a second time he grabbed the end and dived under the water so fast that he almost jerked me out of the boat.

'Typical snide,' Eadie said, as she kept paddling.

It was late afternoon when Eadie steered towards the bank and found a little beach.

'We'll camp here tonight,' she said. 'Where's that fish Ebb gave you? It can be our dinner.'

She helped me out of the reed-boat and settled me on the soft sand. Together we made a fire, and when it was glowing warm Eadie pulled her knife out of her coat, scaled the fish and cleaned it. She tossed the guts into the water and the sleek caught them.

'Guard it,' she said, with a sharp glance at the sleek. 'I'm going to get some sticks.'

There was no need to find sticks. There was plenty of driftwood on the little beach.

'Not for the fire,' she snapped. 'For you. I can't be carrying you around the country like a baby. You've got to take your own weight. That leg should be strong enough by tomorrow.'

As soon as she left, the sleek crept towards me, his eyes on the fish.

'Sit down, Sleek!'

To my surprise, he obeyed me. He sat down and began washing himself.

Eadie returned with handfuls of dried grass, some big leaves and two saplings that forked at the right height to go under my armpits.

'Pack a wad of grass under each arm for padding.'

She wrapped the fish in the leaves and put it on the coals, then she settled herself next to the fire, patting the pockets of her coat.

'That's the only trouble with a coat like this – it has a life of its own, and things are not always where you left them.'

'What are you looking for, Eadie?'

'My pipe, of course. Ah, here it is!'

After she'd lit her pipe, she dived into her coat again and pulled out her story bag.

'Lesson one?' she asked.

'Always open and close your stories.'

'Good waif!'

She took a small handful of sunflower seeds out of her little bag and put two of them in my hand.

'There was once a girl called Blot. She had a birthmark on her face that covered half her cheek.

'This girl was the daughter of a woman of power – a queen, or perhaps you would call her a swamp hag.' She gave me a sidelong glance. 'She lived in a great house on the riverbank. And she was as mean as they come.

'*What a hideous baby*, she cried when the girl was born. *I'll have to find a cure for that face!*

'She went to her remedy room and consulted her library. She had books on everything – how to make tonics, tinctures and potions; recipes for balms and balsams and herbal draughts that could cure any condition. Finally she found the recipe she needed. It was in an old book called *Natural and Unnatural Cures – The Herb Queen's Almanac*. Three drops and the girl's face would be fixed. But the ingredients were rare and some of them grew far away. It would take a long time to gather them all, and the mixture should boil for ten years and a day.'

The sleek stopped washing himself and stared at the fish. I put my hand on him and, when he didn't spit at me, I began stroking his red fur. I was surprised when he purred.

'What is more important, the story or the snide?' Eadie asked. 'If you are my apprentice you must listen with both ears.'

I'm listening, I thought. *And I'm not your apprentice. I'm just travelling with you.*

Eadie ignored this and continued with the story.

'The queen began making the mixture. She collected the ingredients that grew close to home and set them to boil in a big pot on the riverbank. She employed a boy to tend the fire under the pot and an old blind man to supervise the boy. He had to be blind because she didn't want him to see what she was doing. Then she went away to find the other ingredients.

'Meanwhile, the baby grew into a little girl. The old man and the boy looked after her. They didn't mind the birthmark on her face. To them, she was beautiful.

'When Blot was four years old, her mother returned.

'*What's that girl doing outside?* she demanded. *She should be locked up in the great house where no one can see her.*

'The woman shut Blot away and ordered the boy to take food to her once a day. Apart from that, the girl was to see no one until she was cured.

'*If you don't do what I say, I will know it and you'll be punished*, the queen told the boy. She added the new ingredients to the pot and went away again.

'The boy and the old man felt sorry for the little girl, but they were afraid of the hag so they didn't let her out. However, the boy made a gift for the child.'

Eadie put down her pipe and stood up. 'Turn the fish

over, will you?' She walked down to the water and waded in.

'You'll get your coat wet,' I yelled.

She returned with a handful of mud, the bottom of her coat dragging behind her. Then she sat down and closed her eyes.

'What are you doing?' I asked.

'I'm seeing the story in my mind,' she said. Her hands began kneading the mud. 'The boy got clay from the river-bank, and he shaped it into a doll.'

Eadie quickly made a head and a body, and she took the two sunflower seeds from my hand and pressed them into the doll's face for eyes. She looked at what she'd made.

'Perfect,' she said. 'You do the hair. Use grass.'

When I finished pressing in strands of grass to make hair for the doll, Eadie nodded. 'The doll in the story was more lifelike, but we haven't got time to do that. I need to get the story told before the fish is cooked.'

I smiled, and I gave the doll a smile as well. First I drew it on with my fingernail; then I found something better, a curved piece of shell.

'Blot loved the gift,' Eadie continued. 'Every night, when the boy brought her dinner, she gave a little bit of food to the doll. Then, one night, the doll opened its eyes and spoke to her.

'*I am your true friend*, it said. *Tell me what's in your heart.*

'Blot told the doll her deepest fear. *If the brew doesn't clear the mark from my face I think my mother might kill me*, she whispered. *Either that, or I will remain a prisoner forever.*

'*Don't worry*, said the doll. *I will help you.*

'When the hag next came home, six more years had passed and Blot was ten. The queen added the ingredients she'd collected to the boiling brew and stirred it with a paddle. The old man stood back and shook his head and the boy watched sadly as the hag sat by the riverbank and consulted her recipe.

'*On the last day*, she read, *add the girl's most precious thing. Now what could that be?*'

Eadie stroked her chin and gazed into the fire, then she looked at me with her keen eyes. 'The queen knew, of course. She knew about the doll because she had special powers and nothing could be hidden from her.

'On the morning of the ten years and one day she took her daughter to the riverbank and told her to throw her doll into the pot.'

Eadie stopped talking and poked at the fish with a stick.

'It's done,' she said. 'We'll finish the story later.'

'No. Finish it now.'

She pulled the fish from the coals.

'When Blot refused to throw her precious doll into the pot, her mother grabbed the boy.

'*I'll throw him in instead!* she yelled, holding him over the boiling liquid.

'*No!* cried Blot.

'At that moment the little doll leapt from the girl's arms into the brew. Three drops splashed out onto the old man's face – two drops on one eyelid and one on the other. He opened his eyes and saw the pot crack open. The brew burst out all over the queen and she was burnt to ashes.

The old man saw the two children clinging to each other.

'*You will be my grandchildren*, he said. *We will live in the great house, and no door will ever be locked.*

'And that's what they did. Forever.'

'What about the little doll?' I asked.

'She went back to the river,' Eadie replied. 'Her body became mud and her hair became grass, and the two seeds that were her eyes grew into beautiful sunflowers.'

I set the doll on the ground next to me, and she seemed to watch as Eadie put the rest of the seeds back in her little bag and returned it to her pocket. She pulled the fish from the coals, unwrapped it and gave me half.

We ate in silence. The only sound was Eadie sucking the fish bones.

I liked the story. I looked out over the river and thought about Blot. She still had the birthmark, and she'd lost her precious doll but she had a best friend and a grandfather, and she was free. I liked the way the recipe backfired on the herb queen. It didn't fix the birthmark, but it cured the situation. Maybe all the recipes in the book – the almanac – worked that way.

'Did you read any books, Eadie, when you were learning the herbs?'

'It's so long ago I can't remember.' She was licking her fingers clean. 'Glad you liked the story, Peat. Plenty more where that came from. I've got more stories than pockets in my coat.'

She blew into her sleeves, then she stood up and, leaning forward, she began opening and closing the front of her coat very fast. She looked like she was trying to take off.

'What are you doing?'

'Puffing up,' she replied. 'With a coat like this you never need bedding. Trap some air in the pockets and, no matter how cold the night, you're always warm.'

She lay down by the fire. 'One of these days you might own a coat like this, Peat, if you're lucky.'

I settled myself down for the night. Eadie's coat was all right for her, but it wasn't something I would ever want to wear.

Soon Eadie was asleep. Her snore sounded like the rattling purr of the sleek, but it was a hundred times louder.

24

MOTHER MOSS

Eadie woke me early the next morning. The doll had baked dry by the fire overnight.

'Come on,' she said. 'We've got a long way to go.'

She handed me the sticks.

'Goodbye, little doll,' I said, as I made my own way down to the reed-boat. My leg felt steady. I couldn't believe how quickly it was healing.

We paddled all morning, the sleek gliding along in our wake. When we stopped for lunch, he dived under and appeared with some weedy green vegetables he must have pulled from the river bed. He laid them at Eadie's feet.

'Good little snide,' she said.

'He's not a snide, he's a sleek.'

Eadie rummaged around inside her coat and brought out a fish spine, which she must have saved from last night's dinner. She began combing the sleek's tail with it.

'Whatever he is, he's done a good job,' she said.

The sleek closed his eyes and I heard his rattling purr.

The sun shone on Eadie's coat and gave it a reddish tinge. It crossed my mind that perhaps Eadie and the sleek belonged to each other – but as soon as I had that thought the sleek jumped up, spat at both of us, and dived into the water. Eadie stuck the fish bone in her hair.

'Time to go,' she said.

By midafternoon the river had narrowed slightly and I could see the other side: a long shoreline with pale hills behind it.

Eadie stood up in the craft and spread her hands. 'It's grand to be out of the marshes!' she cried. 'Now we must paddle hard.'

—⊱—

Eadie and I spent many days paddling up the river, and the sleek travelled with us. Sometimes he followed along behind. Other times we would round a bend and he'd be there, waiting.

Eadie checked my leg from time to time, and she made sure I had enough to eat. And every night she taught me a story. She had stories about everything – about journeys, places and creatures I had never heard of: rats that spoke human language; fish that swam upstream, leaping waterfalls; birds big enough to steal children; men who were made of salt. She told me stories about the marshes, and how it was one of the few places in the world that was a refuge.

'Once you're there, you're safe,' she said. 'Nothing can touch you . . . Except the other aunties,' she added, and she went on to tell me a funny tale about the time Lily accused Olive of stealing her glimmerweb and how it ended in a mud-wrestling match.

When I asked her about her own story she just laughed and waved me away.

'You wouldn't believe it, Peat,' she said.

The memory of Eadie's face on the night we'd left the marshes began to fade. I didn't want her to own me, but I had come to think that I wouldn't mind being her apprentice after all. I liked learning the stories. And I would have liked to learn the herbs as well. I was already learning the names of flowers. She was pointing them out to me as we went along.

'It's a good life,' she said. 'You can travel around healing people. I've saved thousands of lives, and nearly every person I've treated has told me a story. That's why I've got so many stories in my collection. You'll love this life, too.'

I didn't say anything, but I knew I wouldn't stay with Eadie, not forever anyway.

———✦———

One day, the river forked. We went left, and paddling became harder against a swift current.

'Let's leave the boat and walk along the bank,' I suggested. 'I can use my sticks.'

'The bank won't last,' Eadie said. 'The water is the only way.'

The landscape changed from open country to forest.

'How far is Hub?' I asked.

'Not far.'

We reached a bend in the river and I saw beehives under the trees on the bank. They were like the ones we'd seen before, except these were in good condition. Eadie told me to stop. She pointed further along the bank to a spot where a tree grew way out over the water, its long grey leaves trailing in the current.

'That's a woe tree,' she said. 'The bark is good for sadness. Wait here. I won't be long.'

She waded ashore, but she didn't collect the tree bark.

Instead, she walked quickly along the water's edge and disappeared around the bend.

I decided to follow her. My leg was almost better, and with the help of the sticks I could easily swing myself along.

'Come on,' I said to the sleek. 'I want to see where she's going.'

The sleek and I hurried after Eadie. When we rounded the bend I saw a clearing near the riverbank. A very old lady with long white hair was standing in the doorway of a timber hut that was half covered in pumpkin vines. Her face was as round as the moon and her hands were all white. Next to the hut was a big oven with a domed roof and a chimney pipe out the top. My nose caught the smell of fresh bread. She was a baker, and her hands must have been covered in flour.

'Eadie!' the old lady cried. 'I knew I would see you again!'

I crouched behind a rock and watched Eadie run towards her. They hugged each other.

'Your coat has grown huge,' the lady said. 'And it smells worse than ever.'

Eadie laughed. 'I've got more pockets now, Moss. I've got a pocket for everything.'

'You haven't changed.' The old woman was suddenly worried. 'But why are you here?' she asked. 'Where are you going? It's dangerous for you to be out of the marshes.'

At that moment the sleek made his chirping sound. Both of them turned around and saw me.

'I told you to stay put!' Eadie yelled.

The old lady staggered and gasped. 'Who does that child belong to?'

'No one,' said Eadie. 'She's a swamp waif.'

'Come here, child.' The woman held out her hand. 'What's your name?'

'Peat.'

She looked at me with pity in her eyes, then she glared at Eadie.

'Take her back.'

'Take her back where?' Eadie had switched languages: she now spoke in the western tongue. 'To the marshes? To the wretched place where she came from? She was lost and I found her.'

'Don't do it!' The old lady spoke in the same language. She clasped my hand.

Do what? I wondered.

I quickly looked at the ground and pretended I couldn't understand, which was true in a way: I knew the words, but I had no idea what they were talking about.

'She's injured,' the old woman continued. 'Let her go, Eadie.'

'I will. I'll take the mud cast off tomorrow.'

'That's not what I mean.'

They were silent for a moment, but there was an air of anger between them. Eadie turned to me.

'This is my friend Mother Moss. She used to be a marsh auntie.'

'If you take that child I'm no friend of yours,' said Mother Moss. 'Go and get your skiff, Eadie. You will stay with me tonight, and tomorrow you will go back to the marshes.'

Eadie huffed and turned on her heel.

'Are you her apprentice?' Mother Moss whispered as soon as she was out of sight.

I shrugged. 'Eadie is taking me to Hub, Mother Moss,' I said.

'And where will you go from there?'

I didn't answer. I didn't know what answer to give.

'Come here, little waif.' Mother Moss put a floury arm around me. She smelled of dough and fresh bread. 'Where are you from?' she asked.

'My sister Marlie and I lived at the Overhang, but I can never go back there.'

I wanted to tell Mother Moss everything that had happened to me since I'd run from Alban Bane, but I heard the splash of Eadie's paddle and the reed-boat came around the river bend. There was a landing in front of Mother Moss's place. Eadie tied the boat to it and came ashore.

Mother Moss gave us bread and soup and potatoes baked in the oven for supper, followed by honey buns served with cream.

'Do you own a cow, Mother Moss?' I asked.

'I have Cara,' she replied. 'But I think she owns me, rather than the other way around. You can meet her tomorrow.'

We ate on a bench outside the hut, and when the meal was over I watched Mother Moss stoke the oven. She added more logs and the flames crackled.

'By tomorrow it will be just the right temperature,' she told me. 'I leave the dough to rise overnight and I get up very early and cook the bread. Perhaps you would like to help me?'

'She can't,' said Eadie. 'We will be leaving for Hub tomorrow.'

Mother Moss gave me a blanket and rolled out a mat next to the oven. As soon as I lay down, she began speaking in the western tongue again.

'Don't go to Hub,' she said. 'Go back to the marshes and stay there.'

'I don't want to hide in the marshes forever, Moss. I want to be back in the world.'

'Eadie, you once saved my life, and you know we will always be friends…'

'And I will save many more. Moss, I have to do this.'

'But the child…'

'I know. I like the girl. She's bold and clever. She can remember stories.' Eadie raised her voice. 'It's not easy for me, but I have no choice. I made a bargain and I must keep it!'

'You were so young when you made that deal, Eadie. You hardly knew what you were doing.' Mother Moss stood up. She went inside the hut and didn't come out.

There was silence. I hoped Eadie couldn't hear me in the dark. My thoughts were racing as I tried to make sense of the conversation. I sneaked a look at her. She had lit her pipe and was leaning against the oven, gazing out over the river.

I lay awake for a long time. Eventually the sleek came and curled up against me. After that, I slept.

25

THREADMOSS

I woke the next morning to the sound of Mother Moss humming as she worked. She had a dun-coloured cow tied up outside the hut, and she was carrying a bucket. I saw that the cow's udder hung low to the ground and I was up on my sticks in an instant.

'Can I help, Mother Moss? I'm used to cows.'

'Be my guest,' she said. 'Only watch she doesn't step on your leg. Sometimes she can be a little silly with strangers.'

But Cara didn't find me strange. She gave me a gentle nudge and let me sit with my stiff leg sticking straight out under her. As I milked her, Mother Moss was busy at the oven, taking out loaves of bread with a long flat paddle. I must have been fast asleep when she'd put them in.

'Thank you, Peat. That's a big help,' she said as she put the loaves on the bench. 'The bread boat is coming early today, and I was wondering how I was going to get through the work.'

The smell of the hot bread made my mouth water.

'Go inside and get yourself some breakfast.' Mother Moss waved her hand towards the hut. 'But first, if you wouldn't mind, could you take Cara out the back and let her go? She grazes on the slopes behind the hut.'

I did as Mother Moss asked. Inside, I found a loaf of warm bread on the table, along with a slab of butter and a huge pot of honey. Apart from on the buns last night, I had only eaten honey once before, when Wim had brought some to the Overhang as a special treat. It was a tiny jar, and Marlie and I had made it last for a whole month.

I spread the honey thickly and sank my teeth into it with a sigh. *If only Marlie could share this*, I thought. It was as delicious as the marsh cake I had eaten in Eadie's hide.

Where is Eadie? I asked myself. *Has she had breakfast?*

I thought she might have gone off into the forest collecting herbs, but when I looked outside I saw that the reed-boat was no longer tied to the landing.

'Mother Moss, have you seen Eadie?'

Mother Moss was stacking loaves of bread into a big cane basket. 'I haven't, Peat,' she replied. 'Let's hope she's gone back to the marshes. If she has, you are welcome to stay here with me.'

I helped Mother Moss fill the basket, and when she brought two more out of the hut, I smiled and helped her fill those as well. It was good to be working.

'Did you have enough to eat?' she asked.

'Thank you, Mother Moss. Your bread and butter and honey is marvellous. Do you make cheese as well?'

'I would if I had time,' Mother Moss said.

'Marlie and I made cheese,' I told her. 'We had seven cows, but none of them gave as much milk as Cara, even after the stranger came. They used to only give a tiny bit of milk, but after he came they gave a lot more.'

'Did you have a favourite?' Mother Moss asked.

'Oh yes, Bella was my best cow. I really miss her.'

My chest felt tight. I was about to tell Mother Moss how I missed Marlie as well, and how worried I was about her, when a wooden boat with two men in it drew up to the landing.

'Goodness,' said Mother Moss. 'They're here already!'

'Ahoy, Mother. Got yourself a helper!' one man called cheerfully as he tied up the boat.

The other jumped ashore and came up to collect the baskets. 'The people of Hub are waiting for this,' he told me. 'It's the best bread south of the Western Plains. In fact, there's no better bread in the world – perhaps in all the worlds.'

His friend unloaded some sacks and carried them up to the hut. 'Wheat and rye, Moss. The miller said it's excellent flour.'

'Thanks, Mother,' called the other man as the last basket of bread was loaded. 'See you tomorrow!'

I watched them row the boat upstream. Mother Moss sat on a box next to the oven and wiped her brow.

'Phew!' she said. 'Sometimes I think I'm getting too old for all this work.'

'I'll help you,' I said.

She smiled and stood up. 'Let's wipe out the bread tins and clean up the bench, Peat. Once we've done that and swept up inside, we'll be ready for a cup of tea!'

⌒

Eadie returned at midday. She hadn't left for the marshes after all. She had been to Hub. I was sorry to see her – I'd been having a good time with Mother Moss and I wished I could stay.

'It's all organised,' she said. 'There hasn't been a telling in Hub for a long time, and people are eager to hear us. You will tell first, Peat, and I will follow. We'll perform in a place called the Undercavern.'

'No, you won't!' Mother Moss didn't even bother to speak in the western tongue.

Eadie ignored her. 'Let's get rid of the mud cast, Peat,' she said. She undid the bindweed and gently knocked along the length of my leg with a rock until the cast fell open. I stood up without my sticks.

'You're as good as new!' she said. 'Try it out.'

I walked down the path to the landing. My leg felt fine. I could hardly believe it had been broken. The sleek followed me, but raced ahead when he saw a boat coming around the bend in the river.

'Look!' A shout went up. 'A reed craft!'

The man rowing steered the boat to the landing. 'Does that belong to a marsh auntie?' he called.

I nodded.

'Praise the skies! We need her help.'

He tied up his boat, and a young woman climbed out. She was carrying a child whose head was wrapped in a bloodstained cloth. The man put his arm around the woman and they hurried towards Eadie. A boy followed, leading an old man.

'What happened to him?' Eadie asked as Mother Moss led them all into her hut.

'We were cutting wood and a branch fell on him,' the old man said.

Eadie gently removed the cloth and blood gushed from a wound on the crown of the child's head. She pulled what looked like a mass of tangled hair from one of her coat pockets.

'Threadmoss,' she said. 'I've had it in my coat for years and have never had the chance to use it.'

She pressed it to the wound and the bleeding soon stopped. The boy whimpered in his mother's arms. His eyes were closed and his face was deathly pale. Blue bruises were coming out on his forehead.

'Thank you,' cried the woman. 'You're saving him.' She pressed her lips to the boy's cheek. 'You'll be all right, little one. The lady is helping you.'

Eadie reached into another pocket and pulled out two dried twigs.

'Mother Moss, would you make tea from these? Boondock for the shock and Rockroot to steady him.'

'We are lucky to have found you,' the man said. 'There are so few marsh aunties about these days.'

When Mother Moss had made the tea and sweetened it with honey, Eadie pulled a long stem from under her collar.

'Marsh reed,' she said. 'It's hollow. If he drinks through this he will take in the strength of the marshes.'

The boy's mother held the reed to the child's lips, and to my surprise he sucked greedily. As he did, the colour returned to his face.

'He will live,' said Eadie. 'But just to be sure, I will check with the help of Wiltweed.' She took a withered sprig from inside her coat and held it over the boy's head. I watched in amazement as the limp plant became fresh and green once more.

Eadie smiled broadly. 'Let him sleep. He's out of danger.'

'Thank you, Auntie. May time repay you a hundred-fold.' The old man reached out and touched Eadie's sleeve. 'Do you live here?' he asked.

'No. My apprentice and I are just passing through. We're going to Hub.'

'Ah!' The old man clasped his hands. 'The place where the worlds meet!'

'We are storytellers, and we will be performing there.'

'Perhaps you will tell us a story?'

Eadie reached into her coat and took out the story pouch. She handed it to me.

'My waif will tell you a tale,' she said.

I took the sunflower seeds from the pouch.

'No,' Eadie said. 'Tell the Siltman story. That's the one you need to practise.'

I took out the bent nail and held it up, uncertain of how to begin.

'There was once a warrior...' Eadie prompted.

'His name was Pike,' I said. 'And he was afraid of nothing. Every night he dreamed of fighting, and every morning he woke with the battle light shining in his eyes.'

Eadie nodded encouragement. The sleek came and sat beside me, his chin resting on my leg.

'Pike's enemy was a giant called Scabbard, who lived in a sea cave at the bottom of a cliff.'

I tried to remember what Eadie had told me; to see the story in my mind so the audience would see it, too. I didn't know if I'd seen it all, but when I put the nail back into the pouch the family applauded loudly, and the injured boy woke up and said he was hungry.

26

HUB

The family thanked Eadie again, and they thanked me for the story, then they rowed away as the light was fading.

'You will stay another night,' Mother Moss said to Eadie. 'We need to talk.'

'You've seen what I can do,' Eadie replied. 'What's there to say?'

Mother Moss shook her head. 'It's not such a bad thing to grow old and die, Eadie. It happens to all of us.'

'But not to me,' said Eadie.

Once again I kept my head down. The sleek arched his back, making high whining sounds as if he was trying to block out what was being said. When he jumped onto the bread bench and knocked down some bread tins, Mother Moss stood up.

'Let's eat,' she said, and she served us a dinner of bread and fish, and gave me some honey and milk.

Eadie said little during the meal. She moved the food around on her plate.

'What you're doing is not right,' Mother Moss said. 'And you know it, Eadie.'

Eadie didn't reply.

'Promise me you'll reconsider,' Mother Moss pleaded.

'All right,' Eadie answered. 'I'll sleep on it and decide in the morning.'

I went to bed next to the warm oven. The sleek sat on my chest but he was wide awake and his tail swished from side to side, almost as though he was guarding me. The sounds of the night were all around – frogs, night birds, insects buzzing, water slapping against the landing. Mother Moss and Eadie were talking inside the hut, and after some time their voices grew loud, angry. The river rushed past and I could hear the wind blowing through the leaves of the woe tree – a low moaning sound. For a moment I thought I heard the stranger's voice, in the same low tone.

Go, he said. *Go now.*

I put my hand on the stranger's thread around my neck.

Go where? I wondered.

Go low, he said. *Hide.*

I was just getting up to hide among the trees at the edge of the clearing when Eadie rushed out of the hut.

'We're going,' she hissed. She pulled me to my feet and the sleek leapt away.

'I want to say goodbye to Mother Moss.'

'No,' said Eadie, hurrying me towards the landing. I dug in my heels, but she was much stronger than me.

'What were you and Mother Moss talking about?' I cried.

'That's none of your business.' She picked me up and threw me over her shoulder and the cow charm slipped over my head.

'Put me down!' I yelled.

'Shut up. You're my apprentice and you'll do as I say!'

'I'm not your apprentice!'

She threw me into the reed-boat and jumped in behind

me, then she pushed us away from the shore and began paddling hard. I looked back towards the hut and there was the sleek, on the edge of the landing. He made a trilling sound that ended in a whimper. I held out my arms to him.

'Come on, Sleek,' I cried. But he didn't follow.

'He'll catch up,' Eadie muttered. She paddled steadily, and I kept quiet.

———

The journey to Hub probably only took a couple of hours, but so much went through my mind that it seemed much longer. I should have stayed in Drip Cave and waited for Amos Last to come back for me. I should never have wandered into the marshes. I should never have let Eadie take me away from the other marsh aunties. I wished I was with Marlie and Wim...

'Be quiet,' Eadie snapped. 'I don't want to hear another thought out of you! This is as hard for me as it is for you.'

She gave a panting sort of sob. She was paddling hard, and the river was narrow and fast. I kept looking behind, hoping to see the sleek swimming after us, but the water was dark and there was no sign of him. I thought about jumping in and swimming back to Mother Moss.

'Don't!' Eadie cried. 'The river is dangerous. Trust me. Everything will be all right once we get to Hub. I'll tell you a story with a happy ending.'

I lay curled up in the bottom of the craft and tried not to think. Lights began to appear above. At first I thought they were stars coming out, but it was Hub – the lights of

Hub, twinkling high above like glow beetles. I could hear the sound of a waterfall.

I sat up as Eadie steered the boat into a narrow gorge with tall, steep sides. She paddled close to the edge, where the current was slower. There were boats on the river and I could make out houses in the dark. They were built into the cliffs and they seemed to be heaped on top of each other. Now and then I saw people going past on a walkway that ran along the base of the cliff. They were carrying burning torches. The sound of the waterfall grew louder.

We had to dodge boats tied to platforms jutting out from the shore. They were flat wooden boats and they had huts on them with lights inside the windows. There were tall boats, too, and they made clinking sounds as they rocked about on the water. Some had bright ribbons tied to their masts. Our reed-boat was tiny beside them. I heard snatches of laughter and a man singing in a deep voice – something about a river rolling to the sea. As we passed I listened to the words: 'Where the river meets the sea...you'll meet your destineeee.'

What's that? I thought.

'It's where you end up,' said Eadie. 'Your destiny – your destination.'

She wasn't angry anymore.

'Auntie!' Someone shouted above the noise of the waterfall and threw a rope from the shore. Eadie caught it. 'Welcome, Auntie! We've been waiting for you. Are you performing tonight?'

Eadie put down her paddle as the reed-boat was pulled in.

'No,' she called back. 'My waif is tired. She needs to rest. We'll tell the stories in the morning.'

A long pole with a hook at the end came out of the darkness. Eadie attached it to the boat and we were towed along the edge of the river. The water was choppy and the current so strong it would have been impossible to paddle against it. The roaring grew louder as the pole dragged us further upstream and, although the gorge was dark, there was a dull glow in the sky up ahead.

I had been scared when Eadie was paddling, but now I was petrified – I felt we were being dragged into the heart of something bigger than both of us. The noise was deafening. I cried out in alarm.

'Where are they taking us?'

Eadie didn't hear. She leaned forward, staring ahead.

We came around a corner and I was dazzled by a shock of thundering white water. The gorge ended in a waterfall. There was light behind it – a powerful light that turned everything into bright, swirling turbulence. Our reed-boat bobbed around like a cork on the end of the pole and we were covered in spray. *Surely they're not going to drag us any closer*, I thought.

'They'll tow us in behind the Waterwall,' Eadie shouted. 'The night markets are there, in the Great Hall. Beneath that is the Undercavern and all the tunnels and waterways of Lower Hub.'

As we came nearer I saw a cavern behind the water-fall – a great archway that gaped like an open mouth. The white curtain of water was cascading over it.

Eadie pointed upwards. 'The river is fed by a huge lake, and there's a lookout beyond that. From the lookout you can see a hundred roads and rivers leading in every direction, and they are only the ones above ground.' She was obviously excited to have arrived in Hub.

I didn't allow myself clear thoughts, but somewhere at the back of my mind I knew that if I was going to escape, this was my moment. I didn't dare jump into the wild water, though. Instead, I held tight to the sides of the reed-boat as it slipped behind the waterfall and passed a group of people standing inside the entranceway. It came to rest in a shallow pool. The roar of the water was replaced by the roar of a huge crowd.

'The night markets!' Eadie yelled.

Lamps hung from the roof of the cavern. I smelled smoke and fish oil and burning fat. People were hurrying between rows of market stalls carrying all sorts of things – boxes of vegetables, chickens in wooden crates, trays of little clay cups stacked in towers. A boy ran past with his arms full of silver balls, a stack of bright plates on his head. A man completely covered in birds was blowing a whistle and waving his arms as if he was trying to fly. There were more people and more things in this one moment and place than I had ever seen before in my life. Everyone was talking and yelling at once. It was almost too much to take in, but I had to keep my wits about me if I was to get away.

Eadie grabbed my wrist with one hand and, leaning over the side of the boat, scooped up some white clay with the other. She smeared it across my face, covering my forehead and both cheeks.

'To make you shine in the lights. Everyone must know who you are.'

People rushed towards us, greeting Eadie and touching me on the head, helping me ashore.

'It is our good luck to have a story waif in Hub,' they said. 'We'll all come to hear her.'

Eadie grasped my hand and led me through the markets. As the crowd parted for us, I realised that the moment when I could have got away had passed.

THE NIGHT MARKETS

The markets were vast. There were thousands of people in the Great Hall, and rows upon rows of tables laden with goods. There were bolts of bright cloth, trays of precious stones, small mountains of seeds and beans and spices. A blacksmith was hammering iron. Potters were pedalling their turning-wheels, shaping lumps of clay. Men with big muscles and bare chests covered in tattoos were cooking food in huge vats. Everywhere people were shouting, calling out the names of their wares.

'Wayfinders! Don't leave home without one!'

'Best pottery from the Western Plains.'

'Goats from the distant Mountains of Mirth.'

'Gifts, charms and wise fortunes!'

It seemed everything that *could* be sold was for sale in the night markets of Hub, as well as some things that couldn't be.

'Sayings!' called a woman who sat on the ground with nothing before her except a bright woven mat. 'A saying for the marsh auntie!' She looked Eadie in the eye. 'Many an honest heart beats beneath a ragged coat!' she cried.

'My coat's not ragged,' laughed Eadie. 'It's just stuffed full of herbs.'

And her heart's not honest, I thought, but I didn't know why.

We passed a stack of little square cages made of twigs and wire. 'Glowbirds,' a man called. 'Glowbirds to light your way!'

He noticed me staring and said, 'They look like simple sparrows, but they're not. In the dark they glow like torches.'

As we pushed our way through the crowds, groups of children pressed forward, staring at Eadie, curious but also fearful. Someone reached out to touch her coat. When we came to a clearing in the centre of the markets, a boy gave Eadie a fruit box and she stood on it.

She spent a moment lighting her pipe, and while the crowd gathered to hear her speak she looked over the heads of the people and blew three perfect smoke rings into the air. The first ring was small and hovered above her head. The second ring circled the first, and the third looped itself around both of them. The audience applauded as the smoke rings faded.

'Circles within circles,' Eadie cried. 'Stories within stories. Hub is the centre of the world and the place where the worlds meet. It is the most powerful place to tell a story.'

She pulled me up and held me high above her head. I looked down on a sea of faces. Some of them weren't even human. There was a man near the front surrounded by goats, and they all stared up at me as well. I wished I could disappear.

'People of Hub and Beyond,' she said. 'I present to you my apprentice, the swamp waif Peat. She will be telling tomorrow, in the Undercavern.'

A cheer rose from the crowd.

Eadie put me down and we went on making our way through the stalls. The crowd surged after us, and now many hands were reaching out to touch my head and to stroke Eadie's coat.

Up ahead I saw a flash of red. *The sleek!* I thought. But it was a girl selling skins.

'Cheap fur,' she called. 'Fur to keep you warm in winter.'

When we reached her, she saw me looking. 'Do you like the red?' she asked. 'It matches your hair. This is the pelt of a creature who travels between worlds. It's called a scarlet runner.'

I shuddered as we passed.

Further on, a young woman with braided hair and earrings that looked like seed pods was sitting on the ground. 'Futures!' she cried. 'A future for the marsh auntie and her waif. Let me read for you. No charge.'

She reached up and took the pipe out of Eadie's hand; then, tapping it on the ground, she peered into the white ash.

'Perhaps I had better not,' she said.

'Why not?' Eadie squatted down beside her. 'What do you see?'

'A death,' the ash-reader replied.

'Mine?' Eadie asked.

'If it's your pipe and your tobacco, the death probably belongs to you as well.'

'The pipe is hers but the tobacco came from me,' I said. It was the first time I had spoken since we'd left Mother Moss's.

'Then who can say?' The woman turned to me. 'Put your fingers in the ash, waif.'

I did as she asked.

'There's a place in a blind valley,' she said. 'A place of stone huts and deep shadow. Do you know it?'

I nodded.

'I see a broken settlement,' she said. 'The bell has fallen. The huts are roofless. Cattle run wild among the ruins. Something has happened there – a plague, an illness. The people have died.'

'What?' I cried. 'All of them?'

'Not all.'

'Is this the past or the future?' I asked.

'I think it's the present.' She was about to say more when a little goat ran between us, scattering the ashes. The crowd around us laughed, and Eadie snatched back her pipe and stood up.

'Clear the way,' she said. She pushed forward, and before long we reached the end of the markets. We went through an archway in a rough rock wall, which led us into a smaller – but still vast – cavern. In there, a ladder reached towards the roof. I looked up but couldn't see the end of it. It disappeared into the darkness.

'That's the way to Upper Hub,' Eadie said. 'The ladder has a thousand rungs.'

There were hollows and niches in the walls of the cavern. Eadie led me into an alcove at the far end.

'We'll sleep here,' she said.

28

THE THREE SISTERS

The alcove was dimly lit by a candle at its entrance. There was a pile of blankets stacked inside and straw was spread on the floor. People were sleeping in there; they stirred when we arrived.

'It's the storyteller and her waif,' someone whispered.

Eadie passed me a blanket and lay down, pulling her coat around her. There was rustling in the dimness. People were edging towards us – I could see their faces as they got close. We seemed to be in a circle of light, but I couldn't tell where it was coming from.

'From you,' Eadie said. 'It's your white face.'

I turned to the left and lit a group of people in a soft glow. When I turned to the right they disappeared into darkness and others appeared in front of me. The faces were waiting expectantly.

'I promised my waif a story,' Eadie said. 'You are welcome to listen.'

She pulled herself up and took something from her pouch. She held it towards me – a walnut.

'There were once three sisters,' she began. 'They lived with their old mother in the mountains. One year they had a hard winter. The snow lay thick on the ground. When they were almost out of food, the mother called her eldest daughter and asked her to go out and see what she could find.'

I wrapped myself in the blanket and lay down. I didn't want to listen to Eadie's story.

'The daughter wandered far and wide until, hungry and exhausted, she began to see things that weren't there, or so she thought. She saw a red animal. You call them swamp rats, or perhaps scarlet runners. I call them snides. The creature had fallen in a hole. It was trying to scramble up the sides, but the hole was deep and it was trapped.

'*Don't harm me*, it said. *And I will show you the riches of the world.*'

I was listening now. She was telling a tale about a sleek.

'The eldest daughter thought she was dreaming. She looked closely at the snide.

'*It's not big enough to feed us all*, she thought. *I'll kill it and eat it myself.* And that's what she did.'

I looked at the circle of faces. Everyone was listening keenly. I was glad my sleek wasn't around to hear this story.

'Then the eldest daughter made a rough shelter over the hole so that it had a roof, and she got in and went to sleep. She dreamed she was wandering through a forest. The night was bitterly cold and she needed somewhere to stay. She saw a twist of smoke in the distance and followed it until she came to a clearing. In front of her was a small mud house. It had no windows or doors. She circled the house, trying to find a way in. Then she saw a flash of red on the roof. It was a creature just like the one she had eaten. It disappeared down the chimney.

'The eldest daughter climbed onto the roof and followed the animal. When she was inside the house she found it was bigger on the inside than out. The walls were white and hung with rich tapestries. There was a table set with steaming food, and the plates were made of gold.

'There was no one about, so the girl sat down and ate. When she finished the food she licked the plate clean. And what a shock she got! Because the face she saw reflected in the golden plate was not her own, but a bone-white skull. She was up the chimney in a second. She leapt off the roof and, as she fled, she looked back and saw it wasn't a house at all but an ancient grave mound.

'At that moment the eldest daughter woke up. She had a terrible pain in her guts. She groaned and cried for help, but no one could hear her.'

Eadie paused.

'Go on, Auntie,' came a man's voice.

'When the eldest daughter didn't return the next day, the old mother sent her middle daughter to look for her.

'The middle daughter followed the tracks in the snow for days, until she found her sister half dead in the hole. She was frozen and almost too weak to speak. She used the last of her breath to tell what had happened, then she died.

'The middle sister heaped snow and earth over the grave. She sat for a while weeping for her sister, then she continued on her way.

'She had not gone far when she came across a hole, just like her sister had done. A snide was trapped in it.

'*Don't harm me*, it said. *I'll show you the riches of the world.*

'*I wouldn't dream of hurting you*, said the second sister. She let the snide go, but then when it ran away she gave chase. She followed it across the mountains and over plains and through forests. She chased it through the years of her life until, one day, it led her into a clearing and there was the mud house without windows or doors. When the snide leapt down the chimney, the girl followed just as her sister had done. The table was set and the golden plates were heaped with steaming food.

'The middle daughter didn't eat the food, because she knew what she would see at the bottom of it if she did. Instead, she tossed the food onto the floor and put the plates in her bag.

'As soon as she did this, the rich tapestries disappeared and the room began to shrink. She raced for the chimney but she couldn't fit. The ceiling pressed down, and the white walls became rough, crumbling dirt. Soon she was crouching in a hole no bigger than the one in which she had found the snide.'

Eadie held the walnut in front of her face and gazed at its wrinkled surface.

'Back home, the old mother waited, and when her second daughter didn't return she gave her youngest daughter the last of their food and sent her out to see what had become of the others.

'The youngest daughter followed the tracks of her sisters. She found two mounds and she guessed that her sisters had died. So she continued on. She had not gone far when she came across a snide trapped in a hole.

'*Don't harm me*, it said. *I'll show you the riches of the world.*

'*You poor thing*, the youngest sister replied. *You could have died if I hadn't come along.*

'She only had a small piece of bread, but she gave it to the snide, then she reached into the hole and helped the creature out. The snide did not run away. Instead, it followed her, and when she lay down to sleep it lent her the warmth of its body.

'The next morning, the creature began digging under the tree where they had slept. It dug up a hoard of nuts, and when the sun came out, the nuts shone golden in the light. The youngest daughter filled her pockets and went home to her mother, and together they lived to see many more winters.'

Eadie put the walnut in her bag. I closed my eyes and thought of the golden nuts. I was hungry, and I wished my sleek was with me.

'Did he show her the riches of the world?' someone asked.

'He saved her life with his offering, and then he followed her home and gave her his friendship,' Eadie said.

'Thank you, Auntie.'

'Goodnight, Auntie.'

There was rustling of straw and bodies as people settled back down for the night.

'Wait here, Peat,' said Eadie. 'I'll get you something to eat.'

She got up and left the alcove, returning soon with a bun that reminded me of marsh cake. She had a hot drink for me as well.

'Why didn't Mother Moss want you to bring me here?' I asked.

Eadie looked troubled. She turned her face away. 'Just eat up and go to sleep,' she said. 'You'll need to keep up your strength for tomorrow.'

When I had finished my supper I rolled over and pulled my knees up to my chest. I wished I still had my cow charm. I had a bad feeling about the performance, and I didn't want to do it.

29

THE UNDERCAVERN

When we woke the next morning the alcove was deserted. Outside our sleeping place, I could see a shaft of light shining down to the foot of the ladder. Sunlight. People were stepping off the last rung one after another and heading through an archway that went in the opposite direction to the night markets.

'They're all going to the Undercavern,' Eadie said. 'They'll be lucky to get seats. Come on. Let's go.'

She led me from the alcove to a wide passageway at the far side of the cavern. People stood aside to let us pass.

'What time will you begin, Auntie?' they asked.

'Soon,' she replied.

The passage wound deep under the ground. It was lit by lamps mounted on the wall, and smaller tunnels fed into the main corridor. People streamed in from these. Everyone was going in the same direction.

We entered the Undercavern through two sets of doors. They were huge doors, covered in green felt, and as one set closed soundlessly behind us, the others opened. The air inside was still – not hot or cold – and people lowered their voices as they entered. If there was a ceiling, it was so high above I couldn't see it. The lamps were low, but I could see that the walls of the Undercavern went straight up, like a cliff face. The seating was scaffolding – a rickety structure made of long poles and wooden planks – and people were climbing ladders to take their places high up along the rock walls.

In the centre of the Undercavern was a large flat stone. It was big enough for several people to sit on, but no one went near it. It was lit by a circle of candles.

'That's where we'll be,' Eadie whispered. 'But for the moment we will wait here inside the doors.'

I watched the crowd flow past. I recognised some people from the night markets. The woman selling sayings went by. 'The test of the heart is trouble,' she said to me. 'You can have that one for free.'

When all the seats in the Undercavern were full, Eadie closed the doors. Some of the lights went out and a hush fell on the crowd.

'Tell the Siltman story,' Eadie whispered.

She led me to the stone in the centre and she welcomed the audience, saying something about how it had been a long time since she'd last performed in Hub. I was only half listening. She looked huge in the candlelight. Her nose and chin were brightly lit from underneath and her eyes were in deep shadow. Her coat blended into the darkness, and I couldn't see where it ended.

'Let me introduce my swamp waif!' she declared.

I gasped as she pulled me towards her. The white clay on my face was tight, like a mask. My throat was dry and my legs were trembling. I didn't trust Eadie, and I didn't know why it was so important that I tell the story. There was applause, and then a quiet waiting. Eadie left me standing alone in front of the audience.

'Start,' she said.

I couldn't see the faces of the crowd, but I could feel everyone's eyes on me. For a moment my mind went blank. I couldn't remember how the story began. I couldn't remember anything. Then the first lesson of storytelling came into my mind: *Always open and close your stories. If you don't, the characters can come out into the world.*

The nail. I needed the nail. Eadie had the story pouch. She was standing aside with her arms folded. In the half-light she looked like a great bear guarding the door.

'Eadie, the pouch?'

'Just start,' she said. 'Once, long ago and far from here, there lived a warrior. His name was Pike...'

There was nothing to do but continue.

'Pike slept with a battleaxe tucked in his belt. Every night he dreamed of fighting, and every morning he woke with the battle light shining in his eyes.'

My voice sounded loud in the Undercavern.

'Pike lived in a stone fort at the top of some cliffs, and his enemy, a giant called Scabbard, lived in a sea cave at the bottom. Every day they met on the path and fought. You'd think one would have killed the other, but the two were perfectly matched.'

It was not difficult to tell the story once I had started. And I could feel the audience listening.

'One night Pike dreamed he lost the endless battle. He dreamed Scabbard speared him straight through his heart, and he was so frightened by this that he decided to seek advice.'

I paused and looked into the crowd. Was it only the day before that I had been telling the same story at Mother Moss's? It felt such a long time ago. Now I was performing in front of a huge crowd, and the story seemed bigger as well. My voice became stronger.

'There was a wayfarer who came to that part of the world – an old man known as the Siltman. People would visit him at his camp by the river mouth, because they believed he had knowledge and special powers. Pike decided he would take his dream to this man.'

I described the Siltman. I made him tall and thin, with long grey hair.

'He wore rags that flapped around him,' I said. 'And he travelled with a pack of dogs – wild rangy creatures that were taller than he was.'

I closed my eyes and continued.

'The Siltman had always been old, and he never grew any older. He came each winter, and people knew when to expect him because his footprints and those of his dogs appeared on the beach three weeks before he did.'

As I spoke, I thought of the second lesson of story-telling: *See the picture in your mind and the audience will see it, too.* Now I imagined a beach. I saw the footprints of the dogs and, for a moment, I could hear the sea – but it was probably just the audience breathing. Somewhere a dog barked. It was a muffled sound.

'Pike, the warrior, found the old man sifting silt at the river mouth,' I went on. 'He told of his dream and waited to hear what the Siltman had to say.

'The Siltman's voice was like wind blowing through dry grass, and his eyes seemed to look through to the next world.'

I remembered how Eadie had spoken in the Siltman's voice when she told the story in the marshes, and I made my voice dry and whispery, too. It echoed through the Undercavern.

'*You were right to come to me*, the Siltman said. *You will certainly die, unless I save you.*

'*Save me?* asked Pike. *How?*

'*I must separate your spirit from your body and put it away somewhere safe. If I do that, you can never be killed.*

'*Then do it*, said Pike.

'*There's a price*, said the Siltman.

'*Name your price*, said Pike. *I have a strongroom full of gold.*

'*I don't want gold*, the old man whispered. *I want something more valuable.*'

I paused. The sound of the sea grew louder. I wasn't sure if it was in my ears, or where it was. Perhaps there was a wind somewhere above; or maybe the sound was coming from the passage outside the Undercavern. I raised my voice.

'*Give me a child*, the Siltman said. Your *child.*

I whistled through my teeth the way Eadie had done when she had told the story.

'*It's a deal*, said Pike, who had no children.'

I stretched out my hand.

'The Siltman then reached up and touched the warrior's chest. He took out Pike's spirit and dropped it in a bag at his feet.

'One of the Siltman's dogs had recently given birth and there were puppies in that bag. The spirit went into a puppy. The old man drew out the pup and gave it to Pike.

'*Keep him safe*, he said. *And you will live forever.*'

I stopped speaking, because something was happening outside the doors. I heard a crash, then scratching – loud scratching – and the sound of something tearing.

'Go on!' Eadie said sharply. 'Finish the tale.'

'Pike put the puppy inside his cloak and went home. The next day, when he fought his enemy, a spear passed through him without leaving a scratch and he knew everything the Siltman had said was true.

'Years passed. Pike gave no thought to the bargain he had made—'

Suddenly the doors of the Undercavern burst open. There was a sharp salt wind and the dank smell of wet dog. The candles flickered and went out, and so did the lamps above. The only light was the glow coming from my face, and in that I could see a pack of dogs – a big group of enormous hounds. The audience gasped as the dogs turned their wild, glittering eyes on me. In a moment I was surrounded by huge, grey shaggy beasts.

'Keep still,' someone shouted.

I froze. I thought that in a second they would leap at me. But the dogs circled the stone, around and around. In the hush I heard a dry, whispering voice.

'Drop.'

Immediately the dogs lay down with their heads between their paws. Their eyes were watching me. At the doors, I could just make out the figure of a man standing next to another gigantic hound. He was tall and thin. The man lifted one hand.

'Fetch,' he said in a voice that was like the wind blowing through dry reeds. In one movement, the dogs leapt onto the stone. They towered above me, brushing me with their wiry coats. I stared out through their legs like a prisoner looking through bars, and when they moved, I moved with them. In this way, they steered me towards the doorway.

There were murmurs from the audience, who only now dared to speak.

'Extraordinary…'

'What a telling!'

Someone stood up and yelled 'Bravo'. Then they began to clap, softly at first, as if they were fearing for me, and then with great enthusiasm. They cheered and yelled and stamped their feet. They thought whatever was happening was part of the storytelling.

Through the dogs' legs I saw a pair of bare feet, ancient and gnarled – the worn feet of an old man. His trousers were ragged and so thin that I could see his legs through them, smooth and bone-white, like driftwood.

'You will come with me,' the Siltman said. 'The bargain is complete.'

I felt myself swept up, thrown onto the back of one of the dogs, and the Siltman was behind me, with his hard, bony arm around my waist. The dogs surged towards the doorway. Eadie leaned towards me as we passed. I thought she was going to grab me, but she didn't.

'I'm sorry, Peat,' she cried. 'I had to do it.'

'Do what?' I yelled.

The dogs bounded past, leaping the second set of doors that were lying flat on the floor of the passageway, the green felt shredded, and Eadie disappeared behind me. The roar of the audience's applause faded and the wind roared in my ears instead as we raced away from the Undercavern.

In a moment we came to a place where the passageway forked. The Siltman gave a sharp whistle and the dogs streamed to the left. We were going down, deeper into the earth, instead of following the passage back towards the alcove and the night markets.

I screamed as the pack of dogs careered forward. They were running wildly, weaving in and out and leaping across each other. Their paws thudded on the ground, and the sound echoed through the passage as they charged ahead with their tongues hanging out and a look of mad joy in their eyes. Terrified, I grabbed a handful of hair and tried to hang on.

'Where are you taking me?' I cried. 'Why?'

The Siltman didn't answer.

30

THE SILTMAN

The passage was wide but the roof was low and it grew lower as we ran along the tunnel.

'Head down,' breathed the Siltman.

I leaned forward, pressing my head against the dog's neck as the pack rose and fell around me like a grey sea. The dogs were running like they would never stop. They raced around a bend, and then the ceiling arched above us and I could sit up again.

'Hold!'

The pack slowed and came to a halt, and the only sound was panting. It was cold in the tunnel and I could see the white breath of the dogs curling from their mouths like question marks. They looked to the Siltman, waiting for a command. He slipped to the ground.

'Stay,' he said, and I didn't know if he was talking to me or the dog I was on. He looked over the pack, then he moved among the dogs, patting each one, running his hands over their backs and down their legs, checking their paws, feeling their ears and necks and noses.

'Flank!' he called.

One of the dogs came to him, pushing its way through the others.

'Grey!' The Siltman whistled. 'Fathom!'

Two more dogs followed.

'Drop.'

Except for the three he had called, all the dogs lay down, including the one I was riding. They were focused on the Siltman, waiting for instruction.

I looked back up the tunnel. I could have slid to the ground and run, but my body was frozen in shock. And how far would I get?

'Change.' The Siltman pointed to one of the standing dogs. 'You will ride Fathom.'

The dog pricked its ears at the sound of its name and stepped forward, and then I felt the Siltman's hands on my ribs as he picked me up and threw me onto the dog's back. When he let go I could still feel the prints of his fingers burning into my sides, not hot but freezing cold.

'Grey. Flank. Stay by!' He flicked his hand and the dogs took their places, one on either side of me.

'Away!' commanded the Siltman and the pack was up and running again. This time the Siltman didn't ride. He ran beside one of the dogs with his hand on its shoulder, and he ran like the wind, not like an old man with bony legs.

There were very few lamps in this tunnel. Long stretches of darkness followed short spaces of light. And then there were no more passage lamps at all. The dogs ran freely in the dark, as if they knew where they were going.

'Ease,' cried the Siltman.

The dogs slowed to a steady pace.

'You have nothing to fear,' came his whispery voice. 'You will stay with me and help me with my work. You will sift silt at the river mouth in winter, and in summer you will travel with me to the far north.'

He groomed the dog beside him as he spoke, raking his fingers through its long grey hair. 'When you return, your footprints and those of your dogs will appear on the beach three weeks before you do.'

'No!' I cried. 'I don't want to go.'

'You're the storyteller,' the Siltman said. 'But let me tell you a story. Once, long ago, there lived a young woman called Eadie. She was perhaps a bit older than you, and she was learning the art of healing. In order to protect herself from all the dangerous illnesses she would be called upon to cure, she came to me for advice.'

'*No!* I don't want to hear your story.'

The Siltman took no notice of me.

'I told her there was only one way of keeping safe. I could remove her spirit from her body and hide it away, in my land of the Ever, so she would always be protected.'

'You're telling the wrong story,' I cried. 'Your story is the one about a warrior called Pike.'

'There are many stories,' the Siltman replied. 'I told Eadie she would never catch a disease. She would never be injured. She would never grow old. And that is what happened. For long years she wandered the world, curing the sick and injured. Nothing could harm her. She was immune. But there was a price, and that price was a child...'

'It's not true,' I said. 'I don't believe it! You're telling lies.'

'The Siltman never lies,' he replied. 'When I demanded payment, Eadie fled to the safety of the marshes and she remained there for a very long time. Until you arrived.'

One of the dogs howled and another answered, then the pack was running again.

I closed my eyes and tried to keep hold of my thoughts. The wind roared past. I felt as though my life was a very small thing that was streaming out behind me. I called out to Marlie and to Mother Moss and Wim. Then I called to the stranger and to Amos Last, and to the sleek and Bella and Bright. No one could hear me, but if I could hold onto my friends I would have something. Their names disappeared behind me, though, and soon there was nothing in my mind except the howling of the dogs and the huge hollow made by the knowledge that Eadie had betrayed me.

31

THE SILVER RIVER

If you asked me how long we were in the tunnel, I couldn't tell you. I didn't know if it was night or day. But finally the dogs stopped howling and slowed to a loping sort of trot. They were hot and sweating, and the air was full of their smell as the tunnel narrowed.

'Hold,' said the Siltman. And to me, 'Get down.'

I dumbly obeyed. There was nothing left in me to resist him.

The Siltman ran his hands over the rock wall in the same way he had run his hands over the dogs, patting and feeling.

'See it?' he asked.

The stone had a greenish tinge.

'Closer,' he ordered, and when I moved nearer, the rock glinted in the light from my face and I saw it was shot through with a bright seam of silver.

The Siltman reached into his pocket and took out a tiny hammer. He chipped a piece off the rock and put it in his bag, then he whistled and we were moving forward again. The dogs he had chosen for me stayed close, one on each side and one behind. Up ahead I could hear the others splashing through a creek. The ceiling became very low and soon the dogs were whining as they scrambled on their bellies. I hit my head on a rock and crawled forward on my hands and knees, moving into icy-cold water. One of the dogs grabbed me by the scruff of the neck and hauled me along. The water got deeper, and soon I realised that the dog was swimming, pulling me after him. At one stage my head dipped under the freezing water.

'Here!'

I looked up and saw the Siltman crouched some distance ahead, on dry land. The tunnel was slightly higher there. The dog dragged me to the Siltman and dropped me at his feet.

'Follow me,' he said, and he crawled ahead, moving quickly until we came to a place where the tunnel opened out. He stood up and told me to do likewise.

When I got to my feet my clothes pulled tightly on me, as if they had shrunk in the water.

There was light ahead. We had almost reached the end of the tunnel. The dogs whimpered with excitement.

'Away!' the Siltman whispered, and all the dogs surged forward, some still scrambling on their bellies, others scraping their backs on the low roof of the tunnel. I followed and saw that the light was not daylight but a night sky full of stars, and that there was an expanse of bright water – or perhaps it was mud or wet sand.

The dogs emerged from the tunnel and their backs gleamed silver in the moonlight. They shook themselves, each standing for a moment in a spray of shining water before racing across the mud flats, for that's what they were. The Siltman brushed past me into the open, his arm resting over the last dog.

'This is the Silver River,' he said. 'The tide is out. We'll cross and camp on the other side.'

I could see him clearly for the first time, but somehow he was less distinct than he had been in the dim light of the Undercavern. His tattered shirt flapped around him like a bag hung over a doorframe, and his wispy hair covered half his face. There was no wind; yet everything around him was blowing. He strode ahead with long light steps, and the dogs stopped and looked back, waiting for him. When he had caught up, they followed him in a line, their shadows stretching across the wet sand.

I watched them move away. The ground was shiny and their paw prints filled up with water, leaving a trail of silver dots in their wake. In another time or another life, it might have been a beautiful sight; a scene I would have liked to describe to Marlie. But Marlie was long gone, and I was lost as well.

I gazed after the dogs and realised there weren't as many of them as I had thought. In the tunnel there had seemed to be dozens of them, but now I counted eighteen, nineteen, twenty...I stopped counting and stared. I had reached the end of the line. There were twenty dogs, but twenty-one shadows.

The Siltman looked back.

'Come, Siltgirl,' he called. Then he shouted something and three dogs broke from the line, circling back behind me. One barked. Another made a low growl. They herded me after the Siltman, and he only began moving once I was close behind him.

When we reached the far side of the river bed the Siltman raised his hand. His nails were long and pointy, more like the nails of a dog than a person. He made as if to throw something. Silt blew from the folds of his sleeves into my eyes, blinding me.

'Fetch,' he called.

I heard the dogs yelp and bound away. When I could see again, each had a stick in its mouth. The Siltman made a fire.

'This is for you,' he said in his whispery voice. 'I don't feel the cold and soon you won't, either.'

I looked back the way we had come. A wall of mountains towered above us.

'Is Hub up there?' I asked.

'Hub is a lifetime away. Forget about Hub.' He scooped up a handful of black sand and let it trickle through his fingers. 'Well, not exactly a lifetime,' he muttered. 'But at least a year.'

The sand was fine and sooty, and it blew away before it reached the ground. A strange and empty feeling came upon me, as if I had somehow been left behind in Hub and only my body had arrived in this place. And even that seemed different to me. I looked at my feet, pale and long – they might have belonged to someone else. My trousers were halfway up my legs, as though the bottoms had been cut off. And they were tight. So was my vest. I held out my arms to see if the sleeves of my dress had got shorter as well, and I felt it split at the back. I put my hand to my face. There was no trace of the white clay Eadie had painted on me.

'You've grown,' said the Siltman. 'The journey does that. But now you have arrived you won't grow anymore.'

He sat down a short distance away and all his dogs

settled down around him. A gull flew overhead and they watched it pass. One dog yawned. Another scratched itself behind the ear then rested its head on its paws. The air was salty and I could hear sea booming in the distance. I remembered a snatch of song from what seemed a long time ago: *Where the river meets the sea, you'll meet your destiny.*

'Does this river flow into the ocean?' I asked.

The Siltman ignored my question.

'Now you will tell me a story,' he said, looking beyond me with his strange pale eyes. I glanced over my shoulder to see what was there, but there was nothing except the riverbank.

I didn't reply. I wasn't going to tell him a story. I wasn't going to tell him anything.

The Siltman sighed. 'You'll change your mind in time.' He scooped up more river sand and poured it from one hand to the other. 'And there's plenty of time,' he said. 'Time is like silt. We have all the time in the world.'

He lay down among his dogs and looked at the night sky. After a while I realised he had gone to sleep, although his eyes were still wide open. His dogs were asleep, too. The shaggy hair on their backs rose and fell in time with the Siltman's breathing.

32

THE SILTMAN'S BOY

That night I dreamed of dogs – huge dogs racing through the waves. They were grey and slavering, and their howling was carried on the wind. They turned on me, chasing me along an endless beach. I ran hard, and behind me their paws, thudding on the wet sand, sounded like thunder. I ran inland and found myself in Bane Valley. The dogs were gaining on me. Their jaws snapped and their mouths drooled. I knew Bane Valley ended in the steephead, so I turned and faced the pack.

'Call off your dogs,' I cried.

The Siltman was there – or perhaps it was Hazel, the Great Aunt. It was someone vague and surrounded in mist. They raised an arm and the dogs were still. In the half-light the hounds looked like huge grey stones. I ran through them, heading for the Overhang. The mist dispersed, and with it the spell that was holding the dogs. Their howling filled my ears, and by the time I reached the Overhang they were almost on me. I threw myself into the night cave and looked for the opening in the roof, but it was gone. I was trapped like a rat in a hole.

'Awake! Awake!'

I sat up with a start. A boy was staring into my face.

'Wake to the world and speak!' he demanded. 'Be you true or a piece broke off from Siltboy's dream?'

'What?'

The boy was smaller than me. He had bleached white hair and blue eyes that were wide with fright. There was a scar on his face – three fine lines from his cheek to his chin. He wore a ragged shirt, a silver breastplate and a shiny little helmet. He had a cloth bag slung over his shoulder.

'Speak!' he repeated. 'Be you friend or foe?' He raised a silver spear above his head.

'Friend,' I said hurriedly.

'Friend!' He threw the spear at my feet, and it broke into three pieces. It was a corn stalk. 'Siltboy has no friend – not now, not ever. Where from you come?' he demanded.

I was sitting on the sandy riverbank, where I had fallen asleep. The Siltman and his pack of dogs were gone. The tide was in and a sheet of silver water lay before me, stretching forever. I pointed across the river.

'You lie in your tooth,' he said. 'No one can cross the Silver River.' He stared at me as if he couldn't believe I was real. Then he stepped forward and touched my hair. 'Fire head!' He drew back his hand as if he had been burnt. 'I thought you was a ghost!'

He pointed to my neck. 'Thread,' he said. 'Give it up.' He held out his hand, and when I took off the stranger's thread and dropped it into his palm he smiled, showing a broken front tooth.

'Do you hunger?' he asked.

When I looked at him blankly, he rubbed his stomach and pointed to his mouth. I nodded. I hadn't eaten since Eadie had given me the bun in the alcove, and if I was to believe what the Siltman had said, that was over a year ago.

The boy turned and looked along the edge of the river. He gave a long low whistle.

The day was blustery; clouds blew across the sky. When I saw something moving along the water's edge, I thought at first that it was the shadow of a cloud, then there was a splash and it was gone.

'Come!' the boy shouted.

I could see ripples, fanning out into a V-shape. Something was swimming towards him. Perhaps there was a big fish under the surface.

'Come!' he yelled again.

There was another splash and the surface of the water became smooth. A dark shape moved across the sand towards us. The sun went in and the shape disappeared. A chilly breeze sprang up out of nowhere. I watched the boy reach up and pat the air.

'My hound,' he said.

He made long stroking movements with his hands that reminded me of the way the Siltman had run his hands over his dogs – only there was nothing there.

'His name is Shadow.'

'Shadow? Your dog is Shadow?'

Siltboy gave me a strange look.

'You see him better with eyes shut,' he said. 'Shut up your eyes and look.'

I thought I'd better do as he said. I closed my eyes and saw a faint outline glowing behind my eyelids. It was the shape of a dog, dim at first, but as my eyes adjusted, it grew brighter.

'Hands over eyes is best,' the boy said.

I cupped my palms over my eyes and gasped. The edges of the dog-shape were alive with white flames, and there were lights in the middle of him – hundreds of tiny flickering lights, like stars or fireflies.

'A ghost hound!' I cried. 'He's scary!'

'No scare,' said the boy. 'Shadow is faithful hound and true. He is afraid of nothing and he will fight to the death.'

'But he's already dead,' I breathed.

'Never! Give me your hand. Touch him.'

I stared wide-eyed at the boy as he pulled my hand forward. I couldn't see the dog with my eyes open, but as my hand moved to the spot where he was, the air felt dense and my fingers tingled.

'Feel the strands of him?' he asked.

There was something beneath my fingers, something tangly – string or rope. It slipped through my fingers.

'Hair of dog!' the boy cried. 'Give him pat.'

I did as he said and gasped as the ghost hair parted and my hand went straight through. The boy laughed.

'Shut up the eyes again.'

I closed my eyes, and now there were thousands of tiny flickering lights within the dog's edges. They were swarming like insects.

'See! He likes you!'

The sun came out and I jumped back. Something was moving on the ground beside me.

'Shadow wags his tail,' the boy cried. 'Hold this.'

He handed me the bag, then he turned and ran into the water, diving under. When he came up his helmet had gone soft. He peeled it off and threw it away.

'Not metal-made,' he yelled. 'Fish skin.'

He gave a loud whistle. I couldn't see the dog, but I saw its shadow running to meet him. It must have been the same one that I'd seen yesterday when I'd counted the Siltman's hounds.

The boy dived under again and when he surfaced he had a fish in his mouth. He put both hands in front of him as if he was holding onto something, then he rose out of the water and moved towards me, with his legs apart and his feet not touching the ground. I blinked and stared. He looked like he was riding the air!

'Gob it,' he said, handing me the fish.

I had never eaten raw fish before, but I was hungry, and it seemed best to obey him. He watched me eat, biting chunks of fish meat and swallowing them down.

'Friend,' he said, holding out his hand for me to shake. I was surprised at the strength of his grip.

'Who are you?' I asked, although I thought I already knew.

'Siltboy,' he answered. 'I am his.'

'Whose?'

'Siltman's. I am the Siltman's boy.'

'You are now, but you weren't always.'

'Truth,' he said. 'Siltboy was the son of Pike. He knows the battleways.' He reached into his bag and pulled out a slingshot. 'How many years have you got?' he asked.

I supposed he meant how old was I. 'Nine.'

'I've got nine hundred.'

'Nine hundred! But you're not even grown up!'

Siltboy drew himself up to his full height, which brought him just under my chin. 'Siltboy is grown,' he said. 'He is strong in the legions and brave in the heart. In the old days he would have been a giant.'

He scratched a scab on his leg. 'What for have you come?' he wanted to know.

'Stolen. Like you,' I said. 'I am part of a bad bargain.'

'Stolen!' he cried. 'Where is the thief? Siltboy will get him.' He picked up the broken pieces of his spear, ready for battle.

'It's not a him, it's a her. A marsh auntie. Her name is Eadie. She let me be taken by the Siltman.'

'Where is she?'

'Not here. She's back in Hub.'

Siltboy looked confused. 'Hub?' he asked. 'I never did hear of Hub.'

'It's the place where the worlds meet. From Hub, you can go anywhere.'

He shook his head for a moment, then he shrugged and smiled.

'I have a fort,' he said. 'Do you want to see it?'

I nodded. Siltboy might have been nine hundred years old, but really he was just a little boy. 'Yes, Siltboy. Show me your fort.'

He reached into his bag and pulled out a piece of leather. At first I thought it was a belt. It had a rusty buckle and there were iron studs in it. 'Collar,' he said. 'For hanging on.' He reached up and put the collar on the invisible dog. 'We ride,' he said.

Siltboy threw his leg into the air. When he was sitting upright, he pulled me after him. 'Hold me straps,' he said, putting my hands on the sides of his breastplate, where I felt two pieces of webbing tying it in place.

He reached forward and grabbed the collar, then he whistled and the ghost hound surged forward so fast that I almost lost my grip. We moved swiftly across the wet sand at the river's edge. When Siltboy leaned to one side, we veered away from the water and over the riverbank.

Riding the ghost hound was like riding the wind. He wasn't moving across the ground, he was floating above it, and when I looked down I saw it flashing past beneath me. It made me feel sick, so I looked up instead. There were sand dunes ahead, and beyond them open country stretched before us as far as the eye could see – grasslands, low wooded hills and, very far away, dark plains with mountains behind them.

'This is the Siltman's country,' Siltboy called over his shoulder.

We reached a high point and Siltboy gave a sharp whistle. Shadow stopped so quickly that I fell forward and we both went tumbling headfirst onto the ground. Siltboy's breastplate clanged as he hit a rock.

'Are you all right?' I asked.

He jumped up immediately. 'Always,' he said. 'Nothing breaks.'

Now that I was on solid ground I struggled to get my breath.

We were on top of a hill and below us was a little lagoon with a single tree growing near it.

'You thirst?' he asked.

I nodded.

'Come.'

Siltboy took my hand and pulled me down the slope. The shadow of the dog moved beside us, rippling over the ground. When we reached the water I knelt down to have a drink.

'Wait,' Siltboy cried. 'I have vessel, drinking horn.'

He climbed up the tree and disappeared among the leaves. When he returned he was carrying the longest cow horn I had ever seen. He filled it with water and held it for me while I drank. The end of it was edged with silver, which must have made it even heavier.

'You're strong for your size, Siltboy.'

'True.'

He drank after me, then he poured the rest of the water onto the shadow of his ghost hound.

'My dog don't need to drink but I give him some anyways,' he explained. He put the horn back in the tree and we climbed back onto his hound and were moving again, Siltboy leaning forward and holding the collar and me holding Siltboy.

The land was vast. Some of it reminded me of the country out near the Boulders at the Overhang – rocky outcrops on dry ground. I could see something moving across the plains in the distance: a flock of black goats, or perhaps a herd of cattle. They were the same colour as the earth, and too far away to see clearly.

'Aurochs,' Siltboy told me. 'Horned ones. They is fierce.'

We stopped, and he wrapped his bag around his arm and held his fist up to the sky.

'What are you doing?' I asked.

'*Yeak, yeak!*' he cried, and I heard the same sound from far above. I looked up and saw an eagle circling.

'My battlebird,' Siltboy said. 'She wants your name.'

'You talk to creatures?'

He nodded. 'Siltman taught me.'

The bird wheeled low and landed on his arm in a rush of glossy feathers. Its eyes were gold and its hooked beak was the colour of iron. It was like a bird from one of Eadie's stories – a bird with a huge wingspan and the strength of a horse – the sort of bird that could carry you away.

'I tell her you is stolen,' Siltboy said. 'What name will I give?'

'Peat.'

'*Yeak, yeak.*' Siltboy spoke to the bird. She lowered her great head, then she took off as suddenly as she had arrived, heading out over the hills towards a headland where I could see a tower – or it might have been a chimney.

'Is that the fort, Siltboy?'

'My home,' he said.

———

The fort was a ruin. It stood on a cliff overlooking the sea and all that was left of it were some crumbling walls, a blackened slab of stone that might once have been a hearth, and the remains of a chimney. Siltboy's battlebird was perched there, but when we arrived she took off and flew towards the horizon. Siltboy pulled me to the ground and sat down on a rock that had probably once been the cornerstone of the large building. I sat down beside him and watched the shadow of his hound disappear into the shade of the chimney.

'Tell your tale and tell it true,' Siltboy said.

'What?'

'State yourself. Where from you come? What bargain? Who is your tribe? Say your story.'

'I don't have a tribe,' I said. I thought of Marlie and Wim and the cattle, and I realised I would never see them again. Tears brimmed in my eyes.

'Are you keening?' he asked.

I supposed he meant was I crying.

'Yes. I'm lost. I want to go home.' To say that made me really start crying, because I had no home. The Overhang was far behind me, and so was everything else. 'What will happen to me?' I sobbed.

'Naught,' he said. 'You are in the Ever.' Siltboy stood up and went to the hearthstone. 'Take heart,' he said. 'I'll show you my hoard.'

He pulled the big stone aside, revealing a hole beneath.

'Look under them sacks,' he said.

I peered into the hole and saw a couple of old bags. Siltboy pushed them aside. There were shells underneath – shells and round stones that he probably used for his sling-shot. He picked one up and handed it to me. It was shot through with silver.

'Treasure.'

He reached deep into the hole and pulled out an ancient buckle. Half of it was broken off, but it was still the biggest buckle I had ever seen. It must have come from an enormous belt. He rubbed it on his shirt and it gleamed in the sunlight.

'Gold,' he said. 'It were Pike's.'

I realised then that Siltboy had lost his people just like I had.

'Do you remember your father?' I asked.

'I do. Pike learnt me the battleways.'

'Is the Siltman your father now?'

'No. Siltman is master. He learnt me the language of creatures.'

'What about your mother?' I asked him. 'What did she teach you?'

Siltboy fell silent and stared into his treasure-hole.

'Siltboy misses the mother,' he said softly, then he sniffed and wiped his nose on his sleeve. 'Now two of us is keening.' He sighed and dragged the stone back over the hole. 'When I found you on the shore you had the fright on you and I caught it. Now my hut is made of misery.'

'What hut? What are you talking about?'

'My bone hut, my blood house, wherein beats my heart.'

Siltboy tapped his chest. He had a strange way of speaking and I could barely understand what he meant.

'I'm sorry, Siltboy. I didn't mean to make you cry.'

He sighed again and took my hand. 'Tell your tale,' he said.

33

SIFTING SILT

Siltboy lay down on the grass beside the old hearth and looked at the sky as I told him my story.

'My family was Marlie and Wim and the cows we milked to make cheese. My mother died of a hole in her heart.'

'Speared?' Siltboy sat up. 'Who did the deed? I will revenge him.'

'No one, Siltboy. She was born with it.'

He sighed and lay back down.

'Wim was my mother's sister, and Marlie was my sister.' I was telling the story as if it had happened long ago. 'Marlie and I lived at the Overhang all by ourselves.'

'Overhang was your fort?' Siltboy asked.

'Yes, I suppose it was. The other people lived in a settlement four days' walk away. We weren't allowed to go there. There was a headman, a boss man, who was in charge of everything.'

'Chief,' Siltboy said.

'His name was Alban Bane and he hated me.'

'Enemy chief.' Siltboy nodded to himself.

'One day, when I was out with the cattle, I met a stranger – a good man from far away. He wanted to go to the settlement and I told him the way. But he had the catching sickness, and when it spread, Alban Bane blamed me. He wanted to punish me, and he came for me at night with a mob of people. They had burning torches, Siltboy.'

I remembered how I had crouched on the roof of the Overhang, listening to Alban Bane giving instructions, and how the cattle had run off in terror.

'Siege,' Siltboy said. 'Go on.'

'I had to escape. Marlie gave me her lucky cow charm, and I climbed the escarpment. All night I climbed. I felt like I was climbing up into the sky.'

'Scarpment?'

'It's like a cliff face, Siltboy – a wall of rock. It was behind the Overhang. I nearly fell, but the sleek saved me. He was a wild little creature with pointy ears and a red tail. He bit me, but he helped me, too. Then he stole my cow charm and made me get lost in the marshes...'

I started crying again. Siltboy waited for me to continue.

'And that's where I met Eadie, the marsh auntie. I got caught in her snare. She wore a huge coat covered in pockets, and every pocket was full of herbs, and she had a pouch with special things in it to open and close her stories. She had stories about everything. She told me the story of you.'

'Me? Siltboy?'

'Yes. Your father was a giant warrior called Pike, and Shadow was the pup of one of the Siltman's dogs.'

Siltboy listened wide-eyed, and when I got to the part where Scabbard came to the fort, he raised his hand for me to stop. His face was white and the air seemed very still.

'Steady, Shadow,' he said.

A tremor ran through the ground beneath us and I heard a sound so low and deep it was as if the earth was growling. A loose stone fell from one of the walls.

Siltboy went and sat in the shade of the chimney. He patted the air. 'Go on with the tale,' he said.

I told him the rest of the story about Pike, and when I finished Siltboy shook his head in bewilderment.

'Siltboy is bargain boy?' he asked.

'Yes,' I said. 'You were payment for the bargain your father made with the Siltman. And the same thing has happened to me.'

'Your father made Siltman bargain?'

'No,' I said. 'Eadie did. She taught me the art of story-telling, but she tricked me. The only story she didn't teach me was her own. She made the same sort of deal Pike did. The Siltman hid her spirit away here in the Ever so she could never die, and I was the payment.'

'How do you know?'

'The Siltman told me. Eadie took me to Hub and that's where he got me. Now Eadie is free and she will live forever, and I have ended up here, lost to the world.'

'Not lost. Siltboy has found you. You will live forever just like your muck hag.'

'She's not a muck hag, she's a marsh auntie. And I don't want to live forever, Siltboy. I want to grow up and live my life.'

Siltboy looked surprised, as if he had never imagined himself grown up.

'I want to see Marlie and Wim again. I want to travel the world like the stranger. I don't want to end up nine hundred years old and still be exactly the same.'

Siltboy was quiet for a long time. He stood up and walked around the fort, then he squatted and began drawing in the dirt – four straight lines, and one that went across. He did it over and over again, as if he was trying to add something up in his mind, then he went to his hoard and, scooping up a handful of shells, he let them trickle through his fingers. He looked at his empty hand and closed it into a fist.

'I will save you,' he declared.

'Save me?'

'Upon my honour. I swear it.' He put his hand on his heart. 'Friendship is forged and a promise is made.'

'But how can you save me? You're trapped here just like me.'

'Where is your luck?' he asked.

'What luck?'

'The charm your sister gave.'

'I lost it along the way. Eadie tipped me upside down and it fell over my head.'

'Where is your sleek?'

'I don't know. The last time I saw him was on the boat landing at Mother Moss's.'

'Say him to me,' Siltboy ordered. 'I will call him.'

'What do you mean?'

'Tell him to me. Give me his looks.'

'He's reddish-brown and no bigger than a rabbit. His tail flares right out when he gets angry. His eyes are bright and shiny and he has sharp teeth.'

Siltboy sat down and closed his eyes. He became very still.

'What are you doing?' I asked.

'Silence. I need to blank my mind so I can hear.'

Siltboy was quiet for so long that I thought he had gone to sleep, then he began twitching. His face grew narrow and he made a high-pitched cheeping noise that sounded just like the sleek. The look of him frightened me.

'Siltboy, what are you doing? Wake up!'

He opened his eyes and stared at me as if he had no idea who I was. Then his gaze cleared.

'Sleek is fierce,' he said. 'I ask him to bring the luck, but he bites and spits.'

'He's always like that.'

Siltboy hung his head, disappointed.

'I don't think the sleek could help me anyway, Siltboy. When the tide goes out I will try to go back the way I came.'

He shook his head. 'No way back, Peat. Not once you reach the Ever.' He sighed and became still again. He closed his eyes and sniffed the air.

'Is it the sleek?' I asked. 'Do you hear him?'

'No. The Siltman calls,' he said. 'I must take you to the river mouth.'

'I don't want to go.'

'No choice. Siltman is master. When he calls, Siltboy obeys.'

He whistled, and when I closed my eyes I saw Shadow standing before us, with all the lights moving inside him.

'You ride front,' Siltboy said.

I held the collar and put my leg over the ghost hound, and Siltboy climbed on behind.

'Away!' he said, and we swept towards the cliff. For a moment I thought we would go straight over, but when we reached the edge I saw there was a path cut into the face of the rock – a steep path that zigzagged to a stony beach far below.

A strong wind blew off the sea and I held tight to the collar as we glided down the path. When we reached the bottom Shadow turned to the east and raced along the water's edge, heading for the river mouth.

～～

The Siltman was sitting in front of an old hut that looked as if it would blow away at any moment. He was sifting silt, stopping now and then to pick out flakes of silver, which he put in a tin on the ground beside him. The dogs sat around him, watching, with their backs to the wind.

He didn't look up when we arrived, just gave a low whistle. The dogs surrounded me.

'Inside,' he commanded. The dogs herded me into the hut and the Siltman shut the door. 'Stay!' he said.

Was he talking to me or the dogs?

The hut was made of driftwood and bones. It had a tin fireplace that rattled in the wind. The walls inside were blackened by smoke, and the outside was bleached white. Sand banked against the hut and blew through the cracks. There was no floor, just sand and silt. The hut contained nothing but a shaggy grey mat that might have been a dog skin.

I peered out through the cracks in the wall. Siltboy was by the Siltman's side. He looked different from when we had been at the fort. Now he seemed smaller. If he had been a dog, his tail would have been between his legs and his ears would have been down.

'Fetch water,' the Siltman ordered, and the boy ran away immediately.

'Useless child,' the Siltman muttered, returning to his work. 'Are you watching, Siltgirl? This will be your job soon.'

'My name's not Siltgirl. I don't want the job.'

The Siltman gave a wispy sort of laugh.

I looked at the river, but I couldn't see the other side. The tide was as high as it had been when Siltboy had found me, and that must have been hours ago.

'If you are waiting for the tide to turn, you will wait forever,' the Siltman said. 'Tell me a story, Siltgirl.'

When I didn't reply, he sighed. It was a frightening sound – part breath, part growl.

'You must learn to obey, Siltgirl. I have asked you twice. You will not refuse me a third time.'

I was afraid he was going to ask me again, but then Siltboy returned, carrying water on his back in a skin bag. I wondered what it was made of – a goat bladder? Or perhaps it was the skin of a dead dog.

'Give Siltgirl a drink, then feed her,' the Siltman ordered.

Siltboy poured some water into a tin can. He opened the door a crack and slipped it through, then he was gone again, hurrying along the beach. The sun was going down and the sky was streaked with pink and gold.

The Siltman said nothing more to me. He whistled to himself, and when at last it was dark he walked off into the night, taking his dogs with him. I breathed a sigh of relief.

The door of the hut wasn't latched. I went outside and waited for Siltboy. Now that the Siltman had gone, the wind had dropped. A full moon rose over the sea, and the beach and the river were bathed in silver.

34

THE WARRIOR'S WAY

Siltboy gave me shellfish and seaweed for dinner. He didn't eat anything himself – just sat inside the hut with his head in his hands.

'Nine hundred winters and never a day like this one,' he said. 'I'm sorry, Peat. There is two Siltboys – one bold-brazen, the other full of fright.'

'Anyone would be scared of the Siltman,' I said. 'Even Eadie was scared of him. That's why she hid in the marshes.'

'Fear is not the warrior's way,' said Siltboy. 'I have sworn an oath and I must keep it.'

'Siltboy, I know you want to help me but it's impossible. Even if you were brave enough to stand against the Siltman, there is no escape. The deal is done. The bargain is complete.'

'For shame.' Siltboy stared at the ground. 'I hang up my helmet.'

'Where is Shadow?' I asked.

'Gone. Siltman has taken him.'

'Will he come back?'

'If he can. Shadow, like Siltboy, must obey.' He gave a little moan. 'What to do? The thoughts are clashing in the bonehouse of my head. It aches.'

'I'm getting cold,' I said. 'Let's light a fire.'

We walked along the riverbank, collecting driftwood and small sticks. I set the fire in the little tin fireplace, and Siltboy took a flint from his pocket and lit it. The shaggy mat smelled like wet dog, but I lay down on it.

'Yes, you must sleep,' Siltboy said. 'And I must quiet myself to make brave for the battle ahead.'

'What battle? What are you talking about?'

'I is foiled,' he mumbled. 'And deeply plexed.'

My eyes were closing and sleep was coming over me when the air inside the hut changed and Siltboy clapped his hands.

'Ah! My faithful hound! Shadow has come. Now we have a fighting chance!'

I sat up and looked around. I couldn't see Shadow in the dark, but I could feel his presence, and when I shut my eyes I saw a vague shape sitting next to the fire. His outline was weak and there weren't many lights flickering inside him. I lay back down and listened to the waves crashing on the shore.

———

I didn't sleep much that night in the Siltman's hut. Siltboy was restless. He groaned and sighed, and he paced up and down. Once or twice he went outside to get more wood for the fire. He muttered and cursed to himself, then when he finally fell asleep, he ducked and weaved as if he was dodging blows. And all the time he talked in his sleep. I couldn't make sense of what he said, but it sounded like he was having an argument.

During the night the wind grew stronger. It whistled through the walls of the hut, and I thought the Siltman had come back. I sat up and there was Siltboy, wide awake, staring at me.

'Such a clash and clamour,' he cried. 'But the wit-battle is won!'

I stared at him blankly. Was this ancient boy completely mad?

'Surely Peat heard the clatter and the cry?'

'No. Just the wind and the waves. Although you did talk in your sleep.'

Whatever really happened must have taken place between his ears alone.

'All night Siltboy braved his head-hoard of thoughts,' he said. 'All night he riddled with it, and fought.'

I had no idea what he was talking about.

'Victory is near!' he cried.

He was very excited – but how could victory be near when we were both lost, utterly and forever?

'Come!' he said. 'I'll show you the spoils.'

'What spoils?'

'The spoils of battle.'

He opened the door of the hut and ran to the water's edge, and I ran after him. When I had caught up, he squatted down and began drawing a map. He might have been plotting a course of action in battle. He raked his fingers through the wet sand, making long wavy lines, then he drew a cross on either side.

'This is the Silver River,' he said. 'And them crosses is two worlds – one is the Ever and the other is the world beyond. Do you understand?'

I nodded.

He picked up a flat pebble.

'This is you,' he said. Then he took the stub of a candle from his pocket and, cupping his hand around it, lit the wick. 'Do you know what this is?'

I shook my head.

'The marsh auntie's flame – her spirit.' He placed the candle on the Ever side of the river. 'And this is the deed that is done: the marsh auntie's spirit, safe put and hidden.' He dug a little hole and placed the candle in it.

'And here is the payment, Peat.' He put the stone that was me near the candle, and he drew a circle around it. 'There! All done and forever. The marsh auntie cannot die. But... here is the plan.'

He stood up and walked around his map.

'What if you put the bargain back to front?' he asked. 'What if you turn it round, and take back the deed that was done?' He reached across and snatched the candle from its hiding-hole. 'What do you think?'

I wasn't thinking anything. I didn't understand his plan.

'Steal it,' he hissed. 'Steal it back! Steal the marsh auntie's flame.'

He picked up the Peat pebble and he turned and threw it, skimming it across the surface of the Silver River – the real river, not the one on the map.

'You is free!' he cried. 'Simple!'

The stone bounced across the water seven times. Siltboy sat back on his heels, delighted with himself, and his ghost hound must have been delighted, too, because I could see his shadow careering around us in circles in the moonlight, his tail wagging madly.

'That's good, Siltboy,' I said. 'But we don't know where the Siltman has hidden Eadie's spirit. It could be anywhere.'

Siltboy was crestfallen. He hadn't thought of that. He hung his head for a moment, but when he looked up there was a wild light shining in his eyes.

'Siltman will tell us!' he cried.

'Why would Siltman tell us that?'

Siltboy looked slightly dazed, as if all this thinking had weakened him. 'To turn back the bargain?' It was more a question than a suggestion. 'To get rid of Siltgirl?'

'There's nothing I could do to make the Siltman want to get rid of me. I can't do anything to him.'

'You could tell him a story. You have the craft of it.'

'That's what he wants. He *wants* me to tell him a story.'

'Then do it.' Siltboy stood up, triumphant. 'But make it one he does not want.'

I shook my head in confusion.

'Brave yourself, Peat,' said Siltboy. 'Be trickful and cunning. Now we must rest.'

We went back to the hut. Siltboy fell into a peaceful sleep, but I lay awake for a long time wondering what sort of story I could possibly tell the Siltman to make him want to get rid of me.

35

SWOON

The next morning I woke to bright sunlight and the sound of frenzied yelping. The door of the hut was open. The Siltman was there, his rags flapping. He was shading his face with his hand as he gazed up the river. Siltboy was with him, and the dogs were gone.

'They are hunting, Siltgirl,' the Siltman called, without looking in my direction. 'They have caught the scent of something.'

'I'm not Siltgirl. My name is Peat.'

'Soon you will forget your old name,' he said. 'The dogs are turning. I can hear them.'

I looked along the riverbank. The dogs were racing through the water, driving something in front of them – something small and red.

'*Sleek!*' I cried.

He was heading in our direction, with the dogs on his tail, snapping and whining. He swerved and disappeared into a thicket of tussock grass on the riverbank. The dogs immediately had it surrounded.

'*Stop them!*' I screamed. 'Call off your dogs.'

'Why?' the Siltman asked. 'They love to hunt.'

I turned to Siltboy. 'You shouldn't have called him!'

Siltboy cringed.

The sleek shot out of the tussocks. He flashed past me into the hut and I leapt in front of the dogs.

'Siltman, stop them! Please!'

The Siltman raised his hand. 'Hold.' He didn't speak loudly, but the dogs stopped in their tracks. They looked towards him, quivering. If he lowered his hand or flicked his fingers they would be onto the sleek in a moment. They would tear him to pieces.

'What will you give me?' The Siltman stared in my direction with his peculiar eyes.

'A story,' I said. 'I'll give you a story.'

I hoped the sleek might squeeze through a crack in the back wall of the hut or dig himself out. I had to give him time to escape.

'Stories must be opened and closed,' I said. I put my hand in my pocket and, to my surprise, something was there. It was the bottle of perfume Lily had given me in the marshes. I held it before me.

'Once, long ago, there was a Siltman,' I began. 'He understood the language of birds and animals, and he travelled with a pack of hounds that were as big as horses. The dogs answered his every command.'

The Siltman slowly lowered his hand and the dogs went to him and sat at his feet. He was listening. *The story had better be good. What had Siltboy told me? To be trickful and cunning.*

'Every summer the Siltman travelled north and the dogs travelled with him. Every winter he returned to the mouth of the Silver River, by the sea. Then one day a girl arrived. Her name was Peat.'

My heart was thumping in my chest. I had no idea how

the story would go. I took a deep breath and continued.

'Peat was a storyteller. She could tell a tale and make it come true. She had learned from a powerful teacher who was hundreds of years old – a teacher almost as old as the Siltman.'

I tried to remember the rules Eadie had taught me. *See the story in your mind; then the audience will see it, too.*

'Peat came from the world beyond.'

I glanced at Siltboy. He was twisting the stranger's thread between his fingers and staring at the Siltman with the same rapt attention as the dogs. The thread gave me an idea.

'She was carrying a disease,' I declared. 'A deadly disease.'

I was thinking what to say next when I heard a screech and the sleek jumped from the door of the hut onto my shoulder, knocking the bottle out of my hand. It landed on a rock and smashed, releasing a fine mist. The dogs were on their feet in a second, but the Siltman raised his hand.

'Stay,' he said. 'Go on, Siltgirl.'

The sleek hesitated for a moment before jumping from my shoulder onto the rocks behind me. I saw the white tip of his tail disappear into the dunes.

When I turned back to the Siltman, I noticed a change had come over the dogs. They were no longer looking after the sleek or waiting for a command from the Siltman. They were gazing vaguely at the ground. The dog next to the Siltman put its head on his foot, and the one on the other side slumped against his legs. The air was filled with an acrid scent. It smelled a bit like ants.

The Swoon! I saw my opportunity and seized it.

'It was a sleeping sickness! The disease spread from Peat to the Siltman's dogs.'

'No,' the Siltman breathed. 'That's not true.'

'One by one they sickened and died, and without the dogs, the Siltman was lost.'

I didn't know what had made me say that. Maybe it was the uncertain look on the Siltman's face. He moved his head from side to side and whispered a command to the dog that stood beside him. It gave a little sigh and fell down, almost knocking the Siltman over. He reached around him, feeling for his other dogs, and in that moment I realised he was blind.

'He wasn't lost,' the Siltman muttered. 'He had the boy to lead him.'

Siltboy was still twisting the stranger's thread between his fingers. He looked terrified.

'Siltboy wouldn't help him,' I cried, hoping it was true.

'Boy,' the Siltman ordered. 'Come!'

Siltboy took a step towards the Siltman. He looked at me and stopped. I could see that he wanted to obey his master.

'Boy!' said the Siltman. 'Where are you?'

'Brave yourself, Siltboy,' I whispered. 'Courage is the warrior's way.'

Siltboy stayed where he was.

'Stop,' cried the Siltman. 'Stop the story!'

'I can't finish the story until it reaches the end,' I said. 'It's one of the rules.

'The Siltman had made a bargain, and the bargain was complete. The Siltgirl was his. She would stay in his country forever. The only way he could get rid of her,' I said, 'was to reverse the bargain.'

The Siltman nodded like a person in a trance.

'Yes,' he said. 'Reverse the bargain. You're trouble, Silt-girl. You're wilful and bad. Go back to where you come from.'

'Where are you keeping Eadie's spirit?' I asked. 'If the bargain is to be reversed I must take it back to her.'

'I put it in a plant…a flower.' The Siltman staggered and lowered himself to the ground.

The perfume was starting to work on him the way it had worked on the animals. Lily must have perfected it – or perhaps it was the creature in him that was responding. I stepped back and hoped the wind wouldn't blow the scent in my direction. The Siltman leaned against one of the sleeping dogs with his face turned to the sky.

'Which flower?' I yelled. 'Where?'

But he didn't answer. His breath wheezed in and out and his rags flapped around him. The Siltman was asleep.

I backed away.

'Call Shadow,' I said to Siltboy. 'We have to find the flower and go quickly. I don't know how long the Swoon will hold.'

36

SEARCHING

Coral bells and sea pinks grew in the sand dunes behind the Siltman's hut. Wild poppies, shell-bells and happy wanderer covered the ground near the riverbank. Now that I was looking, there were flowers everywhere, and Eadie's spirit could have been hidden in any one of them.

Shadow took us over the dunes and across some grassy hills, stopping and starting whenever we saw a patch of colour.

'We'd be better off on foot,' I told Siltboy.

'Halt, Shadow,' he cried, and we slipped to the ground.

Dandelions and red-clover flowers were coming up through the grass, along with forget-me-nots and wild thyme.

'There are so many flowers, I don't know where to start,' I said.

'How about battle stars or snapdragons?' Siltboy suggested. 'Or thistles or them heads of spear grass?'

'No. Eadie's spirit wouldn't be in those.'

'If Shadow knows the scent he can help,' Siltboy said. 'How is muck auntie smelling? What is her whiff?'

'Eadie smells of fish and smoke,' I said. 'But no flower smells like that.'

I got down on my hands and knees and parted the grass, finding clusters of tiny white flowers with yellow centres. The more I looked, the more flowers I saw.

'It's going to be impossible,' I said. 'We're fighting a losing battle.'

I felt something brush against me, and when I closed my eyes I saw Shadow was moving restlessly behind us. His head was down, and the lights in him were moving up his neck. I put my hands over my face and saw the lights gathering in his nose, until the tip of it was so bright with them it almost hurt me to look.

'He wants to go,' Siltboy said. 'Maybe he has knowledge.'

We climbed back on and Shadow sped across the countryside.

'Too fast!' I yelled. 'We can't even see what flowers we're passing.'

He took us beyond the hills to a stretch of open country, where boulders were scattered about like a giant's marbles and flat slabs of stone towered above us, standing upright on their ends. Shadow weaved back and forth across the ground.

'He looks,' Siltboy told me. 'He's getting scent.'

'Of Eadie?'

At that moment Shadow took off in the direction of one of the flat stones, heading straight towards it. It crossed my mind that he could probably pass straight through the rock but Siltboy and I would hit it. At this speed, if we crashed, we would be killed.

'Stop!' I cried. 'Make him stop!'

Shadow swerved and Siltboy and I were flung into a patch of fireweed at the base of the stone.

'Ow!' Siltboy cried. 'Like nettle. Like fire. Bad dog!'

I said nothing, because I found myself staring into the wild eyes of the sleek. He must have been hiding there. He looked past me and fixed his gaze on Siltboy.

'Your sleek!' Siltboy cried.

The sleek made an angry chattering sound, and his tail flared.

'Shh. Don't speak. Don't move,' I cried. 'Or he'll attack.'

'He says I should never have called him.' As soon as Siltboy spoke, the sleek leapt. He swiped Siltboy's face and sunk his teeth into his ear.

'No, Sleek. No!' I cried. 'Siltboy is my friend!'

I thought the sleek was going to pounce again, but before he had the chance, the ground began to shake and a low growling filled the air. It was the same sound I'd heard at the fort.

The sleek bristled with fright and looked right and left, trying to work out where the threat was coming from. He arched his back and let out a long wailing cry, because he saw Shadow's collar moving towards him. I thought the sleek would flee, but he leapt at the buckle, locking his teeth on it. I watched him hang upside down; then he was swung from side to side. I didn't need to close my eyes to know what was happening – Shadow was shaking his head, trying to fling the creature off. When the sleek let go and dashed behind the rock, the collar followed him. The growling grew louder, and the ground under our feet shook violently. There was hissing and snarling and the fight ended with an ear-splitting yelp.

'Look out!' cried Siltboy, pointing up. 'The standing stone – it falls!'

He pulled me to the side as the great stone crashed forward.

The sleek had been behind it. He glanced at Siltboy and began washing himself. Shadow's collar was near the ground, and it wasn't moving.

'Who won?' I asked. 'Is Shadow all right?'

I didn't dare shut my eyes. I imagined Shadow lying on the ground, his outline fading and all the sparkling lights inside him going out until he was nothing but darkness. Siltboy, too, didn't look. He kept his eyes wide open and stared at the sleek. Blood was dripping from Siltboy's ear, and an extra scratch had been added to his face. He made angry clicking sounds in the back of his throat, and the sleek replied with the same sound.

'Truce,' Siltboy replied. 'No winner. No loser.'

I sighed in relief. The sleek chittered, staring at Siltboy.

'Sleek very mad,' Siltboy told me. 'He says I make him come so far and bring what I ask, and when Siltman's dogs chase him he drop it.'

'Drop what?'

'The luck.' Siltboy gave a low whistle. 'Now we must find it.'

He reached towards his hound.

'Come, Peat.'

I was surprised when the sleek jumped onto my shoulder. I supposed he didn't want to be left behind. When we took off he dug in his claws and I gritted my teeth.

'Siltboy, where are we going?'

'To mouth of river.'

'No, Siltboy! What if the Siltman wakes up?'

'We is never finding flower without luck,' Siltboy replied,

as we moved across the country, heading back the way we had come.

When Shadow reached the dunes behind the Siltman's hut, he paused. I looked down and saw that the Siltman and his dogs had not moved.

Siltboy put his finger to his lips.

'Them hounds is swooned, Peat,' he whispered. 'We is safe.'

He chittered to the sleek, who spat at him in reply but then slipped from my shoulder onto the ground and began creeping down the slope.

Oh, Sleek! I held my breath.

'What if the dogs get wind of him?'

'Worry not. Their sniffers is full of ant stink.'

As Siltboy spoke, one of the dogs stirred and tried to raise its head. The sleek stopped in his tracks, and his fur stood on end. The dog groaned. When it was still again, the sleek continued. He crept right past the hut; then, with his nose to the ground, he ran towards the wet sand at the river's edge, where he began digging furiously.

The wind lifted the Siltman's hair and I saw his rags flapping around him. His arm was draped over a dog.

'Sleek has found!' Siltboy cried.

The sleek dashed towards us with something in his mouth. As he passed the hut, I thought I saw the Siltman raise his hand, but it might have been the wind. The sleek scrambled up the dune and flung something in my direction.

'The cow charm! Sleek, thank you!' I put it around my neck, and we were moving again, quickly, over the dunes. We passed the lagoon with the tree where Siltboy stored his drinking horn and headed inland away from the coast. As the boom of the waves grew fainter, I thought I heard a voice on the wind – the Siltman's voice – very slow and slurred, with long gaps between the words – *You…won't…get…away…with…this…Siltgirl…*

37

THE FLOWER

'Please help us, Sleek,' I cried. 'You must know what sort of flower we are looking for. Ask him, Siltboy.'

We were on Shadow's back in the open plains, and there were as many flowers here as anywhere else in the Siltman's country.

Siltboy did as I'd requested but the sleek ignored him, and when he asked a second time the sleek glowered and turned his back.

'Then who will help?' I cried. 'It's hopeless!'

'*Yeak, yeak!*'

The sleek flinched at the sight of Siltboy's eagle hovering above us; then he cowered, ran up my trouser leg and hid under my dress.

'Stop it, Sleek. You're meant to be helping.'

'Best he hide,' Siltboy said. 'Battlebird will snatch him.'

The bird circled overhead, riding the air currents.

'She is wide-seeing,' Siltboy said. 'If you give her the look she will find.'

'How can I give her the look when I have no idea what I'm looking for?'

'When I speak to creatures, I blank my mind so I can hear,' said Siltboy. 'Maybe you try that. Blank your mind and your mind's eye.'

I closed my eyes and tried to make my mind empty, but no flowers came into it. Instead I saw Eadie. She was splashing through the dark towards me as I hung upside down in the snare. Then I saw her paddling towards her hut. She climbed the rickety ladder. In my mind, I pulled aside the bag that hung over the door, and I looked around her cluttered hut. And then I saw them – the flowers in a jar on the table.

'Everlasting daisies!' I cried. 'Could they be the ones?'

'Tell them to me,' said Siltboy.

I tried to describe the flowers I had seen on Eadie's table – their dried petals, their bright colours, the size and shape of them. Siltboy looked up and translated everything I said. '*Yeak. Yeak. Yeak.*'

The bird circled higher and higher. When she tipped one wing and swooped towards the west, Shadow followed. I had never travelled so fast before – not even in the tunnel with the Siltman and his dogs. In a few seconds I found myself in a field of everlasting daisies. There were hundreds of them – white ones, orange ones, pink ones and red ones. Where to start?

I looked up. The battlebird was a tiny dot in the sky.

'She is watchbird,' Siltboy said. 'Tarry not, Peat.'

The sleek let go of my leg and slid to the ground, where he began pacing up and down, making anxious yipping sounds.

I walked among the everlasting daisies. Their dry petals rustled in the breeze. So many of them looked exactly the same. How would I find the right one? How would I *know* it was the right one?

The sun was high in the sky. I searched all through the afternoon, and when the sun set I was still searching. One by one, the flowers were closing up for the night.

'Sleek, can you help? Please can you help?'

He laid back his ears, then he turned and groomed his tail, picking grass seeds out of it. I supposed he thought he had already done enough by bringing the cow charm – and perhaps he had, because as I spoke I noticed the everlasting daisy right in front of me. It was large and reddish in colour, and it was still wide open. The centre was gold and the petals had white tips, like the sleek's tail.

'Siltboy, look! This must be the one. I've found it!'

I carefully dug up the plant, cupping it in soil, then I tore a piece off the bottom of my dress and wrapped it around the roots. 'Your plan is brilliant, Siltboy! Now we can take back the deed that was done!'

He didn't answer. His eyes were closed and his face had gone very white.

'What is it, Siltboy?'

'The Siltman calls,' he said. 'Sleep-like, his voice...'

I grabbed Siltboy's hand and the sleek leapt onto my shoulder.

'Don't listen,' I cried. 'Tell Shadow to get us to the river!'

I had to make Siltboy climb onto his dog, pushing and shoving him, but once he was there he did as I asked. He whistled softly and we were moving again.

'We'll cross the Silver River and find the tunnel,' I yelled, hanging on with one hand and holding the flower in the other. 'We can go back!'

'I is fraid, Peat,' Siltboy whimpered. 'Fraid and afeared. I is fraid of behind and fraid of ahead.'

'What do you mean?'

He replied with something I couldn't hear. The wind was howling in my ears.

When Shadow reached the riverbank, Siltboy raised his hand and called out, 'Halt!' We stopped so quickly that the sleek went flying from my shoulder into the water and landed with a splash. I could still hear the howling.

'Let's go,' I cried. 'What are we waiting for? Let's get away!'

Siltboy turned to me with huge, frightened eyes.

'Siltman says if you cross the Silver River you die.'

'It's true,' I told him. 'But first you have a life. Have courage, Siltboy.'

'All my life for nine hundred years, I live in the land of the Siltman,' he said. 'Where to can we go?'

'To Hub,' I said. 'If you want to go anywhere, you must go to Hub first.'

'But Shadow knows not the way...'

Siltboy looked very young just then. He was trembling, and I thought he might burst into tears.

'Siltboy, you are the son of a warrior giant, you are the proud owner of a noble hound, and you are my true friend – the friend of my life,' I cried. 'Brave yourself!'

At that moment there was a cry far above us.

'Watchbird gives warning,' Siltboy whispered.

The howling grew louder.

'The Siltman's dogs!' I yelled.

Siltboy seemed to be frozen to the spot. Suddenly the sleek leapt from the water, impatient with the delay. He hissed at Shadow and nipped Siltboy's ankle before scrambling up onto my neck and biting me hard on the earlobe.

'Make Shadow go!' I shouted.

Siltboy gave an uncertain whistle and Shadow took off over the water. He didn't touch it, he skimmed just above the surface, and when I closed my eyes I saw the sleek sitting between Shadow's ears, talking to him in clicking sounds. The lights in the ghost hound's head swirled for a moment like confused thoughts, then they settled into a pattern that looked a bit like the map Siltboy had drawn in the sand at the river mouth.

'Look, Siltboy,' I cried. 'The sleek knows the way!'

The shore disappeared behind us as we glided out over the water, into darkness. When the moon came up I saw mountains looming in the distance and I thought the sleek would lead us towards them, but he continued to steer Shadow straight out over the river. I couldn't see the other side.

'No, Sleek. You're going the wrong way. You must find the tunnel,' I cried. 'Tell him, Siltboy.'

Siltboy had stopped shaking. He stared straight ahead and the wind blew through his hair.

'I dare not,' he said. 'Sleek comes by his own way. He is fierce and trusty guide.'

I clutched Marlie's cow charm and hoped he was right.

'How far?' Siltboy asked.

'I don't know. It didn't seem far when I came with the Siltman, but the tide was out then.'

'This is tide of time,' Siltboy said. 'Long way and long journey.'

The moon moved over the sky as we travelled across the Silver River. From time to time I thought I could still hear howling. I hoped it was just the wind. The water was choppy beneath us, and as the night wore on the wind picked up and small waves broke against us, splashing my feet. I pulled up my legs.

'Make Shadow ride higher, Siltboy,' I said. 'I'm getting wet.'

Siltboy whistled, but Shadow kept gliding just above the waves, moving steadily forward.

As we journeyed on he sank lower, until half of him was in the water. Now my legs were really wet. Soon I was shivering with the cold.

'He's tiring, Siltboy,' I cried.

'No tire,' Siltboy replied. 'Shadow likes to swim.'

I closed my eyes and saw the outline of Shadow's paws paddling through the water. When I looked behind, his tail glowed and streamed behind him like a wake.

'He's trailing stars,' I said.

'And making bigger, just for us!' Siltboy let go of Shadow's collar. He pulled up his feet and sat cross-legged, and I found I could do the same. 'See how he grows!'

Our ghost hound did seem to be getting larger. Somehow, he was letting himself spread as he sank into the water. Soon he was wide enough for us to sit upon side by side. He rose and fell with the swell, and we rose up and down with him.

'Shadow is rocking, Peat,' Siltboy said. 'He rocks like a ship on the ocean. He is making me think of sea-voyage songs.' Siltboy began whistling to himself. Suddenly he burst into song. His voice was high and clear.

Oh wave beat. Oh wing beat
Oh beat of the oars
Hail the hero…

He hummed a bit of the tune then fell silent. He looked as
though he was trying to remember the words.

'Is it an old song, Siltboy?' I asked. 'Did your mother
sing it to you?'

'Siltboy make it up,' he replied, then he sang some
more.

We're riding the saltways
To seek out our fortune
In far-flung lands
Beyond the shore.

Siltboy hummed to himself some more. After a while he
slumped against me and went to sleep. I held up the flower.
Against the night sky it looked like a dark star.

'Good night, everlasting daisy,' I said, putting it into
Siltboy's bag for safety. I didn't want to fall asleep and
drop it into the water.

The wind off the river was cold but Shadow felt a
little bit warm, as if the lights inside him were giving off
heat. When I lay down next to Siltboy, the warmth seeped
through my damp clothes and into my skin. I sighed and
turned facedown, putting my arms around Shadow's
sides. I could feel his ribs, like the ribs of a boat, and when
I turned my head I thought I heard a heartbeat, very faint
at first but getting stronger.

How could that be? I wondered. *Shadow doesn't have a heart – he lost it when Scabbard speared him through the chest.*

As I dropped off to sleep I decided it must have been my own heart I was hearing, beating in time to the rhythm of Siltboy's song.

38

THE GREAT HOUND

I couldn't have said how long that night-crossing took. It was longer than a normal night, but it didn't seem as though a year had passed, like when I'd come to the Siltman's country. When I woke up it was dawn, and Siltboy and I were lying on cold sand. The sleek was sitting between us, wide awake and flicking his tail from side to side as if he had been waiting for hours.

I sat up and looked about. This side of the river looked exactly the same as the other, except the sand wasn't smooth – there were holes and trenches, and it was dug up in rough heaps.

'Siltboy, we've arrived.'

Siltboy was muttering in his sleep. I hoped he wasn't having another wit-battle.

'Smite him,' he called. 'Smite the Siltman. We have fled from the darksome into the dazzle.'

'You're dreaming,' I said. 'Wake up.'

He rubbed his eyes and sat up, hugging his knees and shivering. Then he blinked and stared at his arms.

'Look, Peat – skin of Siltboy is like skin of bird without feather.'

'Goosepimples,' I said. 'You'll warm up once we get moving.'

'Siltboy never felt cold before.' He jumped to his feet.

'No matter. We is alive and on the far side!'

He gave a shrill whistle. 'Shadow,' he called, looking along the riverbank. He whistled again, and when nothing happened he turned to the sleek and made some strange chortling sounds that weren't at all like the noises the sleek made. The sleek cheeped a reply and ran up the bank, stopping to look over his shoulder.

'What did he say?' I asked.

Siltboy shrugged, and for a moment he looked small and lost. He was shivering so much that his teeth were chattering. I took off my wool vest.

'Put this on. You need to keep warm.'

He put the vest on over the top of his breastplate.

'You could take off your armour,' I suggested. 'The metal is making you cold.'

'Never!' he cried. 'Shadow will make me warm.'

He looked up and down the beach. The sun was coming up over a range of mountains in the distance, and his own shadow was clearly visible. It stretched to the water's edge.

'Come on,' I said, taking his hand. 'Shadow will be around somewhere.' I wanted to get far away from the water as quickly as possible. Just because we had crossed the river didn't mean we were safe from the Siltman.

Siltboy stumbled along beside me, tripping in the rough sand's holes and hollows.

'Hang on,' he cried suddenly. 'Them's not potholes, them's paw prints!'

He let out a whoop and ran ahead. The sleek flicked his ears in annoyance and his tail began to redden.

'Come back!' I yelled, but Siltboy took no notice. He

followed the prints to a spot high on the riverbank, and he crouched there behind some bushes.

'Peat, look!' He beckoned for me to follow.

When I had caught up I found he was trembling, not with the cold but with excitement. He put his finger to his lips and urged me to keep low.

'Behold,' he whispered. 'Through them leaves is a wondrous sight!'

I peered through the bushes.

'Shadow?' I breathed.

The creature was drinking from a small pond not far below us. His paws were the size of upturned cooking pots and his shaggy legs could have been the pillars of a great hall. He was the same colour as the Siltman's dogs – a steely grey – but he was bigger than them, much bigger. He was the size of a draught horse, and his shadow stretched across the water and over the grasslands beyond.

We didn't make a sound, but he raised his great head, sniffing the air; then he turned towards us and let out an ear-splitting bark. The sound must have frightened him as much as it frightened us, because he shied away and cowered for a moment before shaking his head and barking once more. He wagged his enormous tail and the movement created a wind that blew the bushes about.

Siltboy stood up. He was braver than I was.

'Shadow? Is it you?' he asked.

The great hound was before us in a single bound. He lowered his head and sniffed Siltboy, then he yelped with joy.

'It *is* you!' cried Siltboy. Shadow gave him a lick that sent him rolling down the bank, across the sand and splashing into the water.

'No, Shadow. No!' I cried as the gigantic dog bounded after him. Siltboy was laughing, but I could see how dangerous it was to play with a dog that size.

'Drop,' Siltboy commanded, and he smiled when the huge dog lay with his paws stretched in front of him and his head on the sand.

Even lying down, Shadow was taller than a cow. Siltboy gazed up at him as if he couldn't believe it was true. I couldn't believe it, either. I shut my eyes to see what his lights looked like, but there weren't any. He simply disappeared, and when I opened my eyes he was still sitting there, huge and shaggy – a real, live dog.

'Awe hound,' Siltboy cried. 'Most marvellous of mutts.'

He stretched his arms wide and hugged Shadow's nose, and the big dog panted with a 'Ha ha ha' that sounded like laughter.

'Come to him, Peat. He is gentle.'

Cautiously I made my way down the bank. I could see that Shadow was friendly, but he was too big and too much like the Siltman's dogs for me to be easy with him. Nevertheless, I reached up and gave him a pat. Long strands of hair hung over his eyes and he smelled salty. He gave me a solemn look, and his eyes were kind. I heard his tail thumping on the ground.

'He's thanking you,' Siltboy said. 'Shall we climb him?'

Shadow didn't move as Siltboy went to his shoulder and, grabbing a handful of wiry hair, pulled himself up onto the dog's broad back, where he sat with his legs stretched wide.

'Come on, Peat.' He leaned down and gave me a hand up.

Shadow wasn't hard to climb – his coat was so rough and shaggy that it was like pulling yourself up with ropes.

'Shadow, stand!'

I nearly slid off the back when the giant hound straightened his front legs. Siltboy leaned forward and put his arms around Shadow's neck, and I held onto Siltboy, and then we were upright, high in the air.

'Look at his diggings!' Siltboy exclaimed, pointing to the hills and hollows in the sand.

The sleek chittered and ran towards us, staring up.

'What's he saying, Siltboy?'

'Naught. Creature-sounds that make no sense.'

The sleek shook his head in frustration, then he ran behind Shadow and nipped his heels.

'He wants us to go,' I said. 'He's trying to round us up.'

The sleek jumped up onto Shadow from behind, scrambling over my shoulder and over Siltboy and settling himself at the front, sitting on the dog's wide head. He gave three clicks and we were off, following the river.

We were a long way from the ground, but Shadow moved so smoothly that we had no fear of falling. The sleek gave a sharp cry and we left the water, bounding over the riverbank. Open country lay before us – grasslands and rolling hills. Shadow loped along with huge strides, startling birds; they rose around us, beating their wings, and settled again once we'd passed.

The grasslands stretched towards the horizon, and

although the ground passed quickly beneath us, it seemed as though we were moving on the spot because the country did not change. Once or twice I looked back, but there was no sign of the Siltman or his dogs. *They would have lost our scent at the river*, I told myself as I gazed into the distance, pleased there was nothing to see except the pale waving grasses.

The sleek chittered and clicked, first in one of Shadow's ears, then in the other.

'He's telling Shadow the way,' I said.

After a while he left his place on Shadow's head and curled around my neck, resting his nose on my shoulder.

'Good little sleek.' I turned to him as I spoke, but he looked away.

~

We travelled all through the day. By the time the light was fading we had reached forestland and I could see mountains ahead. Shadow moved among tall trees, and the ground underfoot was soft with leaf litter. He didn't tire, but I was growing weary and my stomach was grumbling.

'Let's stop and rest.'

'Rest not,' said Siltboy. 'The Siltman rides my shoulder sure as the sleek rides yours. When the flower is with the muck auntie we are safe, and not before.'

I reached into Siltboy's bag and checked the everlasting daisy. The leaves had wilted, but the flower was still perfect.

~

It was almost dark by the time we reached the foothills of the mountains, and that's when we stopped. We were in a clearing. The sleek sharpened his claws on a tree trunk, then he darted up and perched high in the tree's branches, looking back the way we had come. Siltboy listened with his head on the side.

'Hear anything?' I asked.

'Only wind in treetops,' he said. 'But Sleek will listen for us. He is true and noble friend. He travels far to help, and now he guards from above.'

The sleek looked down and bared his teeth.

The air smelled of moss and rotting bark. Siltboy found berries and mushrooms for our dinner, and Shadow drooled as he watched us eat.

'I know you hunger,' Siltboy said. 'Tomorrow we will find food fit for a great hound.'

Siltboy rubbed Shadow behind the ears, and the dog sighed and closed his eyes. We lay down between his huge paws, and soon we were fast asleep.

———

The next morning we woke to a chorus of birds twittering in the trees. Siltboy cocked his head.

'Bold brassy they sing, but their tweet to me is bird babble.'

'You can't understand them?'

'Not a word,' he said, puzzled.

'Maybe the birds here speak a different language,' I suggested.

Siltboy sniffed the air. 'Smoke.' He got up and peered through the trees. 'Peat, look!'

Ahead of us was cleared land, a farm with crops growing – potatoes, corn and sunflowers. A hut made of rough boards stood inside a brushwood enclosure, and there were other buildings scattered about.

'Stay,' Siltboy commanded his hound.

We left Shadow in the clearing and walked towards the hut, accompanied by the sleek, who may have been a true and noble friend but still bit Siltboy's foot and then glared at me as if daring me to do something about it.

'Poor Sleek,' Siltboy said. 'How few winks did he sleep to make his mood so bad?'

I was suddenly aware that my clothes were dirty and that my hair was matted, with leaves and grass tangled in it. I could have had a wash when we were back at the river, but it hadn't crossed my mind. Siltboy looked worse than I did. His face was grubby and his hair was so stiff with salt that it stood up in peaks.

An old man was sitting outside the hut, talking to himself. He had a blanket around him and he was holding a bowl.

'Eat your breakfast, Pa,' someone called from inside the hut.

The old man looked at the bowl as if he wasn't sure what to do with it, then a woman came out and put a spoon in his hand.

'Eat,' she said. 'I'll be out when I've finished the chores.' She disappeared into the hut.

The man looked blankly at the spoon and continued muttering to himself.

'Fine days and fair weather,' he said. 'Grits and gruel. Have you planted the oats yet?'

He noticed us outside the brushwood fence and waved.

'Mutti, there's children here,' he called. 'Wild ones.'

'Finish your breakfast, Pa,' came the reply.

The old man watched as we let ourselves in through a gate in the brushwood fence, then he let out a gasp. 'Strike me down! A scarlet runner!'

He set the bowl on the ground and the sleek wasted no time in polishing off its contents. 'They're rare, so rare,' the man told us. 'It's a gift to see one these days.'

He watched the sleek lick clean the bowl, then he looked us up and down.

'Where did you two urchins come from?'

'The far shore,' Siltboy said. 'We crossed the Silver River from the Ever land.'

The old man's eyes widened.

'I know it,' he said. 'I'll go there one day. What sort of craft did you come in?'

'A boat without oars.'

'Are you hungry?'

We nodded.

'Mutti!' the old man called. 'They're starvelings. They've come from the Far Shore. And they've got a runner with them.'

'Pa, I'm busy. I'll be out when I can.'

I could hear children inside the hut and the sound of pots and pans.

'Grits and gruel is all you'll get, and maybe some…' The old man stopped mid-sentence. His mouth fell open, and he stared past us. 'Strike me dead with a single blow!' he cried. 'A Great Hound! Mutti!'

I looked over my shoulder. Shadow had followed us. He stood outside the enclosure with his head over the fence. Perhaps he sensed how big and frightening he might seem to the old man, or maybe he was afraid he would get into trouble from Siltboy for not staying put – either way, he wore a questioning expression and his gaze was gentle. He reminded me a bit of Bella, looking down with big soft eyes.

'Mutti! It's one of the old breed.'

The man staggered to his feet and raised his hands. 'A noble hound,' he cried. 'Mutti, Lem, Uncle, Jute, Stringer. Everybody, come at once!'

'Stop it, Pa. You're wandering again.' The woman poked her head out the door. 'What in the halls of Hub!' She dropped the bowl she was holding and it shattered at her feet. 'Lem, get your da. Get Uncle. Get Jute, Marta and the others!'

The sleek was gone in a flash. Siltboy and I soon found ourselves surrounded as the yard filled up with people. Some of them had come in from the fields, carrying scythes and pitchforks. They put down their tools, and there were cries of awe and mutters of disbelief. The children huddled together and one little boy began to cry.

'Mutti,' he sobbed. 'Big dog will eat us.'

His mother picked him up and quietened him.

'I thought Pa was seeing things.' She shook her head. 'I never believed those old stories until now. Far tarnations!'

'What sort of dog is it, Ma?' a girl asked.

Siltboy stepped forward. 'Battlehound,' he said proudly. 'There's none more noble.'

'Should we be afraid of him?' asked a man with sandy hair.

'Fear not!' Siltboy told them. 'He is a fierce enemy but loyal friend.'

'You've got a strange turn of phrase there, boy,' the man said. 'Where do you come from?'

'Beyond the Silver River.'

'There's no river around here, only the ocean, and no one has landed on this part of the coast in my lifetime. It's too wild.'

'He must be a throwback,' another man said. 'Look at his garb. He's wearing some sort of breastplate.'

Some of the children edged towards Siltboy. They wanted to touch him to make sure he was real. Siltboy backed away.

The man with sandy hair turned his attention back to Shadow. 'Well, I never in all my days thought I'd live to see a Great Hound.' He shook his head. 'Let him in.'

Someone opened the gate and Shadow stepped carefully into the yard as the people drew back. He was almost taller than the hut.

'Sit,' said Siltboy, and everyone gasped when the dog sat down on his haunches. 'Drop.' Shadow stretched his great paws out in front of him and put his head on the ground.

'Where are you taking him?' the mother asked.

'Hub,' I said.

'You will make your fortune there. People will pay anything for a Great Hound.'

Siltboy looked shocked. 'Shadow is our true friend. We don't trade him.'

'Let him be our friend, too,' the mother said. 'Lem, come with me to the smokehouse.'

She and one of the older boys disappeared behind the hut, returning with a large piece of meat. It looked like half a goat.

'For you.' She laid it at Shadow's feet and watched with satisfaction as he took it in his mouth.

'He's hungry,' Siltboy said. 'He hasn't eaten for nine hundred years.'

The mother laughed a big open laugh, then she looked at Siltboy and me and decided we needed feeding as well.

'You poor children. You look famished.' She clapped her hands and sent a couple of girls into the hut. They came out with cooked potatoes, oatcakes and green beans for us to eat. I noticed the sleek slip in after they'd left the hut. No doubt he would help himself to the food inside.

After we had finished eating, the mother spread a mat on the ground and laid a bundle of clothes on it.

'Help yourselves,' she said. 'You can't go to Hub in rags.'

'Hub is far from here,' the man with sandy hair said. 'You have a Great Hound, but the pass is steep and dangerous. Do you know the way?'

'They have a scarlet runner,' the old man told them. 'Those creatures can find their way anywhere.'

I chose a pair of cloth pants and a felt jacket. Siltboy picked up a shirt and fingered the fabric.

'What weave is this?' he asked.

'Flax,' the mother replied. 'Linen.'

He put the shirt in his bag and chose some other items from the pile.

'Glads, jerkin and breeches. Have you no helmet?' he asked.

Some of the children giggled and their mother silenced them with a look. She handed Siltboy a woollen cap with earflaps.

'Take this,' she said kindly. 'You don't need a helmet. The battle is over.'

Siltboy put on the cap and picked up two pairs of trousers – one just his size and the other longer than he was. He chose the second pair.

'No, Siltboy,' I said. 'They're too big.'

'Let the lad take the large ones,' the old man cried. 'His people were giants. They set the stones on end.'

One of the bigger girls handed us each a cup of sweet tea. 'To see you on your way,' she said. 'Your visit is our good fortune. I never thought I'd see a Great Hound. May good luck follow you to the ends of the earth.'

We left the farm and Shadow carried us through the foothills. The sleek sat between Siltboy and me, occasionally chirping to give directions but mostly sleeping. His face looked fuller than usual and his belly was tight.

'You're bad, Sleek,' I said. 'To steal from those good people.'

He opened one eye and gave me a shrewd look.

'Let him be,' said Siltboy. 'Sleek has his own way.'

Shadow kept up his steady pace, loping through the trees with long, easy strides. Soon we left the lowlands behind and moved into steeper country. Our hound slowed down and made his way along narrow tracks and animal pads. From time to time I looked back and saw the forest far below, and away in the distance, the farm. The sun was high when the path we were on petered out. Shadow paused, hot and panting, while the sleek slipped to the ground and ran on ahead.

The sleek led us high into the mountains, and he kept going long after darkness had fallen. At times we climbed down as Shadow had to scramble over boulders. At other times, when we were riding, our legs scraped against a rock wall and we knew Shadow was taking us along a narrow ledge.

All night Shadow climbed the mountains, following the sleek. Siltboy and I had to hold on tight to stop ourselves sliding backwards. Sometimes we heard loose pebbles clattering away below and I was glad we couldn't see beneath us. I took Siltboy's bag and put it carefully over my shoulder. I didn't want the everlasting daisy to get battered on the journey.

I wondered where Eadie would be. She might still be in Hub, or she might have taken one of the many roads that led from there. Someone would know which way the marsh auntie had gone.

The sleek picked his way ahead of us, directing Shadow with clicks and low chuckling sounds and sometimes a shriek.

'Are you tired, Siltboy?' I asked.

'Worn,' he replied. 'Battle weary. But that is the way of the great quests.'

When cold gusts of air hit us in the face, we knew we had reached the top. Shadow lay down, panting, and we snuggled into him, sheltering from the wind. The moon came up and its gentle light shone over a bare, rocky plateau.

'Maybe Hub is on the other side,' I said. 'Siltboy, ask the sleek how much further we have to go.'

'Can't,' he replied. 'The gift is gone.'

He looked up at the stars, and he was smiling.

'It must have happened when you crossed the river,' I said.

'True,' he said. 'Small price to pay for finding the way to the world.'

39

SWEET SAGA!

The sleek woke us early the next morning, chittering loudly. My head was buried in Shadow's straggly fur, and I was warm and cosy and would have like to sleep longer, but the sleek wouldn't have it. He nipped Shadow on the ear and the great dog leapt up with a yelp, scattering Siltboy and I. We were lucky he didn't tread on us. The sleek didn't leave us alone till we were mounted on Shadow and he was sitting at the front.

We travelled across the plateau with the cold wind in our faces. The barren ground grew softer, sprouting a carpet of spiky grass. Low shrubs and tiny twisted trees grew here and there, and we heard creatures rustling in the bushes as we passed. Shadow was interested in all the scents and sounds. He kept lowering his head to sniff the ground, but every time he did this the sleek snarled and dug in his claws. Shadow didn't seem to mind much – perhaps he didn't even notice – but when the sleek bit him hard on the back of the neck he turned around and snapped, knocking Siltboy to the ground. The sleek leapt into a tree and crouched there shrieking while Shadow ran off with his nose to the ground.

'Halt, Shadow!' Siltboy called, but the dog took no notice.

I held on tight, hoping Shadow would turn around, but

he didn't. He careered forward, dashing this way and that, then he began whining with excitement. He was on the track of something. I almost dropped Siltboy's bag as I struggled to keep my grip.

'Halt!' I heard Siltboy cry. 'Shadow. Stand!'

His voice faded behind me as Shadow raced across the countryside, splashing through creeks and dodging around the trees. I looked down as the ground flashed past. *Perhaps I should make a leap for it*, I thought. *Who knows where I will end up if I stay on Shadow's back.*

'Please stop, Shadow!' I cried.

I was gathering up my courage, ready to jump, when he began to slow down – not because I had asked him to stop, but because he had found something dead lying on the ground up ahead. The smell of it nearly made me faint. I couldn't see what it was, or what it had been – it was too far gone for that. It had been something big, though – maybe a cow, or one of Siltboy's aurochs. Shadow put his paw on the carcass and pulled up a long strand of gizzard until it snapped, spraying me with a foul-smelling liquid, then he tossed the guts in the air and gulped them down.

I lowered myself to the ground and got out of the way as Shadow tore into his breakfast, bolting down gobfuls of rotting meat and crunching the bones. When he had finished, he lay down and rolled in the mess that remained.

I heard Siltboy calling in the distance. 'Peat, are you all right? Are you hearty?'

'No, I'm not hearty!' I yelled. 'Your dog is disgusting.'

Shadow was on his back, waving his enormous paws in the air. His mouth was open and bits of gore were stuck in his teeth. He looked as though he was grinning.

Siltboy appeared among the trees, running hard. 'Come, Shadow,' he panted. When he was close enough to see what was happening, he slowed to a walk. 'Sit!' he cried, and the big dog reluctantly got to his feet, scratched his ear and looked the other way.

'Drop!'

Shadow lay down at Siltboy's feet, looking a bit apologetic, as if he hadn't meant to cause any trouble. Siltboy held his nose.

'A hundred sorrows, Peat,' he said. 'Shadow is new to the world. He has to learn.'

'But he's older than you are!'

'Yes, but he's not been full-bodied for a long time.'

I looked up at Shadow's back. His shaggy coat was matted with the mess and slime. 'How are we to ride?' I asked.

'We must walk.'

Just then the sleek trotted past with his nose in the air. Shadow went to follow him but Siltboy cried, 'Hound, you stay back. Downwind.'

We followed the sleek along a narrow path, and Shadow walked behind us with his head down and his tail between his legs. The path wound its way through some trees and ended at a small lake, which sparkled in the early-morning sunlight. The water was stained a red-gold colour, and you could see through it to the sandy bottom.

'Into the tarn.' Siltboy pointed, and Shadow plunged in, swimming up and down, barking with delight. Siltboy and I took the opportunity to have a wash as well. Afterwards, I put on my new clothes. I would have liked to keep wearing my old dress, the one my mother had made, but it was torn and tight on me and full of holes. Only the dress the marsh auntie, Olive, gave me had withstood the strain. I rinsed it out and put it back on, with the new pants under it and the felt jacket on top.

My wool dress went in Siltboy's bag; I couldn't see myself wearing it again but I didn't want to leave it behind. Siltboy put his new shirt on under his breastplate and wore my vest over the top, even though it was tatty.

When we were dressed, Siltboy climbed a tree and came back with three eggs. 'One for each,' he said. 'Shadow has no need.'

He handed an egg to me and gave one to the sleek, who took it carefully in his paws and made a hole in it with one sharp tooth before sucking out the contents. When he had finished, he licked his lips and cleaned his paws.

Siltboy lit a fire. 'If only I had helmet,' he said. 'We could boil them.'

He cooked the eggs on a flat stone and we ate them with our fingers. When the sleek appeared with a fish, I was more than happy. We cooked that as well.

'Right, Sleek,' I said when we had finished our breakfast. 'Show us the way!'

The sleek looked at me for a moment, then his eyes turned into slits and his tail began to tremble.

'Calm yourself, Sleek,' Siltboy said. 'She didn't mean to boss you.'

The sleek's tail flared. I bit my lip.

'Sorry, Sleek,' I muttered. 'I meant to say, *When you are ready, if you don't mind... you're the leader.*'

'Always we do your bidding, brother Sleek,' Siltboy said quietly.

The sleek's tail settled and he yawned, then we sat looking at the water for a long time before he finally got up, stretched and decided we could leave. Once we were moving he must have thought we should make up for lost time, because he sat on Shadow's head and urged him forward, down steep slopes and along a track that wound its way off the plateau.

Shadow's breakfast wouldn't have been my choice, but it seemed to have done him good because he ran much faster than he had the day before, bounding over logs and creeks until we were climbing again towards a high ridge. When we reached the top, Shadow stopped. We gasped at the sight before us.

'Sweet Saga!' Siltboy breathed. 'Be it a wheel, a gold brooch, or the spikes of some spidery flower?'

'None of those,' I said. 'I think it's a city. It must be Hub!'

We looked down on a vast settlement built around a lake that shone like a mirror in the sunlight. The water was as golden as the water where we had swum, and there was a huge domed building in the centre of it, which looked like Mother Moss's oven only many times bigger. Four bridges spanned the lake, connecting the building to the rest of the city. North, south, east and west. The surrounding hills were green, and roads and rivers led in every direction, so that the lake and its building looked like the middle of a strange spidery flower.

'Wondrous made,' whispered Siltboy. 'I never seen the likes of it, not even in dreams.'

'Me neither. That must be Upper Hub. I bet there's a ladder inside that dome – a ladder with a thousand rungs.

It goes down to Lower Hub, where the night markets are. That's where we're heading.'

The look of amazement on Siltboy's face turned to worry. 'Shadow is not one for the rung-work,' he said. 'Is there an easy way down?'

I didn't know. I gazed at the marvellous city. A ring road circled the lake, and the buildings around it were every colour of the rainbow. The roofs weren't thatch or sod – they must have been made of something shiny, because they glittered in the sunlight, making the whole scene look like a piece of enormous jewellery.

'This is the centre of the world, Siltboy. From here you can go anywhere you want.' I could hardly believe what I was seeing.

'I don't know where I want, Peat,' Siltboy said in a small voice. 'Will the muck aunt be here?'

'She may be. She might be telling stories, or treating people who are sick; or she might have left for another place. Let's go and find out.'

❧

The sleek didn't take us towards the lake. Instead, he found a track that skirted the city. It wound through a forest of trees that had been planted in rows. The leaves were gold, and the air was bright with birdsong and flickering sunlight.

We came to a crossroads with a signpost full of names. It was as tall as the trees, and there were names all the way up. Hub. Lower Hub. Mirth. Nil. The Deepings, Middle Hub, Holloway. Inroad. The Plains. Way of Fields. Alspith. Glut. Sigh River. Fourth World. Fifth World.

Uplands. Lookout. Mt Hub. Pinnacle Point. Drift Peak.
The Pass...I couldn't read the words at the top.

Siltboy gazed up as I called out the place names.

'You see, Siltboy. The world is bigger than you think!'
I told him.

I would have liked to climb the signpost so I could keep
reading all the way up, but the sleek nipped my ankles and
drove us down the path to Lower Hub. It was a narrow
track and it descended into a gully. Only once did we pass
anyone – a man with a handcart full of oranges.

'Light my lying eyes!' he cried. 'A Great Hound!
I thought your kind had all died out.'

He wheeled his cart to the side of the path so that
Shadow could pass, staring at him in such astonishment
that he barely noticed the sleek flicking several oranges to
the ground and chasing them when they rolled downhill.
He took off his hat and bowed his head. 'Heroes of the
hunt, preserve us!' he said.

Siltboy ran to catch up with the sleek and we had
oranges for our lunch, although the sleek wouldn't let us
stop to enjoy them. He chittered and snapped and hurried
us down the narrow path. I could hear a muffled roaring
sound coming up the gully and wondered if we were
somewhere near the waterfall.

After some time, the path joined up with a level road
that weaved its way through bush and rocks. From time
to time I could hear people – snatches of conversation,
laughter, the murmur of a crowd. Sweet cooking smells
wafted past and set my stomach rumbling. It was puzzling,
because there was nothing around us except boulders and
trees. Then I realised the sounds and smells were coming

through cracks in the rocks. I stopped and listened. The people of Hub were below us – I could hear their voices rising up out of the ground.

The road ended at the entrance to a cave. There were massive stones on either side, with some swirly patterns carved into them. A slab of rock sat over the top, with a symbol on it that looked like a wheel.

'We'd best leave Shadow outside. If we take him into Hub he will attract too much attention,' I said.

We walked away from the track and found a cosy spot for Shadow under some trees by a little stream. He was out of sight of the cave entrance there. Siltboy told him to stay, and he lay down in the shade. The sleek sprang onto his back and nestled into his fur, making himself comfortable. The upset from earlier in the day seemed to have been forgotten.

⸻

The cave was really a narrow passageway. It echoed with voices and the sound of roaring water, but no one was coming or going, except for two boys carrying empty fruit boxes.

'Are the night markets open in the daytime?' I asked.

'Of course,' they replied. 'The night markets never close. This is the back entrance.'

The passage was not like the one I had travelled down with the Siltman and his dogs. This was a short and level thoroughfare and it led straight to the marketplace.

'Strickens!' cried Siltboy, grabbing my hand. 'I never seen such a multitude!'

The markets were just as busy as when I had last been

there. People were calling the names of their wares above the roar of the crowd, and I could hear the waterfall crashing in the distance.

'Boots to walk you to your destination!'

'Spice, cloth and tools!'

'Gemstones from the Uplands. Jewel-rocks from the Lowlands.'

'Pots, pans, skillets.'

Piles of goods were stacked in long rows. The smell of fish oil and burning fat from the lamps above mixed with the scent of flowers and spices. Siltboy coughed and leaned close to me.

'I never believed to see so many peoples all at once in the world!' he whispered.

'Come on. We need to get to the main entrance, to see if Eadie's boat is there.'

We entered the fray, pushing our way through the crowds. I held Siltboy's bag close and wished I'd left the flower with Shadow and the sleek. It was bound to get crushed in the throng.

We passed mountains of fruit, and rows of every type of vegetable that must exist in this world and others. I pulled Siltboy along past tables where sweets were stacked into pyramids, and ornaments made of gold and silver were laid out on silk cloth.

Siltboy was wide-eyed. 'A trove of treasures, Peat. So many wrought things.' He stopped at a stall full of little round mirrors and stared at his reflection.

'What magic is this?' he breathed. 'Fifty Siltboys. Almost an army!'

'Haven't you ever seen yourself in a mirror before?'

'Only in the eye of my battlebird. I is daunted, Peat. And whelmed,' he said.

'It's all right, Siltboy. Stay close. I'll look after you.'

'Glowbirds,' a man with a bare shiny head cried. 'Glowbirds, to light your way!'

Siltboy stopped and stared at the cages. The birds inside sat hunched with their heads under their wings.

'They look like sparrows, but in the dark they glow like torches!' the man cried.

'Don't believe a word he says,' a woman beside him yelled. 'He's a bald-faced liar.'

'Truth?' Siltboy asked the bird-seller.

'Cross my heart and hope to die,' the man answered. 'If it wasn't for the lights above I could prove it.'

Siltboy looked up at the lanterns suspended from the ceiling, then he took back his bag and pulled out his slingshot.

'I'll shoot down them hanging flames,' he said.

'No, Siltboy.' I grabbed the slingshot and the bag and hauled him away.

As we approached the waterfall the clamour grew louder.

'Everyone bragful and boasting their wares.' Siltboy had to shout above the noise. 'My head rings, Peat. And them birds back there is sad.' He sat down under a table laden with melons and put his hands over his ears. 'I'm getting wore out.'

'Wait here and have a rest,' I said. 'I won't be long.'

I left Siltboy and pushed my way through the crowds towards the main entrance. There were many boats on the little shore inside the waterfall, but Eadie's was not among them. When I got back to the melons, Siltboy was gone.

'Did you see a small boy?' I asked the melon-seller.

'The boy in the breastplate? He ran off.'

I looked about in panic, wondering if I should try to find Siltboy in all the confusion of the vast night markets, or whether it would be better to wait by the melons and hope he came back.

A cry went up from somewhere in the crowd. 'Catch them! Stop them!' A few minutes after that Siltboy dived under the table and sat there panting and hugging his knees.

'Siltboy, I told you to stay put!'

He didn't answer. A flock of birds swooped overhead, moving as one, heading towards the light of the main entrance.

'Catch them!' screamed the bird-seller, but the sparrows were gone in a flash, flying over the boats and out through the waterfall.

Siltboy gave a little smile. 'Freedom is everything, Peat,' he said.

'Did he see you?'

He shook his head. 'Siltboy learn from the sleek.'

'Food! Food for the road!' A new voice rose above the din and a sweet, spicy smell drifted past.

'Come, Siltboy. I'll show you how they cook the food.'

I didn't know the way, but I followed the smell until we arrived at a giant cooking pot. The cooks were stirring a bubbling stew with paddles. One large man in an apron was using a ladle as big as a bucket. He dipped it in, scooped up a load and poured it back, releasing clouds of fragrant steam. People were sitting on mats on the ground, eating from flat leaves. A woman with braided hair and long seed-pod earrings waved us towards her.

'You two look hungry. Why don't you sit here next to me?'

We sat down and the cooks ladled out two steaming helpings of lunch.

'You look familiar, young redhead,' the woman said. 'Maybe I once told your fortune.'

'You did!'

'Ah, yes. I remember you. The story waif. I saw you a year ago – or perhaps it was two.'

Two years. How strange. I felt I hadn't been gone more than a week.

'No, it was only a few days ago,' I told her.

She laughed as if I had made a joke. 'Let me pay for your meal.' She pressed some coins into my hand. 'Time flies,' she said. 'Come and see me. I'm still in the same spot.'

⤙

After we had eaten, Siltboy and I headed for the fortune teller.

'I'm mazed,' he said. 'I'm glad you know the way.'

We wandered past stalls full of hanging sausages and people selling bowls of painted eggs. We passed a man with a plate of flat biscuits that were stamped with the same wheel symbol I'd seen above the entrance to the tunnel.

'Wheel-of-the-World biscuits,' he cried. 'None better in the whole of Hub.'

When we passed a stall selling round cheeses, my eyes

filled with tears. They were just like the ones Marlie and I had used to make at the Overhang.

'Ah, there you are!' said the fortune teller. 'Let me tell your future, boy.'

She poured some seeds onto the ground and asked Siltboy to stir them.

'I see sleeping dogs,' she said. 'Let them lie. Stir again.'

Siltboy moved his finger.

'A long and happy life!' she declared. 'Now you, little swamp waif. People are still talking about your performance that day in the Undercavern. Ask a question, any question.'

I put my finger into the seeds but held it still. I didn't want to know my future. I wanted to know about Marlie. Was she all right?

Before I had a chance to ask, the fortune teller spoke. 'I see your auntie. She is on the Plains.'

Eadie was nearby! I remembered the Plains as one of the names on the signpost.

'How far is it?' I asked.

'Not far. And your sister is closer than you think.'

Just then something caught Siltboy's eye. 'Peat, a forge!' He dashed away and I had no choice but to follow him.

There was a blacksmith's stall at the end of the row. The air was thick with smoke and everything around it was slightly blackened.

'Oh, wondrous work!' Siltboy cried.

The blacksmith was a big man with a long black beard that was slightly singed in places. He wore a leather apron and he wielded a hammer, beating a sheet of metal with it. A fire glowed behind him on a low brick box with a tin chimney above it that disappeared into the gloomy reaches of the ceiling.

'Are you making armour?' Siltboy cried.

The blacksmith roared with laughter. 'No, it's flat iron, the base of a boiler. Did you see the cooking pots?'

Siltboy nodded.

'It's the bottom of one of those.'

The blacksmith paused and wiped his brow. 'You're an old-fashioned-looking lad,' he said. 'What's that you're wearing on your chest?'

'Breastplate.' Siltboy opened my wool vest so that the blacksmith could get a better look.

'What the blazes!' the big man cried. He leaned forward and tapped on the breastplate as if he was knocking on a door.

'It rings true,' he said, staring closely. 'But I can't make out the emblem.'

'That's 'cause it's half wore off,' Siltboy told him.

The blacksmith stepped back and looked at Siltboy with his head on the side. 'Would you like to strike a blow?' he asked, handing over the hammer.

There were a couple of thin boys standing near the forge. One was working a big pair of bellows. He didn't look much older than me, but he wore a leather apron like the blacksmith's.

'Bit young, isn't he?' he said, looking at Siltboy.

'I'm nine hundred years old.'

When the boy laughed, Siltboy took offence.

'You think I lie?' he asked. 'I challenge you!' Siltboy held the hammer above his head.

'No fighting, Siltboy. This is not the battle for us.'
I took the hammer from his hand and dragged him away.
'Eadie is nearby. We have to get to the Plains.'

40

LONGREACH

Leaving the night markets was harder than arriving had been, as the back tunnel was now full of people. They were streaming out of the Great Hall, talking excitedly.

'He's magnificent. He comes from the old world.'

'He's one of the ancient breed. A noble hound. He's probably the last one left.'

We had to push our way through the crowd to get outside, and once we were there we couldn't see for the people. I climbed some rocks near the entrance to get a view.

Shadow was sitting on the track and he was surrounded. His head was low and he was glancing uneasily from side to side. He had a hunched look, as if he was trying to make himself small so he wouldn't be noticed. When he saw Siltboy making his way through the crowd, he stood up and welcomed him. People screamed and leapt back, and the great booming sound of Shadow's bark echoed through the tunnel. The sight of the huge dog towering above was too much for one man, who fainted and had to be carried off.

'Keep away!' someone shouted. 'Don't crowd the hound!'

Siltboy pushed his way to the front and Shadow wagged his tail, sweeping the people behind him off their feet.

Some boys climbed up on the rocks beside me. 'He's a Great Hound,' one of them said. 'He's like the dogs we saw in the Undercavern, remember?'

'How could I forget!' another boy answered. 'That storytelling was incredible. I was so scared I had to keep reminding myself it wasn't real.'

A man who had put himself in charge of the crowd began giving directions. 'Place your gifts at his feet. Keep your heads low, and don't touch him.'

People edged forward, cautiously putting packages in front of Shadow, who sniffed the parcels then tossed each one into the air and gulped it down without opening the wrapping. When he had devoured all the offerings, he shook his great head. His ears flapped, and a few long hairs fell to the ground, where they were immediately picked up by people who dashed forward then disappeared back into the crowd.

Somewhere in the throng I heard the voice of the woman who sold sayings. 'Our hands are empty but our hearts are full!'

'His presence is a gift,' someone else said.

'Amazing! The world is full of wonders!'

I knew that voice. I couldn't ever forget it.

A tall man stood at the front of the crowd, staring up at Shadow. His hair was long and fair, and he'd spoken in the western tongue. It was the stranger. And next to him was...

'*Marlie!*' My heart leapt in me.

She turned in surprise. 'Peat?'

I was on the ground in an instant, pushing and shoving my way towards my sister.

'Wait your turn,' people grumbled.

'*Marlie!*' I yelled, and I heard her yelling back, 'Peat, is that you?'

I squeezed through a solid wall of people until I was next to her.

'Peat, it's you! It's really you!'

I hugged Marlie so tight that I must have squeezed the breath out of her, because when she tried to speak, the words were small and crushed.

'Oh, Peat. I was so worried about you.'

'And I was worried about *you*!' I looked up and her tears splashed onto my face. 'Did Alban Bane take you, Marlie? How did you get away?'

She stepped back and wiped her eyes on her sleeve.

'It's a long story,' she said. 'Peat, I didn't expect to see you ever again.'

She cupped my face in her hands, and now I was crying, too. 'I went to the marshes,' I sobbed. 'I got caught in the snare of a marsh auntie. Oh, Marlie, it's so good to see you. I can hardly believe it. What are you doing here?'

'You remember the traveller, Peat? He came back. He wanted to help.'

I looked over Marlie's shoulder. The stranger was right there, standing behind her. His hair was longer now, and his eyes were as clear as ever.

'You *did* help!' I cried. He gave a quiet smile and looked as if he was about to say something when Siltboy pushed in front of us.

'Peat, what ails you?' he cried. 'Why do you keen? Where is the trouble?'

The stranger raised his eyebrows and stepped back.

'No trouble,' was all I could manage to say.

Siltboy turned to the stranger. 'Untie your tongue,' he demanded. 'State yourself!'

'I'm Longreach,' the stranger said softly.

'Friend or foe?' Siltboy demanded.

'Friend!' the stranger replied, and he laughed his high, windy laugh. He held out his hand and Siltboy took it. 'What a grip!' he exclaimed. 'What's your name?'

'Siltboy.'

'I have travelled the wide world, but I have never met anyone like you before.'

Siltboy nodded. 'I is rare,' he said. 'And so is my hound.'

'The Great Hound is yours?'

'He is mine, and I am his.'

'Wonders never cease,' breathed Longreach. 'Tell me, my curious young man, how did you come by that thread around your neck?'

Siltboy pointed to me. 'A gift from my friend.'

Longreach scratched his head. 'I gave that thread to a marsh auntie who saved my life.'

'You gave the thread to Eadie, and she gave it to me,' I told him.

'You know Eadie?'

'I was her apprentice.'

Longreach turned to Marlie. 'Eadie is a healer who can work a marvel,' he said. 'She cured me when I was at death's door. I am so grateful to her. Sometimes the world is smaller than you think!'

Marlie was looking from one face to the next as if it was all too much for her to take in. She hugged me again.

'Wim will be so relieved to see you,' she cried.

'Wim is here?'

'Yes. She's minding the cows on the slopes beyond Outer Hub, at a place called the Plains.'

So the fortune teller hadn't been talking about Eadie – she'd been talking about Wim! And the cattle were here as well!

'We're herders now,' Marlie said. 'We're taking the cows to the high pastures in the mountains beyond Hub – and now that we've found you, we can all go together!'

'Stay away!' yelled the man in charge to some boys who'd gone too close.

Shadow yawned, displaying the roof of his mouth, purple and ridged. There were cries of alarm and the crowd drew back. Shadow licked his chops and lay down, resting his head on his paws.

'Marlie, what happened to you? How did you get away from Alban?'

'It was hard.' Marlie let go of me. She seemed to be searching for the words. When Longreach took her hand, she smiled through her tears. 'But I'm now safe, and you are, too.'

The thought went through my head that I wasn't actually safe, and that I wouldn't be until I had delivered the flower to Eadie.

'So much has happened, Peat,' Marlie told me. 'There was sickness in Skerrick. Many people died.'

'I went back for you girls,' Longreach said. 'I wanted to ask you if you would come with me. When I returned to your country, I found that things had changed. Alban Bane had sickened and died. The settlement was in ruins, almost abandoned. There weren't many people left.'

'It was the catching disease. Those who had worked with the cattle were safe, so I was all right. And Wim was as well.' Marlie shook her head. 'You've changed, Peat. You're taller.'

'You look different, too. You're not thin anymore.'

Marlie's long hair was tied up in plaits and she looked grown-up. She was wearing a dress made of cloth that changed colour in the light – some of it was green and some was blue. She had a bag over her shoulder like the one I had carried the night I left the Overhang, the stranger's bag. And she was wearing soft leather boots.

'You've still got the cow charm!' she cried.

'Your most precious thing. If it wasn't for this charm, I might not be here.' I slipped off the cow charm and put it over Marlie's head. 'Thank you, Marlie. I always hoped I could give it back.'

Just then, someone in the crowd behind us cried out, and we were jostled forward. 'Ouch! It bit me!'

'Ah! Me, too!'

'Well, will you look at that!' Longreach exclaimed as the sleek padded into the open space before Shadow. 'This truly is a day full of wonders. I have heard of such creatures, but I've never seen one. I believe it's a firetail swamp rat.'

The sleek had a large biscuit in his mouth, and his ears were flat against his head. How he had managed to get through the mob without being trampled I didn't know, but I had seen him in worse moods. He sat down and crunched the biscuit, then he stood upright on his hind legs and scanned the crowd, his sharp gaze moving from face to face until it landed on mine. He gave a hiss and sprang through the air, landing on my chest. Marlie jumped back.

'Don't be frightened,' I said. 'He's a friend, although sometimes you wouldn't know it. He's also our guide, and he's impatient to get away.'

'Away? Away where?'

'Marlie. I have to go.'

'Go? We've only just found each other.'

I took the flower out of Siltboy's bag. The leaves were drying, and some of the petals were crushed and broken. The stem was squashed in three places.

'It's hard to explain, Marlie. But I have to deliver this flower.'

'To the marsh auntie?' Longreach asked.

'Yes. How did you know?'

'I *don't* know,' he said. 'It's just that I last saw a flower like that in Eadie's hut.'

'I don't understand...' Marlie began.

'I've got a long story, too,' I said. 'I'll tell you as soon as I get back. Will you wait for me? Can I meet you on the Plains?'

Marlie reached into her bag and handed me a cheese. 'I was bringing this for the Great Hound, but I'll give it to you instead,' she said sadly. 'Oh, Peat, do you really have to go?'

Siltboy took Marlie's hand.

'Sister of Peat,' he said. 'We is not true free. If we was free, Peat would go the cow way with her kith and kin.' He looked down and kicked the dirt at his feet. 'And I would stay here in the Wheel-of-the-World. I could work with that man-of-metal and wield the hammer better than them weed boys.'

Shadow sighed and lifted his head. 'Stand, Shadow!' Siltboy said. The Great Hound rose to his feet and there were cries of awe from the crowd.

I hugged Marlie goodbye, although it hurt my heart to do so. 'I'll see you soon,' I told her. Then I hugged Longreach as well, because he felt like my family.

When I began walking towards Shadow, whispers ran through the crowd.

'It's her. It's the story waif!'

'We're in for another telling.'

'Quick, let's get to the Undercavern. Let's get good seats.'

A few people began hurrying back through the tunnel entrance. Others sat down, as if they expected me to begin a story immediately. For some reason, Shadow raised his hackles. He sniffed the air and whined. The sleek, too, was uneasy. He ran to Shadow and scrambled up his leg and onto his neck, where he stood with his back arched and his tail flared.

'It's all right, Sleek,' I said. 'I'm not going to tell any stories.'

I turned to the crowd. 'There'll be no telling,' I said. 'Not here and not in the Undercavern. We are leaving.'

As I spoke, something in the air changed and a sharp salt breeze blew around my ears. Shadow growled and lowered his head, and Siltboy quickly climbed up his neck, pulling me after him. The breeze grew stronger, and somewhere far away I thought I heard howling. The crowd heard it, too. People turned from us and looked towards the tunnel, because that's where the sound was coming from.

'It's just the wind,' someone said. 'A squall coming up from the gorge. It happens at this time of the year.'

Then Longreach was beside us, stretching up and handing me the cow charm.

'Keep the charm, Peat. Your journey isn't over yet,' he said quietly.

41

STAKED

We headed down a steep slope where the trees grew
close together and the undergrowth was thick. Branches
cracked and twigs whipped our faces as Shadow slid
downhill on his haunches. We leaned forward along his
neck and kept our heads low. The howling faded behind
us, but the sleek crouched on Shadow's head, urging him
forward, and only when we'd reached the bottom of the
hill did his tail settle.

We came to a halt beside a fast-flowing creek. The sleek
slipped to the ground and sniffed the air, his ears twitching. We were in a deep gully, and apart from running
water, there was no sound. The sleek began following the
creek downstream.

'Shouldn't we go back to the signpost?' I said.

I wished I had asked the seed-reader about Eadie. If
a year or more had passed since we were in Hub, Eadie
could be far away. She could have gone anywhere.

'Hush,' said Siltboy.

The sleek shot me a glance over his shoulder.

'I don't think Eadie would have come this way,' I said.
'This isn't a track. We should go back and ask.'

'No back-looking,' said Siltboy. 'Sleek knows. He has
creature-craft and mapwork in his mind.'

'I hope you're right,' I replied as Shadow followed the sleek.

The gully was narrow and dark, and the further we went the darker it seemed to become. I thought it was probably just the trees blocking the light, and the fact that we were near the end of the day, but I didn't like it, and as we travelled along I became more and more convinced that we were going the wrong way.

'You is tired, Peat,' Siltboy told me. 'Today is giant day, so big and brimful. One moment you burst with sister joy, and next moment you is lost again and back on the questing road.'

'We're not even on a road,' I said. 'That's the problem. Let's stop.'

'No talk of stop. We follow Sleek.'

The sleek flicked his ears, irritated by the conversation. His tail twitched.

'How do we know he's heading in the right direction?'

'Settle, Peat,' Siltboy said. 'You is churned.'

'I'm not churned,' I snapped. 'I don't like this valley, and I don't think we're going the right way.'

The sleek stopped and stared at me, then he dived into the creek and quickly reappeared on the far bank. Shadow followed, clearing the water in a single bound.

'Don't doubt Sleek,' Siltboy whispered. 'He goes by shortcut.'

Shortcut to where?

We continued on the far side of the creek. The bank was rocky and Shadow had to pick his way over fallen logs and debris that looked as if it had been left there by a flood. It was evening when the creek met up with a river. It might have been the same river that Eadie and I had travelled to reach Hub, but I couldn't be sure.

'If this is the river Eadie and I came on, the sleek must be leading us all the way back to the marshes,' I told Siltboy.

Why would Eadie have gone back there? That's the very place she wanted to escape.

'Let's find a camp site,' I said. 'It's getting dark.'

As I spoke, the sleek came to a halt so quickly that Shadow almost trod on him. He gave me a killing look, then he leapt up onto some boulders above the riverbank. From there he glared down at me, seething.

Siltboy turned around. 'Get cheese, Peat,' he said. 'Sleek needs peace-offering.'

I took Marlie's cheese out of his bag and broke off a piece. Siltboy reached up, and the sleek snatched it without taking his eyes off me. From where I was I couldn't see what his tail was doing, but I expected the worst.

'You'd better tell Shadow to sit,' I whispered. 'We need to get off.'

'Drop,' Siltboy said.

I climbed to the ground and backed away, and I told Siltboy to do the same.

'Get down,' I said. 'Or he'll go for you instead of me.'

Siltboy didn't move. Instead, he looked up at the sleek and began singing a strange high-pitched tune.

Praise to the sleek,
Bright-wild, with mind of fire...

To my surprise the sleek pricked his ears, listening, and his wild eyes grew calm.

> *Praise to our gallant guide*
> *Who goes by dart and dash*
> *With wit-work flashing*
> *Praise to the sleek!*

The sleek closed his eyes and purred.

'Siltboy, that's amazing!'

I wished I hadn't said anything, because as soon as I spoke the sleek was alert again. He crouched for a moment, then he pounced, landing on Siltboy's shoulder. I cringed, expecting that Siltboy would be swiped in the face, but the sleek's claws were not drawn – and instead of scratching Siltboy, he patted his cheek with a soft paw before taking the lead again.

'Mount, Peat,' Siltboy said. 'Our guide is waiting.'

Shadow turned and gave me a nudge as I climbed back on. I said nothing as we continued on our way.

We had not gone far when the sleek let out a shriek and leapt high in the air. He had been trotting along happily ahead of us at the river's edge, but now his fur stood on end and he showed the whites of his eyes. He backed away, staring at a spot near the water, and when he was close to us he turned and scrabbled up Shadow's leg, sitting behind me, quivering with fear.

Shadow gave a low growl, and I could feel his muscles bunching, but I couldn't see anything ahead except rocks and some soft mud at the water's edge.

Siltboy took out his slingshot.

'Let me look,' he said. He climbed to the ground and crept towards the place where the sleek had been. 'Nothing,' he yelled. 'Just dent in sand.'

'A dent in the sand? Why would that scare the sleek?'

Siltboy shrugged. He whistled and Shadow skirted the spot by the water, keeping as far away as possible. Once Siltboy was back on, he bounded ahead, crashing through sticks and branches that had been washed up on the riverbank.

The moon came up and lit our way for a while before disappearing behind dark clouds. The sleek was restless. He scrambled over me and Siltboy and sat at the front, peering ahead, then he climbed over us again and sat behind, making anxious cricking sounds in the back of his throat. Shadow stumbled in the dark, but he didn't slow down. I closed my eyes and hung on. I was getting tired.

'How much further?' I asked.

'Only Sleek knows,' Siltboy replied. 'He has knowledges we don't. He has wit-ways—'

Suddenly Shadow yelped and came to a halt, raising his front right paw.

Siltboy was on the ground in a second. 'My hound is hurt,' he cried. 'He is staked!'

The sleek hissed and paced up and down, impatient with the delay, as we examined Shadow's paw. A sharp piece of stick was lodged deep between the pads.

'In the Ever my hound could never be hurt,' Siltboy said.

'He'll be all right. It's not serious,' I told him, hoping it was true. I wished I had learned from Eadie. She would know exactly what to do in this situation. She would find the right plant and heal Shadow in two minutes.

I tried to get hold of the end of the stick, but the poor beast howled and pulled away. He limped to the water's edge and had a drink, then he found a bit of clear ground between the rocks and lay down.

'I sorrow for you, Shadow.' Siltboy sat down beside him, stroking his shoulder and staring at the injured paw. 'Wounds is the way of all battles.'

The Great Hound gave him a lick, then he licked his paw and laid his head on the ground with a sigh. Siltboy rubbed his ears. 'We should fire and food, Peat,' he said vaguely.

'Tomorrow,' I replied, as I lay down beside him.

The sleek came and sat nearby, looking peevish.

'We can't keep going, Sleek,' I said. 'Shadow's hurt and we're all exhausted.'

I lay listening to the river rushing past, and I was just dropping off to sleep when Siltboy spoke.

'I is wondering on the tale, Peat. You never made an end to it.'

'What tale?' I yawned.

'The story with me and Shadow and them fighting giants. You didn't finish it.'

'I did. You know how it ended.'

'But what happens to the mother?' he asked.

'I don't know, Siltboy. Eadie didn't tell me what happened to your mother. She must have come back and seen that the fort had been taken over by the other giant. Maybe she searched for her husband's body.'

'But did she look for me?' His voice was tight. He was almost pleading.

'Of course she did. She looked for you everywhere. She went all over the country, but the Siltman had left, travelling north, and he had taken you with him.'

Siltboy was quiet for a long time.

'I wish I asked the seed-reader,' he said. 'She might know where my mother is.'

'The fortune teller sees the future, not the past, Siltboy. And your mother is long past. This all happened in ancient times. You won't find your mother now.'

'You is sure?'

'I'm sure. Sorry, Siltboy, but that's the way it is.'

Shadow gave a little whimper in his sleep, and Siltboy turned and buried his face in the dog's shaggy coat.

42

THE EVERLASTING DAISY

The sleek woke us at dawn. His fur stood on end again and his tail was fully flared. I rubbed my eyes and went down to the water to wash my face, and he jumped up and down on the spot, chittering in agitation. Then I saw what had upset him – a paw print, a big one! I let out a cry and Siltboy came running.

'Be it Shadow's?' he asked.

I shook my head. It was smaller than Shadow's, but still much bigger than a normal-sized dog.

'Hound of Siltman!' Siltboy breathed. 'Maybe that dint I seen yesterday was one like this, only more washed away.' He turned to me in despair. 'Everything is wrong-going, Peat. My hound is hurt. My mother is lost. And now we is lost as well.' He shook his head. 'And the foreteller at them markets said I'd have a long and happy life.'

'Long,' I said, 'but maybe not so happy.'

'I is stricken.' Siltboy's eyes filled up with tears.

I stared at the paw print and tried to think. 'Don't worry, Siltboy,' I said. 'The footprints of the Siltman and his dogs arrive three weeks before he does, and probably longer if he's still got the Swoon on him. We're safe. He's nowhere near us. Let's go.'

I was trying to convince myself as much as Siltboy.

We couldn't ride Shadow with his injured paw, so we walked. The sleek ran ahead, looking over his shoulder and clicking to himself when we didn't keep up. Shadow limped along and Siltboy limped beside him, not because his own foot was sore but because he felt for his hound. Every time Shadow put his paw to the ground, Siltboy winced and gave a little sigh of sympathy.

I was hungry, and I hoped the sleek would let us stop somewhere along the way. We could eat Marlie's cheese, and I thought he might even get us some other food – those weeds from the riverbed or something similar.

The sun had not been up for long when I heard voices on the river behind us. I looked back and saw a boat moving swiftly downstream. The decks were empty, but a man stood at the helm, steering. He was too far away for me to see his face, but I recognised the boat. It was the bread boat!

'Siltboy, we're near Mother Moss's!' I cried.

The man gave a wave as the boat swept past, carried by the current.

The sleek picked up his pace and disappeared without waiting for us to follow. It didn't matter – I knew which way to go.

'Just keep following the river!' I told Siltboy as I ran ahead.

Soon I smelled fresh bread, and when the landing came into view I jumped for joy. I could see the woe tree leaning out over the water and Mother Moss standing next to the oven with her hands on her hips. She looked a little bit older and smaller, but apart from that nothing had changed.

An upturned reed-boat lay on the riverbank. *Eadie!* My stomach clenched, but I was relieved as well – the sooner I gave Eadie the flower, the sooner I could be back with Marlie.

The bread boat was just leaving. The man on the deck saw me and yelled to Mother Moss, 'Your helper has returned, Mother!'

Mother Moss looked bewildered. When the man pointed to me, she gasped and slapped her hand on her heart, releasing a little puff of flour.

'Oh, joy! How is it possible?' She opened her arms and I ran into them. She was warm and soft and she smelled of fresh bread and honey. 'I never thought I'd see you again, Peat!' she cried.

She held me away from her and stared at me as if she was seeing a ghost, then she patted both my cheeks and ran her baker's hands over me, kneading me to make sure I was real.

'Ah! The shock of it. I have to sit down.' Her face broke into a wide smile. 'How you've grown, my girl!' She shook her head in disbelief and hugged me once more. 'But how on earth...?' she whispered. 'I thought you were lost forever. Come, sit by me.'

She led me to the bread bench and pulled up some seats.

'I blamed myself, little Peat. I should never have let Eadie take you.'

'You couldn't have stopped her, Mother Moss.'

Mother Moss shook her head again. She put her big

278

floury arm around me. 'There are things I need to tell you,' she said. 'You're still only a child, Peat, and you can't understand, but there was an old agreement made long ago...'

'I do understand, Mother Moss. I know about the bargain.'

'Eadie told you?'

'No. The Siltman did.'

Mother Moss's mouth fell open.

'Eadie told me he took you, but I scarce believed her,' she whispered. 'She came back here after you were gone.'

'Is she here now? I saw her boat on the bank.'

'No, my dear. Another marsh auntie brought that craft to me. All the rules have changed. There's a new Great Aunt, a woman called Ivy who was living on one of the Hermit Islands in the Far Reaches. The aunties can now come and go as they please.'

'Where did Eadie go?'

'She went back to the marshes. One of the aunties took her, as she was too weak to paddle.'

Too weak to paddle? I couldn't imagine that.

'Was she sick?' I asked.

'Not sick. She was growing old. But tell me, Peat, did the Siltman take you to his realm?' Her eyes looked worried and she pulled me close.

'Yes, he did.' I let myself lean against her. 'He and his pack of dogs. They took me across the Silver River to a country by the sea.'

'But you escaped? How can that be?'

'It was Siltboy who did it. He won the wit-battle, and that's how we got away.' I knew I wasn't making much sense. 'He'll be here soon. Siltboy helped me, and so did Shadow and the sleek. They're my friends.'

I turned and looked up the river.

'Siltboy!' I yelled. 'Shadow!'

Mother Moss gasped and slapped her chest a second time when my companions appeared. 'Goodness,' she cried. 'One miracle follows another. What an extraordinary dog!'

Shadow lowered his head and gave Mother Moss a gentle nudge.

'This is Shadow,' I said. 'He's a Great Hound.'

'I can see that,' Mother Moss replied. 'Oh, but he's hurt.'

'He is staked,' Siltboy said sadly.

Mother Moss carefully lifted Shadow's huge paw. 'Go and get me some horehound, Peat. And some coltsfoot, too, if you can find it.'

I looked at her blankly.

'Didn't Eadie teach you?' she asked.

'I wasn't with her for long. She only taught me the stories.'

Mother Moss gently lowered Shadow's paw and gave him a pat. 'I won't be long, my friend,' she said. 'There's some in Cara's paddock. Peat, would you mind putting the kettle on the fire? I'm going to need hot water.'

Mother Moss's cooking fire was next to the oven. I added some sticks and did as she asked, and by the time she returned the water was boiling. She was carrying a weed with small white flowers and crinkly leaves. She broke off some pieces and put them in a pot, then she poured in the hot water, adding a pinch of salt.

'I learned this when I was in the marshes,' she said, adding cold water and testing it with her finger. I watched her tear a flourbag into long strips to make a bandage. She lifted Shadow's huge paw and placed it in the pot.

'There's a good pup,' she said. 'This won't hurt a bit. Just let it soak for a moment.'

She turned to Siltboy. 'And who are you, my little friend?'

Siltboy pushed out his chest so that his breastplate gleamed in the sunlight. 'Not so little,' he said. 'I is warrior son of Pike. I come from the Ever, and I fight and never give up.'

'Goodness,' Mother Moss said. 'I hope you're not going to fight me.'

He gave a shy smile. 'Is that a forge?' he asked.

'It's an oven. That's where I bake my bread. Would you like some?'

Siltboy nodded.

'Go into my hut and help yourselves,' she said. When Siltboy looked towards Shadow she added, 'Don't worry about your hound. I'll tend to him.'

Siltboy had never tasted honey before. He scooped out spoonfuls and poured it over his bread.

'Running gold,' he said. 'I never seen the likes of it.'

When we went back outside we found Shadow sitting with his paw neatly bandaged. He was eating a side of bacon. Mother Moss was sitting beside him.

'I was keeping that for winter,' she said. 'But one isn't blessed with a visit from a noble hound every day. My word, he has a good appetite!'

Shadow gulped down the bacon, then he walked over

to the oven and lay next to it. He was no longer limping.

'Did you children have enough to eat?' Mother Moss asked. 'Are you full?'

'To the hilt,' Siltboy replied. 'Thank you, Mother. And thank you for helping my hound.'

'You must have been starving. I can't imagine how far you young ones must have come.'

'Far,' said Siltboy. 'Through darkness and dazzlement. Over river, grassland, hummock, forest and hilltop. Over mountain wall, then down by winding ways into the Wheel-of-the-World.'

'He means Hub,' I said.

'Full-folked and teeming, it was. A lofty hall, high-vaulted, hung with flares and packed to the brink with throngs, marvels and all manner of wares. I seen gems and mirrors like fifty eyes of the battlebird, and everywhere the voice-clamour of traders, stealthmen, truth-tellers...'

'Siltboy, you're a sweet child, but I have no idea what you're talking about,' Mother Moss interrupted.

'He's telling you about the night markets,' I said.

'I am full to burst with the sights,' Siltboy cried. 'More things I seen in three days with Peat than in three hundred years in the Ever.'

He was about to say more when Cara bellowed.

'Goodness!' Mother Moss jumped to her feet. 'With all this excitement I've lost track of time. I haven't milked Cara yet.'

'I'll do it, Mother Moss.'

'Thank you, Peat. If there's one thing I need around here, it's help.' Mother Moss handed me a bucket.

'I can help, too.' Siltboy saw an axe leaning against the

wall of the hut. He raced to it and ran his finger along the blade. 'Have you a whetstone, Mother? I'll sharpen him up for you.'

'It's sharp enough, young lad. But you might like to split those logs and stack them next to the oven. Have you wielded an axe before?'

'It comes natural to me,' he said.

Siltboy set to work with gusto. Chips went flying and the wood fell apart on the chopping block.

I had trouble bringing Cara because she baulked as soon as she caught sight of Shadow. Mother Moss had to coax her along with handfuls of oats.

'He's a gentle hound, Cara. Big, but gentle,' she said. 'Don't be nervous.'

Cara mooed a couple of times, then she settled down and the milk began to flow. I pressed my head against her warm flank and squirted the milk into the bucket. I hoped I would soon be milking my own cows – Bella and Pem and Skye and the others.

'What's next, Mother?' Siltboy asked when he had finished stacking the wood.

'Next we clean up the bread bench and wipe out the tins. What a wonderful worker you are, little pikelet!'

Siltboy helped Mother Moss while I finished milking and took Cara back to her paddock. When I returned, Mother Moss made us all a cup of tea and we sat around the fire.

'Now, I want to hear everything, from the beginning,' she said. 'Tell me about this wit-battle business. I don't even know much about the Siltman, except that he never forgets what's owed to him.'

'Siltman is older than time,' Siltboy explained. 'He is full of powers, and we are not yet safe.'

'What?' Mother Moss cried. 'Is he after you?'

'We reckon,' Siltboy said. 'He might not want Peat back, but he will want me.'

'Were you payment for a bargain?' Mother Moss took Siltboy's hand and her soft face grew even softer.

'I was,' said Siltboy.

'And is the person who traded you still living?'

'No. It were Pike, and he's been dead nine hundred years.'

'Then I'd say that bargain is over, wouldn't you?'

She stood up and folded her arms – strong arms from years of kneading dough. She looked as sturdy as the men who stirred the giant cooking pots in the night markets.

'If the Siltman comes this way, he'll be sorry,' she said quietly. 'He'll take you over my dead body.'

Shadow looked from Mother Moss to Siltboy, concerned and ready to help if he was given a command.

'But you already stood up to him, did you, Siltboy?' Mother Moss asked. 'Was that the wit-battle?'

'It were just the workings of it, Mother. Peat was the one that braved him. She lulled him with a tale, and when the sleek broke the smell bottle he were felled.'

Mother Moss sat down again, looking slightly bewildered.

'It were a kind of magic mist,' Siltboy told her.

'It wasn't really magic mist, Siltboy. It was perfume – a scent called Swoon.'

'Not one of Lily's creations?' Mother Moss asked.

'Yes. Lily gave it to me. Do you know her?'

'I knew her when I was a marsh auntie. Her perfumes were always going wrong.'

'When were you a marsh auntie, Mother?'

'Many years ago, Peat. That's how I knew Eadie. She rescued me from a bad situation and took me to the marshes to recover. I stayed there for a long time. Eadie was my friend. She was a good healer and always tried to make people's lives better, but she made some big mistakes.'

Mother Moss sighed and poked the fire. 'Her first mistake was making a bargain with the Siltman, and her second terrible mistake was using you as payment. But, dear Peat, she regretted it almost as soon as she'd done it. She'd thought she would be free to live the old travelling life again when she'd paid her debt, but she was too troubled. She spent a while in Hub, then she came back here. She wanted to go after you but she lost her strength. I don't know why.'

I opened Siltboy's bag and took out the flower.

'An everlasting daisy,' Mother Moss said. 'That's Eadie's favourite flower. It looks worse for the wear. Where did you get it?'

'It's from the Ever. And it's not *any* everlasting daisy. Eadie's spirit is in this plant.'

Mother Moss stared hard at the flower.

'I'm going to reverse the bargain, Mother. I'm taking the flower back to Eadie.'

Mother Moss put her hand to her heart, this time softly, so no cloud of flour rose into the air.

'Do something for me, Siltboy dear. There's a tree that hangs over the river just past those rocks. Please bring me some of its bark.'

Shadow lay down next to the old lady with his head on her feet. He looked up at her and nudged her arm with his nose. Mother Moss stroked his ears and he put his great head in her lap.

When Siltboy returned with the bark, Mother Moss added some to her cup.

'For sadness,' she said. 'Eadie and I have been friends for a long time. You're brave and clever, Peat, but you don't understand everything.' She sipped the tea. 'What you're holding in your hands is not Eadie's life, but her death,' she said. 'How long ago did you dig it up?'

'I don't know, Mother Moss. I thought it was a few days ago, but I seem to have lost track of time. The fortune teller at the night markets said she hadn't seen me for over a year. I think I've been in a land where time stands still.'

I cupped my hands around the everlasting daisy.

'This flower stood out from the others, Mother Moss. It was bright and beautiful, and when all the other flowers closed up for the night, it stayed wide open. But now the leaves are faded and I've broken some of the petals.'

I fiddled with the cloth around the roots, then I put down the flower and ran my fingers through my hair. I was confused. My only thought until now had been to reverse the bargain.

'I could throw the flower away,' I said. 'I could throw it in the river.'

Mother Moss shook her head.

'Take it to Eadie,' she said. 'It belongs to her. She's had her time, and life will not be easy for her now. None of her herbs will make her young again. You were right to fight for your life, Peat. Try to forgive Eadie for holding too tight to her own.' She gulped down the rest of her tea and upended the cup.

There was a long silence. The river rushed past, full of its own conversation, but ours had stopped. Siltboy stared at Mother Moss with the same look on his face as Shadow.

'Can I help you, Mother?' he asked. 'I is strong. I can fight…'

'There's no fighting to be done.' Mother Moss gave a sad smile. 'Look at Shadow. The greatest strength is in gentleness.' She seemed to be talking to herself more than to Siltboy, and after a while she sighed and got to her feet.

'Give me the flower, Peat. I will keep it safe until you go.'

Mother Moss went into her hut. When she came out she looked cheerful again. She was carrying a pumpkin and a large knife.

'We haven't got much time together,' she said. 'Why waste it with sadness? I'm going to cook lunch – soup and seedcake and pumpkin pie. Stoke up the oven for me, will you, Siltboy?' She began chopping the pumpkin on the bread bench. 'Tell me, Peat, what was it like in the Ever?'

I was about to answer when Mother Moss let out a cry. 'Bad little sleek!' she shouted.

'I'm sorry, Mother. I should have put the milk inside.'

The sleek was perched on the edge of the bucket, helping himself. He took no notice of Mother Moss yelling, but when she charged towards him he leapt away, knocking the bucket over and splashing her legs with milk. He ran into the hut and Mother Moss followed.

'Out!' she cried. 'I'll not have creatures taking over my dwelling!'

The sleek shot out of the hut with an oatcake in his mouth and disappeared under some pumpkin vines that were trailing over the wall.

'I'm so sorry, Mother.'

'It's not your fault, Peat. That creature needs to learn some manners. Last time he was here three loaves of bread went missing. The bread-boat boys discovered it when they were unloading their delivery in Hub. He's a real pest.'

'He is, Mother,' I agreed. 'But he's a good sleek, too. He showed us the way back from the Ever, and he's still leading us.'

'Come here, you little rat.' Mother Moss peered into the vines and the sleek jumped into the open and crouched before her, his eyes narrow and his tail beginning to flare.

'No, Sleek. No. Please!' I yelled.

Mother Moss was strong, but she was an old lady and her skin was thin. I couldn't have stood it if the sleek had scratched her.

They stared at each other for a long moment, then the sleek surprised me by lowering his head and coming to sit beside me.

'That's better,' said Mother Moss, as if this was the behaviour she expected. She picked up the overturned bucket. 'Well, there's no use crying over spilt milk,' she said. 'We've got work to do.'

43

SONG FOR A
SCARLET RUNNER

'I don't normally have animals at my table,' Mother Moss said, 'especially thieves, but today we will let bygones be bygones.'

The sleek sat on one end of the bread bench, while Shadow sat on the ground at the other. Siltboy helped Mother Moss lay out the bowls.

'Broth and bread! A fine feast!' he declared.

'What did you eat in the Ever, my boy?' Mother Moss asked.

'Not much. Just that which I found – fish, seaweed, grubs; sometimes berries and roots.'

'Well, you have some catching up to do.'

She gave him two helpings of soup with bread, then she served pumpkin pie and seedcakes followed by a big plate of honey buns with lots of whipped cream. I watched Siltboy eat five, six, seven buns before I lost count.

I kept a close eye on the sleek, expecting he would dart across and pinch someone else's food, but for once he didn't. He seemed to sense that this meal was an important occasion.

After we finished our lunch, Mother Moss filled our cups with warm milk and honey.

'To good company!' she said, raising her cup to her lips. 'And fine food!'

She poured Shadow's milk into a bowl and he lapped it up with big loud slurps. Milk splashed all over the bread bench but Mother Moss didn't seem to mind.

Siltboy wiped his hands on his trousers and stood up to make a speech. 'You mended my hound, Mother. You fed me running gold and fodder like I never tasted before, and now I make you a gift.'

He took off my vest, then he undid the webbing straps that held his breastplate in place and, slipping it over his head, he passed it to the old lady.

'For you,' he said.

'Why, Siltboy, thank you.' Mother Moss took the breastplate in her hands. 'We'll polish it up and it will make a lovely platter. I could serve a grand banquet on this. Are you sure you want me to have it?'

'Certain,' said Siltboy.

'Then I hope you will eat with me often.'

'I will, Mother Moss.' A strange look passed over Siltboy's face, and he hung his head.

'What is it, Siltboy?' Mother Moss asked. 'Speak your mind.'

Siltboy stared at the ground. 'I'm braving myself,' he mumbled. 'I have a question. A great request.'

'Ask away, my young friend.'

When Siltboy looked up, his eyes seemed big in his head. 'Will you be my mother?' he asked.

'My dear, I'm a little old for that!' Mother Moss laughed. 'How about I be your grandmother instead?'

'Would you?'

'I'd be proud to have a grandson like you.'

Siltboy beamed. He cupped Mother Moss's face in his hands and kissed her on both cheeks. 'Grandmother Moss!' he cried. 'I leave my battleways behind. I grow up now in the new world. So many marvels I seen on my travels, but you is the most marvellous.'

Shadow sat up, barking and thumping his tail on the ground.

'Well,' said Mother Moss. 'This calls for a celebration!' She refilled our cups. 'To grandmothers,' she cried. 'And to friendship, health and long life!'

We drank to that, then Siltboy stood up once more.

'I make gift to my grandmother,' he said. 'And now, with banquet and merry-making, I have present for Peat.'

He began to sing in a high sweet voice, and Mother Moss closed her eyes to listen.

Joy to the treasure-giver!
Bold-brave with hair like fire
She runs with the sleek
And shares the wealth of the world!

The sleek blinked and flicked his ears. Shadow sat up and barked his approval, and I missed the next bit of the song – something about *'Siltboy's sorrow'*.

...nine hundred bitter winters
Friendless, except for my Shadow
I wandered the Ever...

Siltboy's sweet voice grew mournful and Shadow picked up the mood, accompanying him with a sorrowful howl. He paused until the Great Hound had finished, then he went on, beating out a rhythm on an upturned bread tin.

Joy to the treasure-giver!
Wit-wise and fleet of foot
She gives me the greatest of gifts –
Courage, freedom and friendship forever!

'It's a true song,' Siltboy said when he'd finished. 'I call it *Song for a Scarlet Runner*.'

The sleek leapt onto Siltboy's shoulder and I held my breath, but the creature didn't scratch or bite – he rubbed his sharp little face under Siltboy's chin.

'Thank you, Siltboy,' I said. 'No one ever made a song for me before.'

My face felt hot and my eyes stung with tears. Mother Moss put her arm around me.

'Well worded,' she sighed. 'It's a beautiful song.'

'But Siltboy,' I said, '*you* gave those things to *me*. You gave me courage. I would have given up on getting out of the Ever. And it was you who won the wit-battle.'

'No, Peat. You braved me. Before you came, I always did the Siltman's bidding. I was a poor boy. My hoard was a shell-heap with a broken buckle.'

He took my hand, and he took Mother Moss's as well. 'Now I am true rich,' he said.

I wished that day could have gone forever, but I knew we had to keep going. The sleek was getting jittery. He had behaved himself well right through lunch, but now he was pacing the length of the bread bench and looking towards the river.

'If only you could stay,' Mother Moss said, handing me the everlasting daisy, which she had wrapped in new cloth and carefully tied up with string.

She gave Siltboy a flourbag full of food. 'There's enough bread and cheese in this, and enough honey cakes, to last for days,' she said. 'Take the craft, and keep near this side of the river. The current will do the rest.'

I turned the reed-boat the right way up and found paddles underneath. The sleek leapt onto the prow and sat there waiting, but Shadow stayed on the riverbank, ponderous, with his head on his paws. I couldn't see how the boat would take his weight, and maybe he felt the same way, because when I pulled it into the water he stood back and howled.

'Come, Shadow,' I said.

He gave a long sad look, as if to say he wanted to help but it wasn't possible, then he sat down next to Mother Moss.

'I'll look after him while you're gone.' She reached up and put her hand on the giant dog.

A sob rose in my throat. I couldn't imagine leaving Shadow behind.

'We'll go another way,' I said. 'We'll go by land.'

'The river is the way to the marshes.' Mother shook her head, and Shadow howled again. I went to him and pressed my face against his neck.

'Lovely hound,' I whispered. 'We will be lost without you.' Then I took a deep breath and told myself to be strong. What had Siltboy said in my song – *bold-brave*?

'Goodbye, Great Hound.'

He gave me a lick that almost flung me into the river.

'All right, let's go,' I said.

Siltboy had the same look of misery on his face as the dog. 'I'm sorry, Peat. I cannot leave my Shadow.'

'What! Must I go alone?'

'You're not alone,' Siltboy said. 'Sleek is with you.'

The sleek jumped into the water and out again, making irritable clicking sounds.

'Please, Siltboy.' I couldn't believe he wouldn't come.

Siltboy looked at the flourbag in his hands. 'I is hamstringed,' he said. 'Half my heart is roped to my hound and the other to my friend. I is pulled split-ways.'

Mother Moss came to his rescue.

'You can't be in two places at once, Siltboy,' she said kindly. 'If you wish to stay here with Shadow, I could certainly use your help.'

Siltboy brightened. 'I can chop wood and work the bread furnace,' he said. 'My grandmother has need of me!'

I wanted to say I had need of him as well, but the sleek fixed me with a stare that made me bite my tongue.

'You is keen, Peat. Be stout and steady.' Siltboy handed me the food bag.

'Go well, my dear,' Mother Moss said. 'Your sleek is waiting. He has no patience for long farewells. May the river carry you safely, and may your return be swift.' She put her arms around me and I sank into her soft belly.

'And if you ever need a grandmother, I'm yours, just as I am Siltboy's.'

'I do need one,' I said. 'Thank you, Mother Moss.'

I turned to Siltboy. 'I'll see you soon, my friend. We'll go to the Plains and meet Marlie and Longreach and Wim, then we'll travel on with the cattle.'

'Peat, friendship is forged, but I'll not sally forth for the herding life. I would stay with Grandmother and work the bread-forge. When she grows small, I will grow big.'

He held out his hand and I shook it like I had when we'd first met on the far side of the Silver River.

'Fare you well,' he said. 'You have your luck and your sleek. We will be friends forever.'

I put the flower at the front of the boat and the sleek sat next to it. As Mother Moss gently pushed us away from the shore the current took the boat, and I was carried around the bend in the river before I knew it.

When I turned to wave, all I could see was the woe tree leaning over the water, its grey leaves trailing in the breeze.

44

THIEF OF TIME

'No back-looking,' I told myself as I was carried down-stream. It began to rain and I couldn't help imagining Mother Moss and Siltboy cosy in the hut.

The sleek jumped in and out of the boat. He didn't care about the rain – he was glad that we were on our way. He glided along beside me, then he scrambled onto the prow and crouched there, leaning into the wind with his fur blown back. He looked perfectly happy.

'It's all right for you, Sleek. You haven't lost anything,' I said.

We passed Mother Moss's beehives, and I watched the trees on the bank change from a solid wall of dark pines to open forest. I wondered how long it would take me to get to the marshes and tried to remember the trip paddling upstream with Eadie. The current was so strong, I didn't know how we'd managed it.

Once or twice the reed-boat got caught in an eddy and was swirled around so that we were facing the wrong way. I tried to keep near the bank but I didn't have much control, so in the end I put the paddle down and let the river take me.

The rain grew heavier, and sometimes the bank disappeared in grey mist. I wondered what time it was. I would need to find shelter and a place to sleep before it got dark. When I saw a spot on the riverbank where I could land I paddled towards it, but the sleek didn't approve. He spat at me, and when I ignored him he jumped onto the shaft of the paddle, ran down to the blade and clung there, making paddling impossible. The spot where I could have stopped sailed past.

'You're trouble, Sleek,' I said.

He flicked his ears and climbed back into the boat. After a while he yawned and went to sleep.

I watched the riverbank gliding past. Feathery trees grew down to the edge of the water, and I could see that the ground was dry beneath them. When the river rounded a bend, the boat was swept out wide towards the shallows. I quietly took up the paddle and steered towards the shore without waking the sleek. As the boat came to rest, he opened one eye, then he gave a sharp cry and dived into the water. He swam back into the flow of the river, glancing over his shoulder as the current took him.

'Come back!' I yelled as he disappeared downstream.

It was raining heavily and I was glad of the shelter of the trees. I gathered a few pieces of dry wood, but then I realised I didn't have Siltboy's flint, so I had no way of lighting a fire. It was getting dark. I hugged my knees and watched the grey water flowing past, and I hummed Siltboy's song to keep myself company. I wasn't hungry, but after a while I thought I would eat something to cheer myself up – some of Marlie's cheese and one of Mother Moss's honey cakes. But when I looked, the bag of food was gone.

'Sleek!' I yelled. 'That's so unfair!'

I doubted that he heard me. He was long gone, and my voice was lost in the sound of the rushing river.

It crossed my mind that the sleek might leave me. He seemed so eager to get to the marshes.

'I don't care!' I yelled. 'I'll find my own way.'

I curled up at the foot of one of the feathery trees and went to sleep.

When I woke the next morning, it was still raining. I was cold and hungry and miserable. I got back in the boat, wishing Siltboy was with me. It was too hard travelling alone like this. I steered out into the current, and the boat was soon moving swiftly.

At least with the sleek gone I could stop and start when I liked, I told myself. Mother Moss had said to keep near the side of the river and the current would do the rest, so I had no fear of getting lost.

By midmorning the rain had stopped and the sun was trying to come out. The river grew wider and slowed down a bit, and when I saw some berries growing on the bank I paddled in to shore and pulled the boat onto a small, sandy beach.

I tasted one of the berries. It was hard and bitter, and I spat it straight out. Eadie would probably have used those berries to make some special medicine, but they were certainly no good for eating.

I wandered into some trees behind the bushes, hoping I might find mushrooms growing beneath them, but I didn't. I began to miss the sleek. How would I eat without him?

I told myself it wouldn't take me long to get to the marshes, and once I was there I could eat. Olive would give me marsh cakes, and Ebb – or Nettie, or whatever her name was – might give me a fish.

I looked up into the trees. Perhaps I could find a bird's nest with some eggs in it. I caught hold of a low branch and swung myself up. I hadn't done any climbing since the night I'd left the Overhang, but I found I was still good at it. Soon I was high above the river.

I found a nest, but it was empty so I climbed down and chose another tree, a tall one with branches that reached out over the little beach. I was near the top when I saw a messy nest above me. I could tell by the bits of dry grass and leaves dangling from it that it was new and fresh, but when I reached it I was disappointed: there were three hatchlings inside. Their eyes weren't open yet and they had no feathers, but they must have heard me and thought I was their mother, because they cheeped loudly and opened their tiny beaks, waiting to be fed.

'Nothing for you, little ones,' I said. 'And I'm not going to eat you, either.'

I sighed and looked down through the leaves to the reed-boat resting on the little beach, then I gasped and almost lost my footing. There were footprints around the boat. Paw prints or footprints? I was too far away to tell.

I quickly climbed down. Once I reached the ground, I crouched behind the bushes and looked right and left. There was nobody around, but as well as my own footprints leading up from the boat, there were others beside them – human footprints and dog prints.

I ran to the boat and pushed it out into the river, paddling hard, and only when I was moving with the current did I put down the paddle and try to catch my breath. My heart was thumping in my chest and it took a long time to slow down.

The sun came out, and the trees on the bank changed again. There were shrubs and low bushes, and in the distance I could see pale hills. By late morning the river joined up with another, bigger one.

'That's right. This is where the river forked,' I muttered.

It seemed a very long time ago that Eadie and I had been paddling upstream in the other direction. I leaned over the side of the boat and had a drink. The river was really slowing down now. Soon I would have to paddle, and I couldn't paddle without food.

⟶

I stopped that night at a grassy place on the bank and fell asleep immediately. I had been looking at the river all day, and now the grey water filled my dreams.

I saw Eadie's coat, floating by with no one inside it. It looked just like the skin of a dead animal, and when I tried to reach for it, it moved away and began swirling around, caught in an eddy. I poked it with a stick to try to catch it, but it was swept downstream, so I followed, running along the bank.

The river in my dream grew wider, and the coat drifted to midstream and got snagged there, collecting weed and sticks until it became a small island. The fur went green, and all the seeds in the coat's many pockets swelled and sprouted. The vine that grew from beneath Eadie's collar took root. Shrubs and saplings followed, and one tree grew up straight and tall, right in the middle of the island.

The shag from the marshes circled overhead and landed in the tree, staring at me accusingly.

'It's not my fault,' I said. 'I didn't make the bargain.'

⁓

I woke before dawn and found apples in the bottom of the boat – small green apples and a pile of leafy weeds that had a sharp, spicy scent. The apples were sweet and crunchy, and once I had eaten half-a-dozen I felt able to go on.

When the sun came up I saw the sleek swimming ahead of me.

'Thank you, Sleek,' I shouted.

If he heard me he showed no sign. After a while he dived under the water and I didn't see him again until late afternoon, when he scrambled into the boat with his mouth full of riverweeds. He spat them out and watched me eat them, then he lay down in the bottom of the boat and fell into a restless sort of sleep, twitching and sighing as if he was having bad dreams.

I stayed on the river that night, paddling into the dark. No moon rose, but the flower began to give out a little light, glowing faintly at the front of the boat as if it was trying to show the way. When I closed my eyes the light grew stronger, and as I went to sleep it seemed to fill my mind.

⁓

The boat must have drifted a long way in the dark, because when the sleek woke me in the morning I found that the river had joined a large body of water and we were far from either shore.

It took half a day to paddle back to land, and when I got close I saw a spot where long grass grew to the water's edge and sunflowers bloomed along the bank. Perhaps it was the place where Eadie and I had camped when she'd told me the story of Blot.

I wanted to collect some sunflower seeds, but the sleek glared at me and hissed a warning, and when I kept paddling towards the bank he leapt onto my arm and bit it, making me drop the paddle. By the time I had fished it out of the water the sunflowers were behind us.

Soon the river was so wide I could no longer see the other side. I kept near the bank, and when we passed the old beehives I knew we were getting close to the marshes.

The sleek didn't bother feeding me that day, and by evening time I was tired and weak and had a headache. I was getting blisters, too, from the paddling.

'Enough,' I said to the sleek. 'I have to rest.'

He gave me a sharp look, then he sniffed the air, wrinkled his nose and sneezed. He began padding around the edges of the boat, as if he was on patrol, stopping from time to time to cock his head and listen. There was no sound except insects and frogs, and every so often a fish jumping; then I heard the cry of a bird, a seagull, or perhaps it was an eagle.

But why would an eagle be out hunting at night? I wondered as I put down my paddle and lay back with my head under the flower. A salt breeze moved over the water and the boat rocked gently beneath me. I was almost asleep when the sleek jumped on my chest. He stared into my eyes; his pupils were huge. He looked from me to the paddle and back again.

'No, Sleek. I've had enough for the day,' I told him.

He growled deep in his throat, and when I closed my eyes he swiped my face.

'Ah, bad Sleek!' I went to swipe him back, but he leapt out of reach and crouched at the far end of the boat, glowering.

'You're not my boss,' I said. 'If I want to sleep, I will.'

I turned my back on him and closed my eyes. I heard the water lapping softly on the sides of the boat – and there was the bird cry again, the gull or the eagle. I thought of Siltboy's battlebird, then a strange feeling came over me...

It must have been the exhaustion that caused it, because I wasn't trying to blank my mind, it just became empty – and next thing I knew, I was gliding above the water, wheeling higher and higher until I could see forever.

I saw a coastline, and the lacy patterns made by the waves breaking on the beach, and I saw the wide mouth of a river with a heap of grey rocks nearby – only they weren't rocks, I realised, because they were moving. I was high above, but when I focused I could see the details: it was the Siltman and his dogs! One dog raised its head in slow motion and looked towards its master. Another staggered to its feet and took a couple of groggy steps before flopping back into the pile. The Siltman raised his hand. He was trying to wake up. I could hear the wind whistling through his teeth, then words came to me – words carried on a salty wind from the sea.

'Siltgirl – thief of time – you won't get away with this...'

The Siltman's voice was like wind blowing through

the reeds. It filled my mind and I was vaguely aware of the smell of ants.

'How strange that I can hear you from this distance,' I mumbled.

'Distance is nothing, Siltgirl. Rest. Sleep, and wait for me to catch up with you.'

'Yes,' I sighed, breathing in the ant smell. 'Rest.'

The salt wind grew stronger, until it was howling around me.

'I won't be long, Siltgirl.'

'No rush,' I murmured.

Then I heard another voice through the howling. 'Peat! Wake up. Time is short.'

'Longreach, is that you?' I muttered.

'Take back the deed that was done!'

That was Siltboy's voice! It sounded small and very far away. I struggled to sit up. Although I was half asleep, I realised what was happening – the Siltman was ahead of himself. He was sending his voice the way he'd sent his footprints and the howling of the dogs. He had sent the salt wind, and he was sending the Swoon as well, to affect me.

I heard the sleek shrieking somewhere in the distance, then I heard my own voice. I didn't know if I was speaking aloud or if the words were in my mind. I was telling myself what Eadie had told me: *The marshes are a refuge. Once you're in the marshes, nothing can touch you.*

The howling faded, and the sound of the sleek grew louder. I held my breath and picked up the paddle. My arms were heavy as lead, but with each stroke I felt stronger and more awake. Soon I was paddling hard and panting the ant smell of the Swoon out of my nose, filling my lungs instead with fresh, clean air.

The sleek sat at the helm and made yipping cries, urging me on, until the boat was caught by a current and we were taken up a channel lined with reeds.

When I saw the burnt-out hut where the shag lived, I knew we were in the marshes and gave an enormous sigh of relief. The shag was standing in his nest. He looked down at me as we passed, then he stretched his long neck in the direction we were going and honked loudly, flapping his wings as if applauding.

The sleek stared at me with huge, frightened eyes. The tips of his ears were trembling. I put my hand on his head.

'Settle, Sleek,' I panted. 'We're safe, and we're almost there.'

A new moon rose that night. The crescent shape reminded me of the horns on my cow charm. I put my hand to the charm and lay down under the everlasting daisy. Now that we were in the marshes, its pale light was stronger.

The sleek lay down beside me, and after a while we both fell into a deep and silent sleep.

45

THE CHURN

We woke the next morning to find ourselves in open water, far beyond the reed fields. I could see islands moving about in the distance, and there was a faint hum of insects swarming somewhere.

The boat travelled towards the droning noise, and as we got closer I realised that it wasn't the buzz of insects, it was singing – a strange low monotonous sort of song. The sleek scratched his ears and shook his head, as if the sound hurt him. When I put him on my lap and covered his ears with my hands, he didn't resist.

We drifted past the islands and I saw a stilt hut up ahead. Eadie's hide! I could tell by the ladder and the bag hanging over the door. The singing was loud and out of tune, and the hut was swaying in time to it.

Half-a-dozen reed-boats were tethered to the walkway below, and there were ropes around the stilt legs of the hut. Above the singing, I could hear arguing.

'Leave me alone, you hags. Get out of my hide. Why can't you give a woman some peace in her old age!'

It was Eadie's voice. She sounded weak but angry. I put my hand on my cow charm and picked up the flower. What had Mother Moss said? *What you're holding is not Eadie's life but her death.*

I had no idea what I was going to do. I sat in the boat and listened.

'We're doing our best to help you, and all you do is complain!' said a voice I didn't recognise.

'It's all right for you, Ivy. You think you can throw your weight around now you're the new Great Aunt, but you can't tell me what to do. Will you lot stop that wretched wailing!'

'If we don't sing, you'll go the wrong way when you die. You won't find your way to the Churn.' That was Flo's voice.

'Don't you fools realise that I can't die! If I *could* die, your dreadful singing would have killed me years ago!'

The singing went on over the top of the argument.

'Give her some more Healbane soup.'

'I don't want your soups and your potions!'

'We've sung ourselves hoarse for you,' Nettie said in a croaky voice. 'You don't appreciate a single note.'

'Shut up!' yelled Eadie.

The singing stopped.

'Ah!' Eadie groaned. 'It makes no difference. Your thoughts are still crashing through my mind like a herd of bog rats through the undergrowth. Can't you still your minds?'

'No,' they said. 'Our minds are always busy.'

My boat glided under the hut and stopped there. I didn't mean to eavesdrop, but what else could I do?

'Light my pipe,' Eadie demanded.

'No. It stinks, and it's not good for you.'

'She's a difficult patient.'

Two pairs of legs suddenly dangled above the ladder. One pair was thick and ended in reed shoes that looked like little boats. The other legs were fine and pale; the feet were bare, and the toenails were painted a shimmering lime-green.

'Eadie has always been difficult. She's been in a foul mood for fifty years.'

'What was she like before that?'

'Bad-tempered.'

A third set of legs joined the others, thin and scrawny with ankles that were bony and shoes made of plaited rope or seaweed.

'The marshes will go to rack and ruin while we spend all our time looking after Eadie.'

The sleek jumped up and spat at the legs, and the conversation stopped. Three heads peered down at me.

'It's the swamp waif!' cried Lily. 'She's returned!'

'Little swamp waif.' Flo clapped her hands. 'Praise be to the marshes. We are saved!'

'The waif is back,' Nettie called. 'She's come to look after Eadie!'

'Your marsh auntie is dying,' Lily sighed.

There was movement above and a face I didn't know looked down at me. 'What are you waiting for? Come up at once. Don't bring the snide. We've got enough vermin in the hut already.'

I took the everlasting daisy and climbed the ladder.

Eadie was lying on the bed. She looked tiny inside her enormous coat. Her hair was silver and her coat had gone grey as well. She was ancient and frail, but her eyes were bright.

'Peat!' she gasped.

Another marsh auntie I hadn't seen before helped Eadie to sit up, and pushed some pillows behind her back.

'I didn't expect to see you, Peat. Never again.' Eadie started coughing, and she struggled to get her breath.

Perhaps I should have felt sorry for her, but I didn't.

'Eadie, you tricked me.'

She looked down and patted her coat pockets.

'Trickery,' she wheezed. 'I believe there's a cure for that – what's it called – Honesty? I don't seem to have it in my collection.'

'I could have been trapped forever in the world of the Siltman,' I said.

Eadie's eyes met mine. 'I'm sorry, Peat. I shouldn't have used you like that.'

'What in the marsh are they talking about?' Flo asked.

'Don't tell them,' Eadie hissed. 'They always want to know everybody's business. Give me my pipe.' Then she added, 'Please.'

Her pipe was sitting on the table and I lit it with a stick from the stove.

'We don't think smoking is good for her,' Lily said. 'But you're in charge of her now.'

Eadie sucked on the pipe and blew out a smoke ring that landed around Lily's neck like a lasso. Lily sniffed. Olive broke into a fit of coughing.

'A dreadful habit,' Myriad muttered.

'Well, we'll leave you to it then,' Flo said cheerfully.

The marsh aunties began clambering down the ladder. They were eager to leave.

'It's been a nightmare trying to look after her,' Lily

whispered. 'We had to hobble her hut, because it kept running away. And Eadie kept trying to escape down the ladder.'

'I wanted to go and collect the buds of Heednot so I could use them as earplugs,' Eadie interrupted. 'I've been a prisoner here, Peat.'

I grabbed Lily's hand as she went out the door. 'Thank you for the Swoon, Lily.'

'Oh, the Swoon?' Lily paused and twisted a strand of hair around her finger. 'I'm afraid I made a tiny mistake with that one. One sniff can lay a creature low for years. Best not to open it.' She flicked her hair behind her ear and climbed down the ladder. 'But I'm working on a new collection,' she said. 'Splash, it's called. Or maybe Flourish.'

'We'll be back, Eadie. Behave yourself.' Nettie pushed past me and followed Lily.

'Don't hurry,' Eadie said.

<hr/>

'Peace at last,' Eadie said once they'd all left. She turned to me and looked me over.

'I may be ancient, Peat, but I can still hear your thoughts. Hand it to me.'

I was holding the plant behind my back.

'You don't want to, but you must.' She sank back into her pillows.

At that moment the sleek appeared in the doorway. He raced past me and jumped on the bed.

'Sleek!' Eadie smiled. 'Soon you will have the place to yourself.'

I wasn't sure what she meant by that.

'Come on, Peat, don't keep me waiting.'

I passed Eadie the plant and she snapped off the flower head and slipped it inside her coat.

'Good waif,' she whispered. 'Now I am ready.'

'Ready for what?'

'The Churn. Can you help me down to the skiff?'

I nodded, but my chest felt tight.

'What happens when you go to the Churn?' My voice was small. I think I already knew the answer.

'You die,' Eadie said.

I took her hand. 'Eadie, I don't want you to die.'

'I can't live well anymore,' she said. 'Besides, there are worse things than death. How would you like to live forever with that mob singing over you?'

She laughed a wheezy laugh. 'It took them a while to catch me,' she said. 'They had to chase my hut halfway across the marshes. Now give me a hand up.'

When I helped Eadie stand, I could see that she had definitely shrunk. Her coat trailed on the floor. She staggered and would have fallen back on the bed if I hadn't caught her. She was so light – the only weight was in her coat.

I picked her up and carried her down the ladder, remembering how she had carried me when my leg was broken. Then I laid her gently in the craft.

'You'd better get the shroud Olive embroidered for me. She'll be offended if I don't use it. It's under the bed.'

I went back up the ladder.

'And get one of those flowers from the bunch on the table,' Eadie added.

A piece of cloth was folded up under Eadie's bed.

I shook it out and saw all the colours of the swamp – greys and greens and blues. It was a map of the marshes, sewn in a thousand tiny stitches. There were names on it – the Far Reaches, the Reed Hut, the Islands of Floatweed, the Hermit Islands. Currents were marked out in shiny blue thread, and the centre was embroidered with a spiral labelled 'The Churn'. I would have liked to study the map for longer, but Eadie was calling from below.

'Come on. I haven't got forever.' She sounded quite happy with the idea.

I chose a flower from the table on the way – a little red bud with white tips.

Eadie seemed to have grown older and smaller in the short time I had been in the hut. I leaned over her and tucked the cloth behind her head. Her eyes were clouding over. I could see the sky in them.

'Goodbye, Peat,' she whispered. 'Push the skiff out. It will find its own way.'

The sleek skittered down the ladder and stood with me on the walkway while I did as she asked.

We watched Eadie drift out over the water. Within a few seconds, she had caught a current and was moving swiftly away.

———✦———

The sleek and I stood there for a long time. We saw the shag fly past. He followed Eadie's craft until it was a dot on the horizon. Then we saw him circling overhead. I couldn't be sure, but I thought I saw smoke from Eadie's pipe, a long twist of smoke rising in a spiral.

'Goodbye, Eadie,' I said under my breath.

The sleek made a rattling sort of sigh and scrambled back up the ladder, leaving me alone.

I gazed across the marshes, and the longer I looked the more desolate they seemed to me. The sky hung low and heavy and I could feel the weight of the clouds pressing down on me.

'I'm sorry, Eadie,' I whispered. 'But it was your life or mine, and you'd already had a good run. You must have been hundreds of years old, whereas I'm only nine, or maybe I'm ten now, or even eleven.'

A deep sigh came out of me, and I sat down on the landing and looked at the bud in my hand. It was more than a bud, really – the outside petals were just beginning to open. *Why did Eadie tell me to choose a flower?* I wondered. But it was too late to ask her now.

When Eadie's boat came back empty, my tears began to flow. I thought of the song I had heard with her when we were outside Hub. *Where the river meets the sea, you'll meet your destiny...*

'My destiny wasn't with the Siltman, Eadie,' I said. 'Now that your bargain is undone, he has no hold over me. I have to follow my own fate, the way you had to follow yours.'

Then I stopped talking, because I realised the boat wasn't empty. Eadie's story bag was sitting in the bottom. As I leaned over and picked it up I thought I heard a voice, Eadie's voice. I wasn't sure if it was in my mind or on the breeze – or perhaps it was in the faint smell of tobacco smoke that rose from the pouch when I opened it.

'For you, Peat. May all your stories have happy endings. If you like that sort of thing.'

I put the bud into the story bag and pulled the drawstring. Then I tied the pouch around my neck.

'Come on, Sleek,' I said, calling back into the hide.

No answer.

'Sleek. Come on!'

He poked his nose out and stared down at me.

'What's wrong? You can't stay here.'

He narrowed his eyes and spat. There was something strange about the look on his face. I had got to know the sleek well in our travels together, but this was something new, a look I hadn't seen before. His ears seemed sharper, and there was something glintier about his eyes. Then I noticed they were the wrong colour. They were yellow, not grey-green. At that moment another sleek appeared next to him, *my* sleek!

Both creatures began chittering, then one nipped the other and they disappeared inside. I climbed the ladder. When my head was level with the floor of the hut, I saw them both on Eadie's bed. One was burrowing under her pillow. There was some squeaking and hissing, and three baby sleeks tumbled out and fell onto the floor. One skidded in my direction and landed on my shoulder. It stared at me in surprise then bit my ear so hard I almost fell backwards. It leapt down onto the walkway.

'Come and get your cub,' I said to my sleek.

He gave a yawn and ignored me. His mate blinked and began washing herself. The tiny sleek sprang into the boat and sat there, waiting.

As I climbed back down the ladder, my old sleek came and rested his chin on the top rung, gazing at me steadily.

'Farewell, my friend,' I said quietly.

I stepped into the boat, and the cub gave me a questioning look as if to say, *Where are we going, Peat?*

'Home,' I said. 'Home to Marlie and Longreach and Wim and the cows. We will travel the world, telling stories and herding cattle.'

The little sleek must have been happy with that idea, because he took his place at the prow, and when I began to row back the way I had come, hoping to catch a current that would take us out of the marshes, he jumped onto my lap and purred.

ACKNOWLEDGEMENTS

Many thanks to my editor, Sue Flockhart, who helped bring this book into being and said, 'Oh no – not the dog!' when I thought of leaving Shadow out of the story. Thanks to the scarlet runner beans for growing so vigorously, and to the everlasting daisies for flowering all summer. Thanks to the quolls for inspiring the sleek, and to Terry for inspiring Amos Last. Thanks to Dale and Ruth for the beautiful cover, and to Angela for the idea of the marsh auntie giving the pouch to Peat – a gift at the end of the story.

ABOUT THE AUTHOR

Julie Hunt lives on a farm in southern Tasmania and is fascinated by landscapes and the stories they inspire. This interest has taken her from the rugged west coast of Ireland to the ice caves of Romania. She loves poetry, storytelling and traditional folktales, and her own stories combine other-worldly elements with down-to-earth humour. Her picture books include *The Coat* (illustrated by Ron Brooks) and *Precious Little* (illustrated by Gaye Chapman). She has written a three-book series called Little Else about a plucky young cowgirl (illustrated by Beth Norling), and a graphic novel called *KidGlovz* (illustrated by Dale Newman, who drew this book's cover).